NEW YORK REVIEW BOOKS
CLASSICS

# DIRTY SNOW

GEORGES SIMENON (1903–1989) was born in Liège, Belgium.
His father was an insurance salesman, easygoing and unambi-
tious; his mother, an unhappy, angry woman whose coldness
and disapproval haunted her son. Simenon went to work as a
reporter at the age of fifteen and in 1923 moved to Paris, where
under various pseudonyms he became a highly successful
author of pulp fiction while leading a dazzling social life in
the company of his first wife and such lovers as the American
dancer Josephine Baker. (He is said to have broken up with
Baker because their affair was a distraction: he had produced
a mere twelve novels in the year.) In the early 1930s, Simenon
emerged as a writer under his own name, gaining renown for
his detective stories featuring Inspector Maigret. He also began
to write his psychological novels—books in which he displays
his remarkable talent for capturing the look and mood of a
place (whether West Africa, the Soviet Union, New York City,
or provincial France) together with an acutely sympathetic
awareness of the emotional and spiritual pain underlying the
routines of daily life. Simenon remained in France throughout
the Second World War, at the end of which he was accused of
collaboration with the Germans; though quickly cleared of
such charges, he moved to America, where he married his
second wife and lived for close to a decade, returning to
Europe in 1955. Having written nearly two hundred books
under his own name and become the best-selling author in
the world, whose stories had served as the inspiration for
countless movies and TV shows, Simenon retired as a novel-
ist in 1973, devoting himself instead to dictating memoirs

JUN     2004

that filled thousands of pages: "I consider myself less and less a writer ... All this is nothing but chatter ... Since dictating has become a need, so to speak, I will dictate every morning whatever comes into mind ... I would like to be able to be silent."

WILLIAM T. VOLLMANN was born in Los Angeles in 1959 and attended Deep Springs College and Cornell University. He is the author of many works of fiction, long and short, including *The Royal Family*, *You Bright and Risen Angels*, *Whores for Gloria*, and *The Rainbow Stories*, as well as an ongoing series of seven novels, collectively entitled *Seven Dreams: A Book of North American Landscapes*, about the collision between the native populations of North America and their colonizers and oppressors. (Four volumes have been published so far: *The Ice-Shirt*, *Fathers and Crows*, *Argall: The True Story of Pocahontas and Captain John Smith*, and *The Rifles*.) Vollmann has also written two works of non-fiction: *An Afghanistan Picture Show*, which describes his crossing into Afghanistan with a group of Islamic commandos in 1982, and *Rising Up and Rising Down*, a treatise on violence. He lives in California.

# DIRTY SNOW

GEORGES SIMENON

Translated from the French by

**MARC ROMANO**

**LOUISE VARÈSE**

Afterword by

**WILLIAM T. VOLLMANN**

NEW YORK REVIEW BOOKS

*New York*

This is a New York Review Book
Published by The New York Review of Books
1755 Broadway, New York, NY 10019

*La Neige était sale* copyright © 1948 by Georges Simenon Limited,
a Chorion Company
Translation by Marc Romano and Louise Varèse entitled *Dirty Snow*
copyright © 1951, 2003 by Georges Simenon Limited, a Chorion Company
Afterword copyright © 2003 by William T. Vollmann
All rights reserved.

Library of Congress Cataloging-in-Publication Data
Simenon, Georges, 1903–
 [Neige était sale. English]
 Dirty snow / by Georges Simenon ; translated by Marc Romano ;
afterword by William T. Vollmann.
    p. cm. — (New York Review Books classics)
 ISBN 1-59017-043-1 (pbk. : alk. paper)
 I. Romano, Marc. II. Title. III. Series.
 PQ2637.I53N4313 2003
 843'.912—dc21
                         2003013762

ISBN 1-59017-043-1

Book design by Lizzie Scott
Printed in the United States of America on acid-free paper.
10 9 8 7 6 5 4 3 2 1

September 2003
www.nyrb.com

# CONTENTS

# DIRTY SNOW

PART ONE
# TIMO'S CUSTOMERS

# 1

I<small>F NOT</small> for a chance event, what Frank Friedmaier did that night wouldn't have had much meaning. Obviously Frank couldn't have foreseen that his neighbor, Gerhardt Holst, would pass him in the street. But Holst did pass by, and he recognized him, too, which changed everything. And yet that, and all that later followed, Frank accepted.

That was why what happened that night by the tannery wall was very different, both then and in the future, from, for example, what losing his virginity had been like.

Because at first that was how Frank thought about it, and the comparison amused and disturbed him at the same time. Fred Kromer, his friend—though Kromer was already twenty-two—had killed someone again last week, coming out of Timo's. Just a few minutes earlier, Frank had also been at Timo's. Now he stood waiting, pressed against the tannery wall.

But did Kromer's dead man really count? Kromer had been heading toward the door, buttoning his coat with his usual air of importance, a big cigar between his thick lips. He was shiny. He was always shiny. He had thick coarse skin like an orange's, skin that always seemed to be sweating.

Someone had compared him to a young bull that never got enough. At any rate, it was something sexual that his heavy shiny face, moist eyes, and full lips brought to mind.

A skinny little man, pale and feverish like so many others you saw, especially at night, had stupidly blocked Kromer's way. You wouldn't have thought he had enough money to be at Timo's, by the look of him. Taking hold of Kromer's fur collar, he had begun to yell.

What had Kromer sold him that he wasn't happy about?

Very dignified, puffing on his cigar, Kromer had pushed him aside. But the hungry little man, perhaps because he wanted to impress the woman he was with, had followed him out onto the sidewalk, shouting.

In Timo's street, people weren't much startled by shouting. The patrols passed by that way as seldom as possible. Still, if one of their cars did happen to go by somewhere near, then they would be sure to stop to see what was going on.

"Go home!" Kromer had said to the gnome, who had a head too large for his body and a crop of bright red hair.

"Not before you hear what I have to say . . ."

If you had to listen to everything people wanted to say, you'd find yourself in the loony bin before long.

"Go home!"

Was the redhead drunk? He looked more like he was on drugs. Perhaps Kromer had gotten them for him, and they'd been stepped on one time too many. It didn't matter anyway.

Kromer, in the middle of the dark alley between the two banks of snow, took the cigar out of his mouth with his left hand. He punched with his right, just once. Then two arms and two legs were in the air, just like a marionette, and then the black form sank down into the pile of snow along the sidewalk. The strangest thing was that there was an orange peel beside the head—something you probably wouldn't see anywhere in town except in front of Timo's.

Timo came out without his overcoat or cap, dressed just as he had been at the bar. He poked the marionette and stuck out his lower lip.

"He's had it," he growled. "In an hour he'll be stiff."

Had Kromer really killed the redhead with a single punch? That's what he wanted people to believe. The little runt wouldn't say one way or the other. At the suggestion of Timo, who wasted no time, he had been carried some two hundred yards away and dumped in the Old Basin, where the sewers drained and kept the water from freezing over.

So Kromer could claim he'd killed his man. Even if Timo was right, even if the marionette, which had had to be tossed into the air over a little brick wall, hadn't been quite dead.

Proof that Kromer didn't attach too much weight to the incident was that he continued to tell the story of the strangled girl. Only that hadn't happened in town or anywhere anyone knew. There was no evidence. And in that case, anyone could boast about anything.

"She had big breasts, practically no nose, and blue eyes," he always said.

On these points he never varied. But he added fresh details each time.

"It was a barn."

Okay. But what had Kromer, who'd never been a soldier and hated the countryside, been doing in a barn?

"We were going at it in the straw and the whole time bits of straw kept tickling me and making me mad . . ."

Kromer always told the story while chewing on his cigar and staring straight ahead with an absent look, as though out of modesty. Another detail that never changed was something the woman said.

"I want you to get me pregnant."

He claimed it was this remark that had started everything. The idea of having a child with that stupid, dirty girl he was kneading like a piece of dough had seemed grotesque, unacceptable.

"*Completely un-ac-cept-able.*"

And she had kept getting more tender and clinging.

He had reached a point where, without closing his eyes, he could see the monstrous head, blond and pale, of what would have been his and the girl's child.

Was it because Kromer himself was dark and hard as a tree trunk?

"It disgusted me," he always concluded, letting his cigar ash fall.

He was good. He knew what gestures to use. His little mannerisms made him interesting.

"I thought it safer to strangle the mother. That was the first time. And let me tell you, it's very easy. Not in the least upsetting."

It wasn't just Kromer. Everybody at Timo's had killed at least one man—in the war or wherever. Perhaps by informing on someone, which was the simplest way. You didn't even have to sign your name.

Timo, who didn't brag about it, must have killed piles of people, or else the Occupation authorities wouldn't let him stay open all night without bothering to check on what was going on. Even though the blinds were always closed, even though you had to come through the alley and say who you were before you were allowed in, they weren't so stupid as not to know.

Losing his virginity, his actual virginity, hadn't meant very much to Frank. He had been in the right place. Others made it a story they still talked about years later, adding flourishes like Kromer did with the girl he strangled in the barn.

And for Frank, who was nineteen, to kill his first man was another loss of virginity hardly any more disturbing than the first. And, like the first, it wasn't premeditated. It just happened. As though a moment comes when it's both necessary and natural to make a decision that has long since been made.

No one had pushed him to do it. No one had laughed at him. Besides, only fools let themselves be influenced by their friends.

For weeks, perhaps months, he had kept saying to himself, because he had felt within himself a sort of inferiority, "I'll have to try..."

Not in a fight. That would have been against his nature. To have it count, it seemed to him, it would have to be done in cold blood.

Now the opportunity he'd been waiting for had presented itself. Was it because he had been on the lookout for it?

They'd been at Timo's, at their table near the bar. Kromer was there in his coat that he kept on all the time, even in the hottest places. And with his cigar, naturally. And his shiny skin. And his huge eyes that seemed almost bovine. Kromer must have thought he was made of different clay from everyone else, since he never bothered putting his money away in a wallet. He just stuffed the bills, big crumpled wads of them, into his pockets.

There was a man with Kromer Frank didn't know, someone from another crowd, who introduced himself to Frank by saying, "Call me Berg."

He must have been at least forty. Cold and mysterious. He was somebody. The proof was that Kromer's manner toward him was almost fawning.

Kromer told him the story of the strangled girl, but without making a big deal of it, as though it were unimportant, just a funny story.

"Frank, look at the knife my friend here just gave me."

Kromer took the knife out of his warm coat, like a jewel that seems even more impressive because it's taken from a rich jewel case. He laid it on the checkered tablecloth.

"Feel that edge."

"Yes."

"Can you read the trademark?"

It was made in Sweden, a knife with a folding blade, so pure of line, so sharp, that you got the feeling the blade was actually intelligent and could find its way all by itself into someone's flesh.

Frank asked, ashamed of the childish tone he adopted despite himself, "Lend it to me, will you?"

"What for?"

"Nothing."

"Things like this aren't made just for nothing."

The other man smiled a bit indulgently, as though listening to the boasting of boys.

"Lend it to me."

It wasn't just for nothing, of course. Yet he still didn't quite know what it was for. But then he happened to see, at the corner table under the light with the lavender silk shade, the fat noncommissioned officer, already red in the face—it was violet because of the light—take off his gun belt and set it down among the glasses.

Everybody knew the noncommissioned officer. He was almost a mascot, a sort of family pet you get used to seeing around the house. He was the only one among the Occupation forces who came to Timo's regularly and openly, without taking precautions, without bothering to be discreet.

He must have had a name. Here, they called him the Eunuch—because he was enormous, so fat that his flesh bulged out of his uniform, forming great rolls at his waist and under his arms. He made you think of a matron who has taken off her corset, leaving marks on her flabby flesh. There were more rolls of flesh around his neck and under his chin, and on his head a few stray hairs, colorless and silken.

He always sat in the same corner, invariably with two women, it didn't matter who so long as they were brunettes and skinny. They said he liked them hairy.

When customers entered and were startled by the sight of his uniform—that of the Occupation police—Timo barely lowered his voice to say, "Don't worry. He isn't dangerous."

Did the Eunuch hear him? Did he understand? He ordered brandy by the carafe. One woman on his lap, another beside him on the bench. He would whisper stories to them and laugh. He drank, he told stories, he laughed, he made them drink, his hands busy under their skirts.

He must have had a family somewhere in his own country. Nouchi, whom he had allowed to go through his wallet, claimed it was stuffed with photographs of children of all ages. He called his girls by nicknames. It amused him. He bought them food. He loved watching them eat expensive dishes that could only be found at Timo's and a few other places that were even harder to get into, reserved exclusively for high-ranking officers.

He practically forced them to eat. He ate with them. He would paw at them in front of everyone. He would look at his wet fingers and laugh. Then, like clockwork, at a certain moment he would unbuckle his gun belt and set it on the table.

On the belt was a holster containing an automatic.

In itself none of this was important. The noncommissioned officer, the Eunuch, was just a lecherous fat man no one spoke about without laughing—even Lotte, Frank's mother.

She knew him, too. The whole neighborhood knew him, since to get to town, where his office must have been, he would cross the streetcar tracks twice a day and head to the Old Bridge.

He didn't live at the barracks. He boarded at Madame Mohr's, an architect's widow, two houses beyond the streetcar line.

He was a neighbor. He was seen at certain hours, always pink and well groomed despite his nights at Timo's. He had a certain smile that seemed knowing to some, but which was perhaps only a baby's.

He would turn to look at little girls, complimenting them and sometimes giving them the candy he always carried in his pockets.

"Bet we'll be seeing him up here one of these days," said Lotte, Frank's mother.

Her business was illegal. She had the right, of course, to run a nail salon here in the Old Basin neighborhood, but it was obvious no one was going to climb three flights of stairs in a building crammed with tenants to have their nails done.

Everybody in the street, in fact everyone in town, knew that there were rooms in back.

The Eunuch, who belonged to the Occupation police, must have known it, too.

"You'll see, he'll come."

Just by looking down at a man from her window on the third floor, Lotte could tell whether or not he would finally come upstairs. She could even predict how long it would take him to make up his mind, and she was usually right.

Embarrassed and awkward, the Eunuch finally did show up one Sunday morning—because of his office hours. Frank happened to be out, and he was sorry he was, because he could watch through the transom by climbing onto the kitchen table.

But he heard about it. There was nobody that day but Steffi, a big gawky girl with dark skin, who just lay there, opened her legs, and stared at the ceiling.

The noncommissioned officer was disappointed, probably because with Steffi there was nothing to be done if you didn't go all the way. She wasn't even artful enough to listen to the stories he told her.

"You're nothing but a hole, my poor girl," Lotte often said to her.

The Eunuch must have expected something else. Maybe he was impotent. In any case he had never left Timo's with a woman.

Or perhaps he got off while fooling around with the girls at Timo's. That was possible. With men anything was possible, as Frank knew from the education he had gotten by standing on the kitchen table, looking through the transom.

So wasn't it natural that—since he had to kill someone sometime—he would choose the Eunuch?

First of all, he knew he had to use the knife that had been

slipped into his hand. It was a handsome weapon, and you couldn't help wanting to try it out, to feel what it was like when it sank into flesh and slipped between bones.

There was a trick he'd been told about—you twisted your hands a little, like turning a key in a lock, once the blade was between the ribs.

The gun belt was on the table, the automatic smooth and heavy in its holster. The things you could do with a pistol! The kind of man you became just having one in your hand!

Then, too, there was this forty-year-old, this Berg, one of Kromer's pals, someone you knew was certainly the real thing. Frank wanted to impress him.

"Lend it to me for an hour and I'll break it in. I bet I'll come back with a pistol."

And so, at that moment, that was all there was to it. Frank knew where he could lie in wait. In the rue Verte, which the Eunuch would have to take to get to the streetcar line from the Old Basin, there was an abandoned old building that was still called the tannery, although nothing had been tanned there for fifteen years. Frank himself had never known the tannery when it was running. People said that once, when it was on contract for the army, as many as six hundred men worked there.

It was nothing now but great bare walls of black brick with high windows, like a church's, opening at least six yards above the ground and with the glass all broken.

An unlit blind alley a yard wide led from the tannery to the street.

The nearest working streetlight—the city was full of twisted, broken ones—was far away, near the streetcar stop.

So it was all too easy, not even exciting. He was there in the alley, his back against the brick wall of the tannery, and except for the shrill whistles of the trains on the other side of the river, around him was nothing but silence. Not a light in a window. Everyone was asleep.

He could see, between the alley walls, a bit of the street, and it looked just like it had always looked in winter months. The snow along the sidewalks formed two grayish banks, one on the side of the houses, the other on the side of the street. Between the two banks was a narrow blackish path that people kept clear with salt or ashes. In front of each house this path was crossed by another leading to the street, which was deeply rutted with tire tracks.

Nothing to it.

Kill the Eunuch.

Men in uniform were killed every week, and it was the patriotic organizations that got into trouble, the hostages, councilmen, notables, who were shot or taken God knows where. In any case, they were never heard of again.

For Frank it was a question of killing his first man and breaking in Kromer's Swedish knife.

Nothing more.

The only problem was that he would have to stand there up to his knees in the crusted snow—since no one had shoveled the alley—and feel the fingers of his right hand slowly stiffening in the cold. He had decided not to wear a glove.

———

He wasn't scared when he heard footsteps. He knew they weren't the Eunuch's, whose heavy boots would have made more of a crunching noise in the snow.

He was interested, nothing more. The steps were too far apart to be those of a woman. It was long after curfew, and while for various reasons that didn't bother people like himself or Kromer or any of Timo's customers, no one in the neighborhood was in the habit of walking around at night.

The man was nearing the alley, and already, even before seeing him, Frank knew, or guessed, who it was, which gave him a certain satisfaction.

A little yellow light was flitting over the snow. It was the electric flashlight the man was swinging as he walked.

That long, almost silent stride—at once soft and astonishingly rapid—that automatically evoked the figure of Frank's neighbor Gerhardt Holst.

The encounter became perfectly natural. Holst lived in the same building as Lotte, on the same floor. The door to his apartment was just opposite theirs. He was a streetcar conductor whose hours changed each week. Sometimes he would leave early in the morning before it was light; other times he would go down the stairs in midafternoon, invariably with his tin lunch box under his arm.

He was very tall. His step was noiseless because he wore homemade boots of felt and rags. It was normal for a man who spent hours on the platform of a streetcar to try to keep his feet warm, yet for whatever reason Frank never saw those shapeless boots of blotting-paper gray—they seemed to have the texture of blotting paper, too—without feeling uncomfortable.

The man was the same grayish color all over, as though made of the same material. He never seemed to look at anyone or to be interested in anything but the tin lunch box under his arm.

Yet Frank would turn his head to avoid meeting the man's eyes; at other times he would make a point of staring Holst aggressively in the face.

Holst was going to pass by. And then?

There was every chance he would keep going straight along, pushing before him the bright circle of his flashlight on the snow and the black path. There was no reason for Frank to make a noise. Pressed against the wall, he was practically invisible.

Then why did he cough just when the man was about to reach the alley? He didn't have a cold. His throat wasn't dry. He had hardly smoked all evening.

In fact, he coughed to attract attention. And it wasn't even a threat. What possible interest could he have in threatening a poor man who drove a streetcar?

Holst wasn't a real streetcar conductor, though. It was obvious that he had come from somewhere else, that he and his daughter had led a different kind of life. The streets and the lines outside bakeries were full of people like that. Nobody turned to look at them anymore. And because they were ashamed of not being like everybody else, they assumed an air of humility.

Still, Frank had coughed on purpose.

Was it because of Sissy, Holst's daughter? That didn't make sense. He wasn't in love with Sissy. She was a sixteen-year-old girl who didn't mean anything to him at all. He meant something to her, though.

Didn't she open the door when she heard him coming up the stairs, whistling? Didn't she run to the window whenever he went out, hadn't he seen the curtain stir?

If he wanted to, he could have her anytime he felt like it. Maybe it would require patience and a show of good manners, but that wasn't hard to pull off.

The astonishing thing was that Sissy certainly knew who he was and what his mother did for a living. The whole building despised them. Not many people said hello.

Holst didn't say anything to them either, but then he never said anything to anyone. Out of pride. No, more out of humility, or because he couldn't be bothered with other people, because he lived with his daughter in a little circle from which he felt no need to step outside. Some people were like that.

He wasn't even mysterious.

Had Frank perhaps coughed out of childish impulse? That was too simple, too pat.

Holst wasn't scared. His step didn't falter. It never occurred to him that someone might be waiting for him in the alley. That was odd, too, since a man would have to have a good reason for flattening himself against a wall in the middle of the night, with the thermometer at ten degrees below freezing.

As he passed the alley, Holst raised his flashlight for an instant, just long enough to light up Frank's face.

Frank didn't bother to raise the collar of his coat or turn his head aside. He stood there in plain sight with that thoughtful and resolute air that he usually had, even when thinking about the most trivial things.

Holst had seen him and knew him. He was no more than a hundred yards from the apartment building. He was taking the key out of his pocket. Because he worked nights, he was the only tenant who had one.

Tomorrow he would learn from the papers—or simply while standing in line in front of some shop—that a noncommissioned officer had been killed at the corner of the alley.

Then he would know.

What would he decide to do? The Occupation authorities would offer a reward, as they always did when one of their own was in question, especially an officer. Holst and his daughter were poor. They couldn't afford meat more than a couple of times a month, and even then only odd scraps they boiled with turnips. From the odors escaping through the doors, you could tell who in the building ate what.

What would Holst do?

He definitely couldn't be happy to have a business like Lotte's going on just across the hall from his apartment, not with Sissy there all day long.

Wasn't this a chance to get rid of them?

Yet Frank had coughed, and not for a moment did he consider abandoning his plan. On the contrary—for a second he mouthed a sort of prayer that the Eunuch would turn the corner of the street before Holst had had time to enter the building.

Holst would hear him, would see him. Perhaps he'd wait a moment with his key in his hand and even see the thing done.

That didn't happen. Too bad—Frank had been excited by the idea. It seemed that there was already a secret bond between him and the man now climbing the stairs in the dark building.

Of course it wasn't because of Holst that he was going to kill the Eunuch. That had already been decided.

It was just that, at that moment, his act had made no sense. It had been almost a joke, a childish prank. What was it he had said? Like losing his virginity.

Right now there was something else he wanted, that he accepted with open eyes.

There was Holst, Sissy, and himself. The noncommissioned officer fell into the background; Kromer and his pal Berg were completely unimportant.

There was Holst and himself.

And it was really as though he had just chosen Holst, as though he had always known that things would turn out this way, because he wouldn't have done it for anyone but the streetcar conductor.

———

A half-hour later, he knocked at Timo's, on the little door at the back of the alley, just like everyone else. Timo himself opened the door. There was hardly anyone left, and one of the girls who had been drinking with the Eunuch was vomiting into the kitchen sink.

"Has Kromer left?"

"Ah! Yes . . . He said to tell you that he had an appointment in the Upper Town . . ."

The knife, carefully wiped, was in Frank's pocket. Timo paid no attention to it and went on rinsing glasses.

"You want something to drink?"

He almost said yes. But he preferred to prove to himself that he wasn't nervous, that he didn't need alcohol. Yet he had had to stab the noncommissioned officer twice because of all the fat larding his back. Now the automatic made a bulge in Frank's other pocket.

Should he show it to Timo? There was no danger. Timo would keep quiet. But that was too easy. It's what someone else would have done.

"Good night."

"Are you sleeping at your mother's?"

Frank was in the habit of sleeping almost anywhere, sometimes in the little building behind Timo's where the girls boarded; sometimes at Kromer's, who had a nice room with a couch; sometimes with others, if things turned out. But there was always a cot for him in Lotte's kitchen.

"I'm going home."

That was dangerous because of the body still lying across the pavement. It would be even more dangerous to make a detour by way of the main street—toward the bridge—since in that direction he might run into a patrol.

The dark heap was still on the sidewalk, half on the path, half in the pile of snow, and Frank stepped over it. It was the only moment he felt frightened. Not only of hearing footsteps behind him but of seeing the Eunuch get up again.

He rang and waited some time for the concierge to push the button at the head of his bed and open the door. He went up the first flights quickly, then slackened his pace, and finally, just as he reached Holst's apartment, where a light showed under the door, he began to whistle to let Holst know it was him.

He didn't go in to see his mother, who was a heavy sleeper. He undressed in the kitchen, where he had turned on the lamp. He lay down. The room smelled so strongly of soup and leeks that it kept him awake.

So he got up, cracked the door into the back room, and shrugged.

Bertha was sleeping there that night. Her big, unappetizing

body was hot. He shoved her aside and she grunted, stretching out her arm, which he had to move to one side to make room for himself.

A little later, when he was about take her, since he couldn't fall asleep, he thought of Sissy, who must be a virgin.

Would her father tell her what Frank had done?

# 2

WHEN BERTHA got out of bed, he woke up a little, opening his eyes just enough to see great flowers of frost on the windowpanes.

In her bare feet, the big girl went to turn on the switch in the kitchen, leaving the door open so that the bedroom was faintly illuminated by the reflected light. And he could hear her at the other end of the room, putting on her stockings, her slip, her dress, then finally going out and closing the door. The next sound would be the scraping of the poker over the grate on the other side of the partition.

His mother knew how to train them. She always made sure one of them slept in the apartment. Not for the clients, since nobody came up after eight o'clock in the evening, when the outside door was locked. But Lotte needed company. What she really needed was to be waited on.

"I starved enough when I was young and stupid to deserve a little comfort now. Everyone gets their day."

It was always the stupidest and poorest girl she kept in the apartment, with the excuse that the girl lived too far away, that there was a fire here, and that she would have a good dinner.

For each of them there was the same dressing gown of violet flannel that usually dragged on the floor behind them. They were invariably between sixteen and eighteen. Older than that, Lotte didn't want them. And, with rare exceptions, she never kept them more than a month.

The clients liked variety. It was pointless to tell the girls in advance. They thought they'd found a home, particularly the ones who were fresh from the country, the ones who almost always came to live in the apartment.

Lotte must have been lying in bed, too, listening like Frank, who was only half asleep, aware of the time, of where he was, of the noises in the apartment and in the street. He was unconsciously waiting for the clatter of the first streetcar, which he would hear a long way off in the frozen emptiness of the streets, picturing its big yellow headlight in his mind's eye.

Then almost immediately came the clank of the two coal scuttles. Mornings were hardest for the girls on duty. One of them—and she had been a strapping big girl, too—had even left because of this forced labor. They had to take the two black iron scuttles down three flights of stairs, down another flight to the cellar, then bring them, full, all the way back.

Everybody in the building got up early. It was like a house of phantoms, since power restrictions and the frequent outages forced people to use only the dimmest electric bulbs. In addition, they had no gas—just the barest flicker, hardly enough to heat their acorn coffee.

Each time the girl went out with the coal scuttles, Frank listened, and Lotte must have done the same from her bed.

Each tenant had his own cellar with a padlock. But who else had any coal or wood?

When the girl came up the stairs with her scuttles full, arms strained and face puffy, doors cracked open as she struggled by. Hard looks were cast at her and her scuttles. Women exchanged loud remarks. Once a tenant on the third floor— he had since been shot, but not for that—had kicked over the scuttles, growling, "Whore!"

From the top of the barracks—and the building really did look like a barracks—to the bottom, they were all muffled up in overcoats and two or three sweaters, most of them wearing gloves. And there were children who had to be gotten ready for school.

Bertha went down. Bertha wasn't afraid. She was one of the few who had held out for more than six weeks, perhaps because she was strong and docile.

But she was worthless for sex. She let out such a strange howl that men were put off.

"A cow," thought Frank.

As, about Kromer, he thought, "A young bull."

They ought to be mated. Bertha lighted the fires in the two stoves as well as one in the bedroom, leaving the door to the kitchen once again ajar. There were four fires in the apartment, more than in all the rest of the building together, all for them alone. Maybe one day people would stand with their backs against the apartment's outer wall to steal a little of their heat.

Did Sissy Holst have a fire?

He knew how it was—he knew about the little blue flames coming out of the gas burners, and only between seven and eight in the morning.

People warmed their fingers on the teakettle. Some rested their feet on the heater or pressed themselves against it. All of them bundled up in whatever old clothes they could find, piling them on their backs, anything on top of anything.

Sissy? Why had he thought about her?

In the building across the street, an even poorer one than theirs since it was older and more dilapidated, people had stuck wrapping paper over the windows to keep out the cold, leaving only small holes in the paper for light and to see outside.

Could they see the Eunuch? Had the body been found?

There wouldn't be any fuss. There never was. Many people had already left for work, and now the women were going out to stand in lines.

Barring an unlikely patrol—they almost never came to the

rue Verte, which led practically nowhere—the first ones, the early risers, who had seen the dark mass lying undisturbed in the snow had probably hurried on to the streetcar stop.

The others, now that it was light, would be able to make out the color of the uniform. They would be in an even greater hurry to get away.

It would be one of the concierges. They were all functionaries of a sort. They couldn't pretend not to have seen anything. Each had a telephone in the hall of his apartment building.

An odor of burning kindling came from the kitchen. Then there was an avalanche of ashes in the other stoves and, finally, the hum of the coffee grinder.

Poor fat stupid Bertha! A little while ago she had stood in her bare feet on the carpet, rubbing her body to smooth away the marks of the sheets on her skin. She hadn't put on her underwear. She was sweating. She was probably talking to herself. Two months earlier, at this same hour, she would have been feeding chickens and probably talking to them in a language they understood.

The streetcar again—its sudden stop at the corner to pour sand on the rails so the brake would hold. You got used to it, and yet you still waited in suspense for it to go away again with its noise like the rattle of scrap iron.

Which of the concierges would be frightened enough to telephone the authorities? Concierges lived in fear. It was their vocation. You could picture this one or that gesticulating in front of two or three carloads of Occupation police.

There was a time when they would have sealed off the entire neighborhood and searched the houses one by one. They'd have taken hostages, too. That time was long past. Men had become philosophers, it appeared, on both sides of the divide. But was there still a divide?

Well, they would go on pretending.

A fat letch was dead. What difference could it make to

them? They must have known he was worthless. The disappearance of the pistol would disturb them much more, because whoever had taken it might have ideas about using it against them.

They were frightened, too. Everybody was frightened.

Two cars, three cars passed, then passed again. Another was going from house to house.

It was for effect only. Nothing would happen.

Unless, of course, Holst decided to talk. But Holst wouldn't talk. Frank had faith in him.

That's it! Now he had the explanation. It wasn't the precise expression perhaps, but it gave an idea of what he had dimly thought the night before: he had faith in Holst.

Holst must be asleep. No. By this time he was up and getting ready to go out. When he wasn't working he stood in the lines.

They had to stand in line, too, at Lotte's, for a few commodities. One of the girls did, that is. But not for everything. There were certain things that were well worth fetching yourself.

All the doors inside were open. The kitchen stove radiated heat through the rooms. If necessary, it would have been enough to heat the whole place. Then the smell of real coffee filled the apartment.

On the other side of the kitchen, opening onto the landing, just to the left of the stairs, was the nail salon. The stove there was always lit.

And each stove, each fire had its own particular smell, its own life, its own way of breathing, its own particular noises. The one in the salon smelled like linoleum and lit the room with its well-polished furniture, upright piano, and embroidered or crocheted doilies on side tables and on the arms of chairs.

"The worst lechers," Lotte always said, "are the bourgeois. And the bourgeois like to do their dirty business in an atmosphere that reminds them of home."

That was why the two manicure tables were so small as to be invisible. And why Lotte taught the girls to play the piano with one finger.

"Like their daughters, you understand."

The bedroom, the big bedroom, as he called it, where Lotte was sleeping at that moment, was swathed in carpets and curtains and strewn with bric-a-brac.

Another thing Lotte always said was, "If I could only hang portraits of their fathers and mothers, wives and children in there, I'd make millions!"

Had they finally taken away the Eunuch's body? Probably. The coming and going of the cars had stopped.

Gerhardt Holst, his long nose blue with cold, shopping bag in his hand, was probably standing motionless and dignified in line somewhere in the neighborhood. Some people accepted that sort of thing, others refused to. Frank hadn't accepted it. He wouldn't stand in line for anything in the world.

"Everyone else does but you," his mother had said to him. She thought he was too proud.

Could anyone imagine Kromer standing in line? Or Timo? Any of those people?

Didn't Lotte have coal? And when Lotte got up in the morning, wasn't food her first thought?

"In my house you eat!" she had once replied to a girl who had never been a prostitute before and was asking how much she would earn at Lotte's.

And it was true. You ate. You didn't just eat, you stuffed yourself. You stuffed yourself from morning to night. There was always food on the kitchen table. A whole family could have survived on their leftovers.

It had become a sort of game to think up dishes that were the most difficult to prepare, dishes full of fat or other ingredients that were almost impossible to find. It was a sport.

"Bacon? Go ask Kopotzki, and say I sent you. Tell him I'll bring him sugar."

And if they wanted mushrooms?

"Take the streetcar and go to Blang's. Tell him . . ."

Each meal was a game. A game and an act of defiance, since everyone in the building got whiffs of the cooking floating through keyholes and under doors. People were almost tempted to leave their doors open. Meanwhile the Holsts put up with a bone garnished with turnips.

What made him keep coming back to the Holsts? He got up. He was sick of lying in bed. He went to the kitchen, rubbing his sleepy eyes. It was eleven o'clock. A girl he didn't know had just arrived, a new one, quiet and proper-looking, who hadn't taken her hat off yet and who was wearing a white, feminine blouse.

"Don't be afraid of helping yourself to sugar," Lotte urged, still in her dressing gown with her elbows on the table, drinking her coffee in little sips.

It was always that way at first. They had to be tamed. In the beginning they didn't dare touch a thing. They looked at a piece of sugar as though it were something precious. It was the same with the milk, with everything. And after a certain time they had to be sent away because they stole from the cupboards. Although, granted, they would have been sent away in any case.

They were well behaved. They sat with their knees together. Most of them wore little tailored suits like Sissy, with dark skirts and white blouses.

"If only they stayed like that!"

That's what the clients liked.

None of this early-morning sloppiness, for instance. Still, who knows? There they were, one big happy family, unwashed, their faces shiny, drinking coffee, eating anything they liked, smoking cigarettes, doing nothing.

"Will you iron my pants?" Frank asked his mother.

And, because the outlet was in the salon, Lotte set up the ironing board there between two armchairs.

What about the Eunuch?

Some of the neighbors were in a panic because of what he'd done, the ones who had seen the body in the snow that morning. Because of it, they wouldn't have an easy moment all day.

Frank's only worry was the automatic. At about nine he had climbed out of bed for a moment with the idea of putting it in the pocket of his overcoat and hiding it later.

But where? And who should he be hiding it from?

Bertha was too easygoing to let anything slip, except out of stupidity.

The other one, the little one in the suit whose name he didn't yet know, would keep quiet because she was new, because she was in their house, and because she was hungry.

As for his mother, he didn't worry about her. He was the boss. She tried to rebel at times, but in the end she knew that she would always do what Frank wanted.

He wasn't tall. In fact, he was short. Once—but that was a long time ago—he had worn high heels, almost as high as a woman's, to make himself look taller. He wasn't big either, though he was well built and square-shouldered.

He was fair-complexioned, like Lotte, with blond hair and blue-gray eyes.

So why were the girls afraid of him? He wasn't even nineteen. There were moments when he seemed like a child. Perhaps he was capable of tenderness. For the most part he didn't bother.

And what was most surprising, given his age, was his poise. When he was still a baby, hardly able to walk, with a big head and yellow curls, people used to say that he looked like a little man.

He never seemed to get excited. He never gesticulated. It was rare to see him in a hurry or angry, and rarer still to hear him raise his voice.

One of the girls, whose bed he had often shared, took his head in her arms and asked him why he was so unhappy.

She refused to believe him when, pulling away, he answered curtly, "I'm not unhappy. I've never been unhappy in my life."

Perhaps it was true. He wasn't unhappy, but he felt no desire to laugh or joke around. He always stayed calm, and maybe that disconcerted people.

And now, thinking about Holst, he was perfectly calm, without the slightest anxiety. He was barely even interested in Holst.

Here everyone drank coffee with sugar in it and real cream. They spread butter and jam and honey on their bread. The bread was almost white. The only other place in the neighborhood to find it was at Timo's.

What did they eat in the apartment across the hall? What did Gerhardt Holst eat? What did Sissy eat?

"You've hardly had any breakfast," remarked Lotte, who had gorged herself as usual.

In the old days, when the others had food, she had often been so hungry that now she was afraid of his not eating enough. She wanted to stuff him like a goose.

He hadn't enough energy to get dressed. Besides, at this hour there was nothing to do outside. He sat around. He watched Lotte carefully ironing his trousers and removing some spots with the tip of her painted nails. Then he followed the new girl with his eyes. He watched her set up the little table with the manicure implements she didn't know how to use.

On the nape of her neck, which was still thin, with very fine white skin that reminded him of a chicken, there were a few stray hairs she kept twisting in an unconscious gesture.

Sissy did the same thing when she was going up or down the stairs.

The new girl called him "Monsieur Frank." Lotte had told her to. Out of politeness he asked her what her name was.

"Minna."

Her skirt was well tailored, the material almost new, and she seemed clean. Had she slept with men before? Probably, or she wouldn't have come to Lotte's. But she probably had never done it with anyone for money.

Later on, when a customer showed up, Frank would climb on the kitchen table. He was sure that after she had taken off her dress she would turn toward the wall. She would finger the straps of her slip for a long time before making up her mind to take it off.

Sissy was just across the landing. At the top of the stairs, there was a door on the right and another on the left before you came to the corridor where there were still more doors. Some tenants had a whole apartment. Others only had one room. There were three more stories above them. You could hear people going up and down the stairs all the time. The women carried shopping bags and packages, and as time went on they had more and more trouble climbing the stairs. There was one who couldn't have been more than thirty, and yet she had fainted on the stairs a few months back.

He had never been in Holst's apartment. He had seen inside many of the others, since the tenants sometimes left their doors open. Some women did their washing in the halls, although it was forbidden by the landlord.

Everywhere during the day reigned a painfully raw, almost frozen light, since the windows were high and wide, and the stairs and halls were painted white, so that the snow outside glared throughout the building.

"Do you play the piano?" Lotte asked the new girl.

"A little, madame."

"Well, then, play something for us."

Lotte had used the formal *vous*. Tonight she would begin to use the familiar *tu*, but she always started out with *vous*.

Lotte was a reddish-gold blonde without a single gray hair; her face was still young. If she didn't eat so much, if she hadn't let herself go, she would still have been very beautiful.

But she didn't care about her figure. On the contrary, she seemed almost delighted to be getting fat. She probably left her dressing gown half open on purpose to reveal her large, very soft breasts, which trembled whenever she moved.

"Your pants are ironed. Are you going out?"

"I don't know."

He would have liked to sleep all day. That was impossible because the bedrooms had to be made up. Sometimes the bell would ring as early as noon. He never met his friends before five o'clock. Nobody he knew really got started until the end of the day, so for hours on end he would lie around doing nothing.

Often, in a bathrobe, uncombed and unshaved, he would sit in the kitchen with his feet against the oven door, reading any book that happened to be lying around. If he wanted to, he would climb on the table when he heard voices in the bedroom.

Today, almost unconsciously, he hung around the new girl playing the piano, and not too badly, either. But actually she wasn't the one on his mind. His thoughts kept coming back to Holst and Sissy, and that annoyed him. He hated when ideas teased him like that, like a fly buzzing around in a storm.

"Somebody rang the bell, Frank."

The piano had almost drowned out the sound. Lotte put away the ironing board and the iron, glanced around the room to see that everything was in order, and said to Minna, "Keep playing."

Then she opened the door a little. Recognizing the caller, she murmured, without enthusiasm, "Oh, it's you, Monsieur Hamling. Come in. Minna, you can go."

And, holding her dressing gown closed with one hand, she pushed a chair forward for the visitor.

"Sit down. Hadn't you better take off your galoshes?"

"I won't stay long."

Minna had joined Frank in the kitchen. In the next room

Bertha was making the bed. The new girl was nervous and uneasy.

"Is it a client?"

"It's the chief inspector of police."

That frightened her even more. Frank remained calm and a little scornful.

"You needn't be scared. He's a friend of my mother's."

It was almost true. The inspector had known Lotte since she was a young girl. Had there been anything between them? Possibly. In any case he was now a man of fifty, well built but without any excess weight. He probably wasn't married. If he was, he never mentioned a wife and didn't wear a wedding ring.

Everybody in the district was afraid of him, except Lotte.

"You can come in, Frank."

"Hello, Inspector."

"Hello, young man."

"Frank, you might offer Monsieur Hamling a little drink. And I'll take one, too, please."

The chief inspector's visits were always the same. He really did seem to have dropped in like a neighbor or a friend. He accepted the chair he was offered and the little glass. He smoked his cigar, unbuttoned his black overcoat, and let out a tiny sigh of satisfaction, like a man delighted to be able to rest for a moment in a cozy atmosphere.

He always seemed to be about to say something or to ask a question. The first few times, Lotte had been sure he was trying to find out what went on in her apartment.

Even if they had been friends in the past, they had been out of touch for years. After all he was the chief inspector of police.

"That's very good," he said, putting his glass down on a small table.

"It's the best you can get these days."

Then he fell silent. The silence never discomfited Hamling. Perhaps he did it on purpose because he knew that it disconcerted others, especially Lotte, who only stopped talking when her mouth was full.

He looked calmly at the open piano with its absurdly homey air, at the two little tables with their manicure sets. He had caught a glimpse of Minna as she left the room to go into the kitchen, and must have known she was a new girl. He had heard the piano from the landing.

What did he think? Nobody knew. They had often discussed it.

He obviously knew about Lotte's activities. Once he had come in the afternoon—that had never happened before—when a client was there, and there was no mistaking the sounds that reached the salon.

Making some excuse about a stew on the stove, Lotte had gone to the kitchen and warned the man not to come out until she gave him the signal.

That time, unexpectedly, Hamling had stayed for two hours for no reason, without any excuse, and with his usual air of paying a polite call.

Did he know Minna? Had her parents been to the police?

Lotte was all smiles. Frank, on the contrary, looked at him coldly and without trying to hide his disdain. Hamling's features and body were hard—he was a man of granite—but the contrast with his eyes, glittering with irony, was striking.

"Those fellows had some work to do in your street this morning."

Frank didn't betray any emotion. His mother only barely kept from glancing at him, as though she sensed her son were somehow involved.

"A fat noncommissioned officer was killed near the tannery. He lay all night in the snow. He had come from Timo's."

All this was said as if casually. He picked up his drink again, warming it in the palms of his hands and sipping it slowly.

"I didn't hear anything," Lotte said.

"There was no gunshot. It was done with a knife. They've already arrested someone."

Why did Frank immediately think, *Holst*!

It was stupid. Even more stupid because the streetcar conductor had nothing to do with anything.

"You might know him, Frank, a young man about your age who lives in the building with his mother. On the second floor, at the end of the hall on the left. He's a violinist."

"I've sometimes seen a young man with a violin case."

"I forget his name. He insists he didn't leave his apartment last night, and his mother, naturally, says the same thing. He says, too, that he's never set foot in Timo's. At any rate, it doesn't matter to us. Those gentlemen are in charge of the investigation. All I've heard is that his violin was a sham, that most of the time the case is full of documents. Apparently he's a member of a terrorist group."

Why did Frank wince? He lit another cigarette. "He seemed sick to me," he said.

It was true. Several times he had passed a tall, lanky young man on the stairs, always dressed in black, wearing a too-light overcoat and holding a violin case under his arm. He had red spots under his eyes and overly red lips, and he would often stop on the stairs to cough his lungs out.

Hamling had said "terrorist," like the occupiers. Others said "patriot." But that meant nothing. Especially when it was an official talking. It was hard to guess what he was thinking.

Did Hamling despise them, his mother and him? Not because of the girls—that was no concern of his. But because of everything else, their coal, their being in with so many people, and because of the officers who frequented the house.

Suppose Kurt Hamling wanted to make trouble for Lotte, what could happen? Lotte would go see some people she knew in the military police, or else Frank would speak to Kromer, who had influence.

In the end the chief inspector would be summoned and ordered to keep quiet.

That was why Lotte wasn't really frightened. Did Hamling know that?

He was sitting in her apartment, warming himself at her fire, drinking her brandy.

What about Holst?

It was easy to tell what most of the tenants thought. They detested and despised Frank and his mother. Their lips curled angrily when they went by.

For some, it was just because Lotte had coal and more than enough to eat. Perhaps they would do the same if they could. For others, especially women of a certain age and fathers with families, it was because of the nature of Lotte's business.

But other cases were different. Frank knew it and felt it. They were the ones who never betrayed what they thought. They never looked at either of them, pretended to ignore their existence.

Was Holst one of them? Was he, like the young man with the violin, a member of the underground?

It wasn't likely. Frank had believed it for a moment because of his calm, his apparent serenity. And also because he wasn't a real streetcar conductor, because he seemed to be an intellectual—perhaps a professor who had been dismissed due to his opinions. Or had he left his post voluntarily because he was unwilling to teach against his convictions?

Outside his hours at work he never left the building, except to stand in lines. No one came to see them.

Did he already know the violinist had been arrested? He would hear about it. The concierge, who knew, would tell all the tenants except Lotte and her son.

Meanwhile, Hamling continued to sit there without saying a word, thoughtfully chewing on his cigar and exhaling little puffs of smoke.

Even if he knew or suspected something, what difference did it make to Frank? He wouldn't dare say anything.

What did count was Gerhardt Holst, who must have returned from his shopping by now and was holed up with Sissy in the apartment across the hall.

They probably had some vegetables, turnips of course, and perhaps a tiny piece of rancid bacon, the kind that was rationed out from time to time.

They saw no one and spoke to no one. What could they have to say to each other, the two of them?

Sissy was always looking out for Frank, parting the curtains to watch him walk away down the street or opening the door a crack when she heard him whistling on the stairs.

Hamling sighed and stood up.

"Another little drink?"

"Thank you. I have to go."

From the kitchen came a tempting odor. He sniffed at it unconsciously as he left, and it floated after him down the hall, perhaps slipping beneath the Holsts' door and into their apartment.

"That old bastard," Frank said calmly.

# 3

FRANK HAD come in to avoid waiting in the street, but he hated places like this. Two steps down and then a tiled floor like in a church. There were old beams in the ceiling, wooden paneling on the walls, an ornately carved bar, and massive tables.

He knew the owner by name, Monsieur Kamp, and Monsieur Kamp must have known him, too. He was a bald little man, quiet and polite, who always wore bedroom slippers. He must have been stocky once, but now his paunch was beginning to hang and his pants had grown too big for him. In this kind of place, which obeyed the regulations or at least seemed to do so to anyone passing by, you were lucky if you could get sour beer to drink.

He felt like a trespasser. At Kamp's there were always four or five regulars, the old men of the neighborhood, who smoked their long porcelain or meerschaum pipes and fell silent when you came in. The whole time you were there they kept their mouths shut, smoking their pipes and staring.

Frank was wearing new thick-soled shoes made out of real leather. His overcoat was warm. Any of these old men could have lived for a month, and his family, too, for the price of his fur-lined kid gloves alone.

He was watching for Holst through the little square windowpanes. It was because of Holst that he had left the building, because he wanted to see him face-to-face. Since the streetcar conductor had come home at twelve the night before, and since it was Monday, he would come down at half past two so as to be at his depot by three.

What had the old men been talking about when Frank came in? It made no difference to him. One of them was a shoemaker with a shop a little farther down the street, but for lack of materials he hardly worked anymore. He must have been eyeing Frank's shoes, appraising them, indignant that the young man didn't even bother to wear galoshes over them.

There were places you could go, no doubt about it, and places where you'd better not set foot. Timo's was the place for him. Not this. What would they say about him when he left?

Holst, too, was one of those big men who had shrunk. They were a race apart and you could spot them at a glance. Hamling, for example, was big but solid. Holst, much taller and with shoulders that must once have been broad, was all droopy now. And it wasn't only his clothes that were worn out and hung loose. His skin had also grown too large. It probably hung from his body in folds, just like it did from his face.

From the very onset of the present situation—and he had been barely fifteen at the time—Frank had felt contempt for abject poverty and for those who submitted to it. It amounted to a revulsion, a sort of disgust, even for the girls, thin and pale, who came to his mother's and threw themselves on their food. Some of them would weep with emotion, fill their plates, and then be unable to eat.

The road where the streetcar ran was black and white, and the snow on it was filthier than anywhere else. As far as the eye could see it was transected by the streetcar rails, black and shining, curving together where the two lines met. The sky was low and too bright, with a luminosity more depressing than any uniform gray. That whiteness, glaring, translucent, had something menacing about it, something absolute and eternal. Under it, colors became hard and mean, the brown or the dirty yellow of the houses, for example, or the dark red of the streetcar that seemed to float in the air. And, opposite Kamp's, in front of the tripe seller's, stretched a long ugly line of people waiting, the women in shawls and the little girls with their skinny legs stamping their wooden soles on the pavement, trying to keep warm.

"What do I owe you?"

He paid. The amount was ridiculous. It was really almost too much trouble to unbutton his coat for so little. The prices in these cafés were absurd. Though it was true—you got what you paid for.

Holst was standing on the curb, all gray, with his long shapeless overcoat, his muffler, and those boots of his tied around his ankles with string. In other times, in other countries, people would have stopped to stare at him, decked out like that, with newspapers stuffed under his clothes for warmth, probably, and that tin lunch box he clasped so tightly under his arm. What kind of food could he be carrying in it?

Frank joined him, as if he, too, were waiting for the streetcar. He paced up and down; a dozen times he came face-to-face with Holst and looked him straight in the eye, exhaling puffs of cigarette smoke. If he threw away the butt, would Sissy's father pick it up? Perhaps not in front of him, for the sake of dignity, although in town people often did, people who were neither beggars nor workingmen.

He had never seen Holst smoke. Had he smoked before?

Frank, annoyed, felt like a loud little dog trying to catch his attention. He prowled around the tall gray figure, and the other man, motionless, seemed unaware of his presence.

Yet last night, Holst had seen him in the blind alley. He knew about the death of the noncommissioned officer. He knew, too, it was almost certain—the concierge had drawn the tenants into his apartment one by one—that they had arrested the violinist from the second floor.

Well, then? Why didn't he do something? Frank was almost

tempted to speak to him, out of defiance. Perhaps he might have, in the end, saying anything that came into his head, if the dark-red streetcar hadn't arrived at that moment with its usual clatter.

Frank didn't get in. There was nothing to do in town at this hour. He had simply wanted to see Holst, and he had—as much as he wanted to. Holst, who had taken his place on the front platform, turned and leaned out for a moment as the car started. He didn't look at Frank but at the building, at his own window, where you could make out the white blur of a face between the folds of the curtains.

This was the way father and daughter said good-bye. After the streetcar had left, the girl remained at the window because Frank was in the street. And Frank suddenly made a decision. Taking care not to look up, he went back into the building, unhurriedly climbed the three flights, and, a weight in his chest, knocked at the door directly opposite Lotte's.

He wasn't prepared, didn't know what he was going to say. He had simply decided to put his foot in the doorway to keep it from closing, but the door didn't close. Sissy looked at him, surprised, and he was almost as surprised to find himself there. He smiled. He didn't often smile. He was more apt to scowl, looking straight ahead with a hard expression on his face even when he was alone. Or else he assumed an air of such indifference that people were chilled by it.

"And yet, when you smile," Lotte would say, "there's nothing people wouldn't do for you. You have the same smile you had when you were two years old."

His smile wasn't intentional; it was because he was embarrassed. Sissy was hard to make out against the light. On a table near the window he noticed some little saucers and some brushes and paint pots.

He entered without speaking because he couldn't help it. He said, no longer looking for an excuse or an explanation for his visit, "You paint?"

"I decorate china. I have to help out my father."

He had seen saucers, cups, ashtrays, and "artistic" candle-holders like these in some of the shops in town. They were bought mainly as souvenirs by the Occupation soldiers. They had flowers painted on them, or a woman in peasant costume, or a cathedral spire.

Why was she staring at him the whole time? If she didn't look at him, everything would be easier. She was devouring him with her eyes, so innocently that it was embarrassing. It reminded him of the girl this morning, Minna, the new one, who was probably busy at that very moment—the way she kept staring at him with a sort of stupid respect.

"Do you do a lot of work?"

She replied, "The days are long."

"You never go out?"

"Sometimes."

"Do you ever go to the movies?"

She blushed. Immediately he seized his chance.

"I'd like to take you to the movies sometime."

Yet it wasn't Sissy who interested him, he now realized. He looked around, sniffed the air, exactly like Hamling when he had come to see them. The apartment was much smaller than Lotte's. The door led straight into the kitchen, where there was a folding cot against the wall. Was that where her father slept, his feet sticking out at the bottom? Through an open door he glimpsed a bedroom, probably Sissy's—the proof was that she looked embarrassed when she saw him glancing that way.

There was a transom like the one in their kitchen, but because it looked into the neighbor's it had been covered with a piece of cardboard.

They were still standing. She had been too scared to ask him to sit down. For something to do, he offered her his cigarette case.

"Thank you. I don't smoke."

"You don't like it?"

There was a pipe on the table and a tin box full of cigarette butts. Did she think he didn't understand?

"Try one of these. They're very mild."

"I know."

She had recognized the foreign brand. These cigarettes meant more than banknotes, and everybody knew what they were worth.

She gave a start when someone knocked on the door. Frank had the same idea she did. Had Holst come back for some reason or other, perhaps because he'd seen the young man at the streetcar stop?

"Excuse me, Mademoiselle Holst . . ."

It was an old man Frank had seen before in the hall, a neighbor, the one whose apartment was on the other side of the transom. He eyed Frank with barely disguised contempt, like something the cat had left on the floor. On the other hand he was gently paternal toward Sissy.

"I came to ask if you might have a match."

"Of course, Monsieur Wimmer."

But he didn't leave. He stood there, holding his hands over the stove, which was going out. He said, in an offhand way, "We're going to have more snow before long."

"That's likely."

"Some people don't have to worry about the cold."

That was for Frank, but Sissy showed him she was on his side by giving him a little wink.

Monsieur Wimmer was about sixty-five and his face was thickly covered with white bristles.

"We'll certainly have more snow before the end of the week," he repeated, waiting for Frank to leave.

Then Frank trumped him: "Excuse me, Monsieur Wimmer . . ."

A minute before Frank hadn't known his name, and the old man stared at him, taken aback.

"Mademoiselle Holst and I were just going out."

Monsieur Wimmer looked at the young girl, convinced she was going to say it wasn't true.

"We are," she said, taking down her coat. "We have an errand to run."

That was one of their best moments. They almost burst out laughing. They were just two children now, playing a prank—and indeed Monsieur Wimmer looked like a retired schoolteacher despite the brass collar-button that could be seen under his Adam's apple. He didn't have a tie to hide it.

Sissy closed the damper on the stove. She retraced her steps to get her gloves. The old man didn't move. It looked like he was going to let himself be shut up in the apartment by way of protest. He watched them go down the stairs, and he couldn't have failed to admire the splendid youthfulness of their steps.

"I wonder if he'll tell my father?"

"He won't."

"I know Papa doesn't like him, but . . ."

"People never tell."

He said this with conviction, because it was true: he knew it from experience. Had Holst turned him in? He was tempted to talk to Sissy about it, to show her the automatic that was still in his pocket. He was risking his life carrying a firearm on him, and she didn't suspect a thing. Once in the street, she asked, "What are we going to do?"

There had been one really extraordinary, completely unexpected moment—when he had replied to the old man and she had taken her coat and they had raced past the unhappy old fellow and down the stairs as if they were going to start dancing there and then.

At that moment she might quite naturally have taken his arm. But now they were in the street and the moment was gone. Did Sissy realize what had happened? They didn't know where to go. Luckily, Frank had mentioned the movies. He said, much too seriously, "There's a good movie at the Lido."

It was across the river. He didn't want to take a streetcar. Not because of her father but because he wouldn't have known how to act. They had to cross over the Old Basin. On the bridge the wind kept them from talking, and he didn't dare take her arm, although she instinctively walked very close to him.

"We never go to the movies."

"Why not?"

He was sorry he'd asked. Because it cost too much, of course. And thinking of money suddenly troubled him. He would have liked, for example, to take her to a pastry shop. There were still a few where, if they knew you, you could get anything you wanted. He even knew two places where you could dance, and Sissy would no doubt have liked that.

She had probably never danced. She was too young. Before it all began, she had been just a little girl. She had never tasted liqueur or an aperitif.

He was embarrassed. In the Upper Town he took her to the Lido, where the electric lights were already on, like fake daylight.

"Two box seats."

And it shocked him to say it. Because he came here often. His friends did the same. When you were with a girl, you took a box at the Lido, everybody did. They were very dark, with sides high enough to make it safe to do almost anything you liked. There were several times when he'd procured girls for Lotte that way:

"Do you have a job?"

"The workshop closed last week."

"Would you like to make a little money?"

Sissy followed him like the others, thrilled to be in the warm theater, to be shown to a box by an usher in uniform wearing a little red cap with the word "Lido" on it in gold letters.

That was going to ruin his mood: she was like all the others. She was acting exactly like all the others. In the dark she turned toward him, smiling because she was happy to be there and because she was grateful, and she said nothing, she hardly even trembled when he put his arm around the back of her chair.

In a bit, that arm would be around her shoulders. She had skinny shoulders. She was waiting for him to kiss her: he knew it, and he did it almost regretfully. She didn't know how to kiss. She kept her mouth half open, and it was all wet, a little sour. At the same time she grabbed his hand and squeezed it hard, and then held on to it as if it belonged to her.

They were all alike. She believed in the picture. She shushed him when he whispered in her ear, because she was trying to understand the movie, having missed the first part, and at certain moments her fingers tightened around his because of what was happening on the screen.

"Sissy . . ."

"Yes . . ."

"Look . . ."

"What?"

"In my hand . . ."

It was the automatic, shining faintly in the half darkness. She shuddered and glanced around. "Be careful!"

It had produced an effect, but she didn't seem that surprised.

"Is it loaded?"

"I think so."

"Have you used it?"

He hesitated. He told the truth.

"Not yet."

Then he seized the occasion to put his hand on her knee, to lift her skirt a little.

Again she didn't object, just like the others. And then suddenly he was gripped by dumb anger—with her, with himself, with Holst. Yes, with Holst, too, though it would have been difficult for him to say why.

"Frank!"

She had said his name. So she knew it. She said it again, on purpose, when she tried to push his hand away.

Now he felt nothing. No, he was furious. Images were dancing before his eyes, enormous faces appeared on the screen and disappeared, black and white, voices, music. What he wanted to know, what he had to find out no matter what she did, was whether she was a virgin, because there was still that to cling to.

That forced him to kiss her, and each time he kissed her she let herself go, she softened, and he gained ground on her bare thigh, where a hand feebly pushed at his, which was groping along the rough groove of her stocking.

He had to find out. Because if she wasn't a virgin, Holst would lose all meaning, all value in Frank's eyes. He would be ridiculous. Frank, too. Whatever had possessed him to have anything to do with either of them?

Her skin must be very white, like Minna's. Chicken skin, as Lotte said. Chicken thighs. Was Minna, at this moment, stark naked in the bedroom, standing in front of a gentleman she had never seen before?

It was warm. His hand crept on. She hadn't the strength to resist forever, and when she lost ground, her fingers would squeeze Frank's gently, like a prayer.

She put her lips close to his ear and stammered, "Frank . . ."

And in the way that she pronounced that word, which he hadn't even had to teach her, she admitted she was beaten.

He would have thought it would take weeks at best, and already he was almost there. It was only a question of inches; the skin grew smoother, warmer, moist.

She was a virgin, and he suddenly stopped. But he felt no pity. He was unmoved.

She was like all the others!

He told himself it wasn't Sissy who interested him, but her father, and it was preposterous to think of Holst while he had his hand where it was.

"You hurt me."

"Pardon me," he said politely.

And suddenly he became formal again, while, in the darkness, Sissy's face must be full of disappointment. If she could have seen him it would have been worse. When he was formal, he was terrible, calm, cold, absent—no one knew how to handle him. At such moments even Lotte was afraid of him.

"At least get mad!" she would say, exasperated. "Go on, yell, hit me, do something, anything!"

Too bad for Sissy. She no longer interested him. Several times lately he had caught himself thinking of those couples walking down the streets, thigh pressed to thigh, of their warm, interminable kisses at every corner. He had sincerely thought that it might be exciting. One detail, among others, had always intrigued him—the steam issuing from the lips of two people, under a streetlight, as they drew close to each other to kiss.

"How about a bite to eat?"

All she could do was follow. Besides, she'd be happy to have some pastry.

"We'll go to Taste's."

"They say it's always full of officers."

"So?"

She would have to get used to the fact that he wasn't just a young man you exchanged love letters with. He hadn't even let her see the end of the movie. He had dragged her out. And when they were outside the pastry shop with its lighted windows, he saw her glancing at him stealthily, with a curiosity already full of respect.

"It's expensive," she ventured again.

"So?"

"I'm not dressed to go there."

He was used to that, too: the too-short, too-tight coats with their sewn-on, hand-me-down fur collars. She would find Taste's full of girls like her. He might have replied that they always showed up there like that, the first time.

"Frank . . ."

It was one of the few doors that still had a neon light around it, this one a very soft blue. The dimly lit hall was thickly carpeted, but here the lack of light wasn't due to poverty. Instead it conveyed an air of luxury, and the liveried doorman was as well dressed as a general.

"Come on."

They went upstairs. There was a shining copper strip on each riser, and the lights along the stairway were imitation candles. From behind mysterious curtains a young woman stretched out a hand to take Sissy's coat. And meekly Sissy asked, "Should I?"

Like all the others! Frank was at home. He smiled at the cloakroom girl, gave her his coat, and stopped in front of a mirror to run a comb through his hair.

In her little black wool dress Sissy looked like an orphan. Frank drew back one of the hangings and disclosed a warm, scented room, pulsing with soft music, full of well-dressed women whose complexions vied with the bright braiding of the men's uniforms.

For a moment she felt like crying, and he knew it.

Who cared?

———

Kromer arrived very late at Timo's, at ten-thirty. Frank had been waiting for him for more than an hour. Kromer had been drinking, which the unnatural tautness of his skin, the brilliance of his eyes, and the violence of his gestures immediately made obvious. He almost knocked over his chair when he sat down. His cigar smelled wonderful. It was even better than the ones he usually smoked, and he always bought the best available.

"I've just had dinner with the commanding general," he announced in a low voice.

After that he was silent to let the meaning of his words sink in.

"I brought you back your knife."

"Thanks."

He took it without looking and dropped it into his pocket. He was too preoccupied with his own doings to think much about Frank. But remembering their conversation yesterday, he asked out of politeness, "Did you use it?"

Frank had returned to Timo's the night before, after it happened, for no other reason than to show Kromer the pistol he had just acquired. He had shown it to Sissy. There were a good many people he would have shown it to willingly, and yet, without quite knowing why, he answered, "I didn't get the chance."

"Perhaps that's just as well. Tell me—you don't know where I could find some watches, do you?"

No matter what Kromer talked about, he always seemed to be discussing important and mysterious matters. He was the same way with everyone he knew, the people with whom he ate and drank. He seldom mentioned names. He would whisper, "Someone very high up. You understand, very, very high up . . ."

"What kind of watches?" Frank asked.

"Old ones, preferably. Piles of them. Watches by the shovelful. You don't get it, huh?"

Frank drank a lot, too. Everybody drank a lot. First of all, obviously, because they spent most of their time in places like Timo's. And because good drinks were scarce, hard to find, and fantastically expensive.

Unlike most people, Frank's face never got red, he never spoke in a loud voice, never waved his arms. Instead his face turned paler, his features more pointed, and his lips so thin that they looked like a line drawn by a pen across his face. His eyes would grow small, with a hard, cruel light in them, as though he hated the whole human race.

That was probably true.

He didn't like Kromer and Kromer didn't like him. Kromer, who so easily took on a genial, cordial manner, didn't like anyone, but was ready to humor people who admired him, keeping his pockets full of all sorts of things, rare cigars, cigarette lighters, ties, and silk handkerchiefs, that he would offer when least expected.

"Go on, take it!"

Frank would have trusted Timo sooner than Kromer. And he noticed that Timo didn't place too much confidence in Kromer, either.

Kromer did a lot of trafficking, of course. Some of his deals got talked about, and he filled you in on the details because he needed you, and in that case he would hand over a very fair share of the profits. He had lots of connections among the Occupation forces. That, too, was profitable.

Exactly how far did he go? How far would he be capable of going if he had to, if his interests were at stake?

No, Frank wouldn't mention the automatic. He preferred to discuss watches, because the word had awakened memories in him.

"It's for the person I just mentioned, the general. Do you know what he was just ten years ago? A worker in a lamp factory. He's forty now and a general. We drank four bottles of champagne between us. Right away he began talking about his watches. He collects them. He's crazy about them. He claims he has several hundred. 'In a town like yours,' he said to me, 'where there have always been a lot of rich bourgeois, officials, people with independent incomes, there must be piles of old watches. You know the kind,' he said, 'made of silver or gold with one or more cases. Some of them strike the hour. Some of them even have little people that move around...'"

While Kromer was talking, Frank was thinking of old Vilmos's watches; he could see old Vilmos again in that room, always dimly lit, where the sunlight trickled in through the closed blinds, winding up the watches one by one, putting them to Frank's ear, making them strike, making the tiny automata move.

"We could get anything we wanted out of him," sighed Kromer, "considering his position, you understand ... It's his passion. He practically drools over them. Somewhere he read that the king of Egypt has the finest collection of watches in the world, and now he'd give anything for his country to declare war on Egypt."

"Fifty-fifty?" Frank asked bluntly.

"You know where to find watches?"

"Fifty-fifty?"

"Have I ever tried to cheat you?"

"No. But I'll need a car."

"That's more difficult. I could ask the general, but that might not be a smart thing."

"No ... A civilian car. Just for two or three hours."

Kromer didn't ask for details. He was a lot more prudent than he liked people to think. Since Frank was offering to get the watches, he preferred not to know where they came from, or how Frank was going to get them.

Still, he was curious. What he was even more curious about was Frank himself, the way he had of making a decision so calmly.

"Why don't you just pick one up in the street?"

Naturally that would have been the simplest thing to do, and at night, for the fifteen or twenty miles he would have to drive, there'd be practically no risk. But Frank didn't want to admit he couldn't drive.

"Just find me a car and someone you're sure of, and I'm almost positive I can get the watches."

"What did you do today?"

"I went to a movie."

"With a girl?"

"Of course."

"Did you feel her up?"

Kromer was a letch. He chased girls, especially poor ones because that was easier, and he liked them very young. He loved to talk about it, nostrils twitching, lips thick, using the crudest terms, relishing the most intimate details.

"Do I know her?"

"No."

"Will you introduce me?"

"Maybe. She's a virgin."

Kromer wriggled in his chair and moistened the end of his cigar. "Do you want her?"

"Not particularly."

"Then let me have her."

"I'll see."

"Is she young?"

"Sixteen. She lives with her father. Don't forget about the car."

"I'll give you the answer tomorrow. Meet me at Leonard's around five."

That was another bar they went to, in the Upper Town, but because of where his place was, Leonard had to close at ten every night.

"Tell me what the two of you did at the movies . . . Timo! A bottle. Go on, tell me."

"The usual. Her stocking, her garter, then . . ."

"What did she say?"

"Nothing."

He was going home. There was a chance his mother had kept Minna in. Lotte didn't like to let them go out the first few days, because some of them never came back.

He would go to her, and, after all, it would be just like it was Sissy. In the dark he wouldn't know the difference.

# 4

HE WALKED with his hands in his pockets and his coat collar turned up, his breath visible in the cold air, along the brightest street in town, but even here there were great patches of darkness. The meeting was in half an hour.

It was Thursday. It had been on Tuesday that Kromer had spoken to him about the watches. Wednesday, when Frank had joined him at five o'clock at Leonard's, Kromer had asked him, "Do you still want to do it?"

To older people, it must have seemed strange to see them, so young and talking together so seriously. God knows they were deciding serious things! Frank caught sight of himself in one of the mirrors of the café, calm and blond, his overcoat well cut.

"Did you get the car?"

"I'll introduce you to the driver in a second. He's waiting across the street."

It was a cheaper and noisier establishment, but you could still get pretty good drinks here. A man stood up. He was twenty-three or twenty-four, very thin, and in spite of his leather jacket he looked like a student.

"That's him," Kromer said, indicating Frank. Then he said, "Carl Adler. You can trust him. He's all right."

They had a drink, because that's what you did.

"And the other guy?" Frank asked in a low voice.

"Ah! Yes. Will he have to . . ."

Kromer hesitated. He hated to speak plainly and there were

certain words it was better never to say, words that people had, out of superstition, erased from their vocabulary.

"Will there be any . . . rough stuff?"

"Not likely."

Kromer, who knew everybody, glanced around the café, found a certain face in the smoke, and disappeared onto the sidewalk, taking someone with him. When he came back, he was accompanied by a young fellow who looked working class. Frank didn't catch his name.

"What time do you think you'll be through? He has to be back at his mother's by ten o'clock. Later than that and the concierge won't open the door, and his mother is sick and often needs him in the night."

Frank had almost decided to give the project up, not because of this second man, but because of the first, Adler, who hadn't opened his mouth the whole time they were alone together. Frank wasn't sure, but he could have sworn he'd seen him with the violinist from the second floor. Where, he couldn't remember. Maybe it was only an impression. It was enough to bother him.

"When do you want to meet?"

"As soon as possible."

"Tomorrow? What time?"

"Eight o'clock in the evening. Here."

"Not here," Adler interposed. "My car will be in the back street, opposite the fish market. All you'll have to do is hop in."

When they were alone, Frank couldn't help asking Kromer, "You're sure they're okay?"

"Have I ever introduced you to anyone I wasn't sure of?"

"What does he do, this Adler?"

A vague gesture. "Don't worry about it."

It was odd. You suspected someone and trusted him at the same time. Perhaps it came from the fact that people had, more or less, a hold on one another, and everyone, if you looked hard enough, had something on his conscience. In short, if you hadn't been betrayed, it was because the other fellow was afraid you'd betray him first.

"And the little girl? Have you thought about it?"

Frank didn't answer. He didn't tell him that on that very day, Wednesday—he had taken her to the movies on Tuesday— he had seen Sissy again. Not for very long. And not right after Holst had left. He had watched him from the window going toward the streetcar stop.

He had waited until four o'clock. Finally, shrugging his shoulders, he had said to himself, *We'll see.*

He knocked on the door as though he was just passing by. On account of the old fool lying in ambush on the other side of the transom, he had no intention of going in. He simply said, "I'll wait for you outside. Will you comedown?"

He didn't have to wait long. She came. She ran the last few yards over the sidewalk, glancing up automatically at the windows of the building, then, automatically too, slipping her hand through his arm.

"Monsieur Wimmer didn't speak to my father," she announced right away.

"I was sure he wouldn't."

"I can't stay out very long."

They never could stay on the second day.

It was just beginning to grow dark. He drew her into the blind alley. She offered her lips to him and asked, "Have you been thinking about me, Frank?"

He didn't do anything to her. He just slipped his hand inside her blouse because the day before, at the Lido, his mind wasn't on her breasts and he still didn't know what they were like. The question had crossed his mind at night, when he was in bed with Minna, who hardly had any.

Was that it, curiosity, that had prompted him to knock at Sissy's door and ask her to come down?

He had seen her again today at the same time, but today he said, "I only have a few minutes."

She didn't question him, though he knew she wanted to. Making a little face, she murmured, "Do you think I'm ugly, Frank?"

Again, just like all the others, though he would have been at a loss to say whether he found any young girl ugly or not.

Well, it didn't matter. He wouldn't promise Kromer anything, but he wouldn't say no. He would wait and see. Minna insisted she was in love with him, that she was ashamed now of what she had to do with the clients. She hadn't been lucky with the first one. More complications! Frank had done his best to calm her. On top of everything else, she was worried about him. She had seen the gun, and it had terrified her.

Today he had had to promise to wake her up, no matter what time he came in.

"I won't go to sleep before then," she promised him.

She already smelled like the other women in the house. Probably due to the regime Lotte put them through and the soap she provided. Whatever the case, the transformation was quick. And all morning she had wandered around the apartment in a black chemise trimmed with lace.

He had made up his mind to meet Adler and the other man without seeing Kromer again, but at the last moment he didn't. Not so much because of Kromer but because he felt the need to cling to something stable, familiar. The crowds in the streets always frightened him a little. You saw, in the light of the shop windows and streetlamps, faces that were too pale, with features too drawn and eyes that had a fierce, vacant look. Most were a mystery. But worst of all were the dead eyes. As time went by, you saw more and more people with eyes that were dead.

Was he thinking of Holst? It wasn't exactly the same thing. Holst's eyes weren't full of hate, and they weren't empty. But you felt no contact was possible and that was humiliating.

He pushed open the door into Leonard's. Kromer was there with a man who looked different from both of them. It was Ressl, editor in chief of the evening paper, always accompanied by his bodyguard with the broken nose.

"You know Peter Ressl?"

"I know his name. Everyone does."

"My friend Frank."

"Delighted."

He held out a long, bony, very white hand. Maybe yesterday evening it had been Carl Adler's hands that had upset Frank. They looked like Ressl's.

Ressl's family was one of the oldest in town, and his father had once been a councillor of state. They had been ruined even before the war, but it was in their mansion that the Occupation authorities had set up headquarters. Not a month went by that those gentlemen didn't ask for something.

It was said that Councillor Ressl, who could be seen slipping among the houses like a shadow, had never spoken a word to them, and that anyone else in his place would have been shot or hanged by this time.

Peter, a lawyer who had once had something to do with the movies, was quick to accept the post of editor in chief of the evening paper. He was probably the only person in the whole region to have obtained, for some mysterious reason, a permit to cross the border. He had gone to Rome, Paris, London. The dark suit he wore that evening had come from London, and he was ostentatiously smoking English cigarettes.

He was a nervous, unhealthy-looking fellow. Some said he took drugs. Others said he was a homosexual.

"I thought you had urgent business," said Kromer—obviously very proud to be seen with Ressl but worried by Frank's presence at this hour. "What'll you have?"

"I only stopped in for a minute to say hello."

"Have something to drink. Bartender!"

A few moments later, when Frank was leaving, Kromer took something out of his pocket and slipped it into his hand.

"You never know . . ."

It was a flat bottle full of brandy.

"Good luck. Don't forget about the little girl"

———

They barely exchanged a word. The car was in fact a small truck. Carl Adler was waiting in the driver's seat, his foot on the clutch.

"Where's the other guy?" Frank asked uneasily.

"Back there."

Of course. He had seen the reddish glow of a cigarette in the darkness in the rear of the truck.

"Where to?"

"Cut through town first."

They caught glimpses of familiar places as they passed. They even drove by the Lido, and for a moment Frank thought of Sissy sitting under her lamp, painting flowers and waiting for her father to come home.

The man in the back was probably a worker, as Frank had noted yesterday. He had big, dirty hands and a face that, with a good wash, would have resembled Kromer's, except that it was franker and more open. He wasn't nervous. Though he had no idea what they were going to do, he didn't ask any questions.

Carl Adler didn't, either. But he had an unpleasant way of only looking straight ahead. The profile he presented to Frank was too self-consciously indifferent, with an expression of dislike, and certainly of condescension.

"And now?"

"Take a left."

Since no car could drive around without a permit from the authorities, who were tricky to deal with, Adler must work for them. Lots of people played a double game. One had just been shot. He had been seen every day in the company of high-ranking officers, and was so notorious that the children used to spit on the sidewalk when he went by. Now they called him a hero.

"Take another left at the next intersection."

Frank was smoking cigarettes and passing them back to their friend in the rear, who must have been sitting on the spare tire. Carl Adler said he didn't smoke. Too bad for him.

"When you see a pylon, go right and up the hill."

They were coming to the village now, and Frank could have found the rest of the way with his eyes closed. He might have said "his" village, if there had been anything anywhere in the world that belonged to him. It was here that he had been raised, where Lotte, who had had him when she was nineteen, had put him out to nurse.

There was a fairly steep hill beyond which lay what they called the lower houses, almost all small farms. Then the road widened out into a sort of large square, paved with cobblestones that made the truck bounce. The church was behind the pond, really nothing but a large water hole, with the cemetery, where the gravedigger—was it still old Pruster?—always struck water with his shovel less than a couple of feet down.

"I don't bury them, I drown them!" he would say after a drink or two.

The headlights illuminated a pink house with two life-size painted angels on the gabled roof. The whole village was painted like a plaything. There were pink houses, green houses, blue houses. Almost all had a little niche with a porcelain virgin in it, and there was a feast day once a year when candles were lit in front of all the statuettes.

Frank was emotionless. He had decided, when Kromer had

spoken to him about the watches, that it wasn't going to mean anything to him.

It was, instead, a stroke of luck. He owed those people nothing, he owed nothing to anyone. It was easy to give a child candy and to talk to him in a ridiculous baby voice.

He had lived here until he was ten, and his mother had come to see him every Sunday, in summer at least—he remembered her big white straw hats. There wasn't a more beautiful woman in the world. His wet-nurse, every time Lotte came, would cross her red hands over her stomach in an ecstasy of admiration.

Lotte didn't always come alone. Five or six times there had been a man with her—a different one each time, with a reserved air, at whom she glanced uneasily. She'd say with affected gaiety, "And this is my Frank!"

It never seemed to work out, for one reason or another. When she put him in school in town as a boarder, Frank had understood, and begged her not to come see him anymore in the visitors' parlor, although she always brought him presents.

"But why?"

"No reason."

"Have your little friends said something to you?"

"No."

She wanted him to be a doctor or a lawyer. It was an obsession.

Luckily the war had come and the schools closed for a few months. When they reopened, he was past fifteen.

"I'm not going back to school," he announced.

"Why, Frank?"

"Because."

He never knew whether it was because he reminded her of someone, but even as a small boy he had noticed that when he assumed a certain expression, his mother wouldn't insist. As if terrified, she would let him have his way.

His "closed" expression, she always called it.

Since then, life had been so complicated for everyone that Lotte didn't mention his education again. They had got into the habit of saying, "Later, when it's all over."

And it went on. And he was a man now. It wasn't so long ago that, during an argument in which he was the calmer of the two, he had tossed back at her, quite calmly, with his eyes like two pinpricks, "Whore!"

Now just as calmly he ordered Adler, "Stop."

A little off the square. There was a street to the right where a car wouldn't be noticed. Anyway, there was no one around. Hardly any lights shone in the windows, since the villagers kept their shutters tightly closed. You could scarcely imagine any life going on inside. The windows of the school were dark, too. How many panes of glass in those five windows had he broken with a ball!

"Coming?" he said to the man in the back.

And the latter, rough but friendly, replied, "Call me Stan." Then, slapping his empty pockets, he added, "Your pal said not to bring anything. That right?"

Frank had his automatic, which was enough. Adler would wait for them in the car.

"You sure?" Stan asked, trying to catch his eye.

Adler sneered as if disgusted and said, "That's what I'm here for!"

The snow crunched under their feet more noisily than in town. Gardens could be made out behind the houses, pine trees, hedges silvered with ice. The Vilmos house was to the right, set back a little from the square.

The house showed no light, but the rooms where they lived were in the back.

"Let me handle this."

"Fine."

"We may have to frighten them."

"Sure."

"We may have to get a little rough."

"Okay!"

It was years since he had been here, but it was impossible for his feet not to follow in his old footsteps. The watchmaker Vilmos and his watches, and his famous garden, these were perhaps his most vivid childhood memories.

Even before reaching the door, he seemed to recognize the smell of the house, which had always had old people in it, since as far as he was concerned the watchmaker Vilmos and his sister had never been young.

Frank took a dark handkerchief out of his pocket and tied it around his face below his eyes. Stan was about to protest.

"You don't need one. They don't know you. But if you like . . ."

He handed him a similar handkerchief; he had thought of everything.

He still remembered Mademoiselle Vilmos's cakes, like nothing else that he had ever eaten, tasteless, thick, decorated with pink-and-blue sugar. She always kept them in a box with pictures from the adventures of Robinson Crusoe on it.

And she insisted on calling him "my little angel."

Vilmos must be over eighty now, his sister around seventy-five. It was hard to tell exactly, since children have a different way of judging age. For him they had always been old, and Vilmos had been the first person he had ever seen who could remove all his teeth at once, since he wore dentures.

They were misers, brother and sister, each as bad as the other.

"Should I ring the bell?" asked Stan, who was uneasy standing there in the deserted square under the moonlight.

Frank rang, surprised to find the bell rope so low, when once he had had to stand on tiptoe to reach it. He held his automatic in his right hand. His foot was ready to keep the door from closing, like the first time he had gone to Sissy's. Footsteps could be heard inside, a sound like in a church. He remembered that, too. The hall, long and wide, with dark walls and mysterious doors like those of a sacristy, was paved with gray tiles, and two or three were always loose.

"Who is it?"

It was the voice of old Mademoiselle Vilmos, who was afraid of nothing.

"The priest sent me," he replied.

He heard the chain being pulled back. He pushed his foot against the door as it opened, his pistol at his waist. He said to Stan, who suddenly seemed awkward, "Go on!" Then to the old woman, "Where's Vilmos?"

God, how tiny and gray she was! She clasped her hands and stammered in her cracked voice, "But, my good sir, you know very well he's been dead for a year."

"Give me the watches."

He remembered the hallway, the dark-brown wallpaper that was supposed to imitate Cordova leather and where traces of gold were still visible. The shop was to the left, with the workbench where Vilmos used to sit, bent over his watches, the little jeweler's glass with the black rim screwed in his eye.

"Where are the watches?" He added, nervously, "The collection." Then, raising the automatic, "Get it now!"

Could it all go wrong? He hadn't foreseen that Vilmos might be dead. With him it would have been easy. The watchmaker was such a coward that he would have given up his watches without a word.

The old bag was made of different stuff. She had seen the automatic, all right, but you felt that she was still looking for a way out, that she wouldn't give in, that she would fight to the end, taking her last chance.

Then he heard a voice, Stan's—Frank had forgotten about him. From deep in his throat, he drawled, "Maybe we could help her remember."

He must have done this before. Kromer obviously hadn't

chosen a novice. Maybe he hadn't been entirely sure about Frank.

The old woman had flattened herself against the wall. A pitiful yellowish-gray lock of hair hung over her face. She had held out both arms, her hands flat against the imitation-leather walls.

He repeated almost mechanically, "The watches . . ."

He hadn't had much to drink and yet things seemed to be happening as if he were drunk. Everything was blurred, confused, with only certain details standing out, exaggeratedly clear: the lock of yellowish-gray hair, the hands flat against the wall, the old hands with their big blue veins . . .

Usually so deliberate, he must have moved too quickly turning to say something to Stan, and the handkerchief slipped down. Before he could pull it up over his face, she exclaimed, "Frank!" Adding immediately—it was really too ridiculous—"Little Frank!"

He repeated, his voice hard, "The watches!"

"You'll find them. You always got what you wanted. But don't hurt me—I'll tell you . . . Oh God! Frank! Little Frank!"

She seemed reassured, but at the same time even more frightened. She had lost her immobility. Her mind was beginning to work again. She trotted off down the hall, toward the kitchen, where Frank noticed a wicker armchair with an orange cat curled up in a ball on a red cushion.

She seemed to be talking to herself, or praying, her bony limbs rattling about in her baggy old clothes.

Was she just stalling? She cast a furtive glance at Stan, probably wondering if it wouldn't be easier to rouse his pity.

"What do you need them for? When I think about my poor brother, he used to be so happy to show them to you, he used to hold them up to your ear and make them strike one after the other, and I always had candy for you . . . There's no candy to be found anymore . . . You can't find anything . . . I'd be better off dead . . ."

She began to cry, the way she always did, but it could be just a trick.

"The watches!"

"He moved them from place to place, with all the things going on. He's been dead a year and you never knew! If he were here, I'm sure..."

What was she so sure of? It was too absurd. It was time to put an end to it. Adler must be getting impatient and would be likely to leave without them.

"Where are the watches?"

She still found time to poke at a log in the fireplace and turn her back on him, intentionally he was sure, before spitting out, "Under the tile..."

"Which tile?"

"*You know perfectly well.* The cracked one. The third."

---

Stan stayed in the kitchen to watch the old woman while Frank went to look for something to pry the tile loose. She had offered him coffee. Frank vaguely heard her saying, "He used to come almost every day, and I always had cakes for him in that box over there." Then she added, lowering her voice as if she hadn't been talking to a man with a handkerchief tied around his face, "My Lord, monsieur, can he have become a robber? And armed, too! Is the pistol loaded?"

Frank had found the watches, all in their cases, covered with old sacking. He called out sharply, "Stan!"

It was over now. They only had to leave. Stupidly, the old woman stammered, "You don't think he'd like a cup of coffee?"

"Stan!"

She clung to them, following them into the hall.

"Oh Lord, who ever would have thought! I who..."

They only had to leave, to go back to the car that was

waiting two hundred yards away. Even if she could shout loud enough to rouse the neighbors, it wouldn't matter, since there wasn't a car in the village that had any gas, and the telephones didn't work at night.

He cracked open the door and saw the square bathed in moonlight, without a trace of life. He said to his companion, "You go on ahead . . ."

And the other knew what that meant. The old woman had seen Frank's face. She knew him. There were times when you could count on the protection of the Occupation forces. Other times, you never knew why, they wouldn't lift a finger to help you, and the police were quick to take advantage. No matter how well you thought you knew them, their behavior remained a mystery.

No one was safe.

Stan started walking away, holding the sack full of watches in his arms. You could hear the crunching of the hard snow.

The door closed behind him. He must have heard a dull report. Then the door opened again. He saw a rectangle of yellow light that narrowed before disappearing altogether.

Footsteps came up to him. A hand out of the darkness took hold of the sack again.

Then, just before reaching the car, while there were still only the two of them, Stan said, "An old woman!"

His remark found no echo, and in the car Frank passed back his pack of cigarettes and curtly ordered, "Back to town."

He was going to have a bad time, but he knew it wouldn't last long. He had been all right until he got into the car. Until then he had kept his nerves under control.

He went to pieces suddenly. Not badly. The others didn't notice. It was inside him, a sort of trembling, a spasm. He had to make an effort to keep his hands from shaking, and it seemed like there was a bubble of air trying to escape from his chest.

He rolled down the window. The cold air on his forehead made him feel better. He breathed greedily.

Only the appearance of lights when they neared town began to calm him. And he hadn't touched the flask of brandy Kromer had slipped into his pocket.

It was almost over. It had been purely physical. He had almost felt the same thing with the Eunuch, but not as strongly.

He was satisfied. He had had to go through it once and for all, and now it was done. With the Eunuch it didn't count. It hadn't meant anything. Just practice, you could say.

And it was odd, but it seemed to him now that what he had just done was an act whose necessity he had felt for a very long time.

"Where do I drop you off?"

Did Adler suspect what had happened? He couldn't have heard the shot. He hadn't asked any questions. He had just pushed the sack at their feet aside so he could drive.

Frank was about to say, "My place."

Then prudence got the upper hand again.

"Timo's. But not too near."

He thought about it and decided not to go to Timo's first. It would be better not to give Kromer all the watches at once. His haul would be safer in the house behind Timo's, where the bar girls lived.

Just before they reached town, he thrust his hand into the sack, groped around for some of the cases he'd recognized, pulled one out, and slipped it into his pocket.

He was feeling fine. He would be glad to see Kromer. He would be glad to have a drink.

The car barely stopped, then pulled away again without him. He walked down the alley, went into the room of one of the girls who would be away at Timo's. He pushed the sack under the bed after slipping his gun in. He hadn't had time to clean it.

The moment was almost solemn. He recognized the lights, the faces, the smell of wine and brandy, Timo waving to him from the bar.

He walked slowly, looking short and squat in his big, thick overcoat, his face relaxed, a subdued light in his eyes. Kromer wasn't alone. He was never alone. Frank knew his two companions and preferred not to talk in front of them.

He leaned over Kromer.

"Can I see you for a moment?"

They went into the bathroom, and without a word Frank put the case with the watch in it into Kromer's hand. In spite of the darkness in the car, he had chosen the right one. It was the big blue case containing a watch with a porcelain face and a shepherd and a shepherdess engraved on the back.

"Just one?"

"I have at least fifty, but you'll have to talk to him first and find out where we stand."

Had the evening left its mark on him? In the car on the way back, Adler had avoided looking at him, and their shoulders hadn't brushed even once.

Kromer too seemed different, embarrassed. He was afraid to ask questions and avoided Frank's eyes, glancing at him surreptitiously.

The other times they had discussed a job, he had been the boss. He had been careful to let Frank know it.

But now he didn't argue. He was in a hurry to get back to the main room. He said tamely, "I'll try to see him tomorrow."

Then, as he was sitting down again, "You want a drink?"

As a matter of fact, Frank had forgotten to return his flask of brandy. He hadn't touched it, and now, handing it over, he looked him straight in the eye.

Did Kromer understand?

Then he went home to Minna's bed and made love so furiously that she was frightened.

She understood, too. They all did.

# 5

HE SPENT the day in the kitchen with his feet on the oven, unshaved, unwashed, reading a Zola paperback. Did his mother suspect anything? Ordinarily by noon she was urging him to wash up because there was only one bathroom and in the afternoon it was needed for the clients and the girls.

Yet today she said nothing. She must have heard the racket that he had made in the night with Minna, and Minna looked tired and very worried. She spent her time either at the window, as though expecting to see the police, or with her eyes fixed on Frank, amazed that he was worried only about the cold he said he'd caught.

As for him, he swallowed some aspirin, put drops in his nose, and stubbornly returned to his book.

Sissy must be waiting for him. Several times, especially after Holst left, Frank had found himself looking at the alarm clock over the stove, but he hadn't stirred. There had been a lot of coming and going in the apartment as usual, voices behind the doors, noises he knew so well. But he wasn't curious enough to climb onto the table and look through the transom. Minna, completely naked, her hand on her belly, face haggard, had come to get a hot-water bottle but couldn't attract his attention.

He got dressed at last, once night had fallen. He went by the Holsts' apartment. He could have sworn he saw the door move, that Sissy was there ready to open it, but he went calmly downstairs, smoking his cigarette, which tasted to him like menthol.

Kromer didn't arrive at Leonard's until after seven. He tried to hide his excitement.

"I've seen the general."

Frank remained stock-still.

Kromer named a very large sum. "Half for you and half for me, and I'll take care of the others."

Already Kromer was trying to treat him the way he used to, acting like an important man, very busy.

"I want sixty percent," Frank decided.

"All right."

Kromer figured that it really didn't matter, since Frank wouldn't see the general and wouldn't know how much he really paid.

"On second thought, fifty percent as agreed. Only I want a green card."

Kromer didn't have one. If Frank asked for one, it was because it was the hardest thing to get. It was extremely rare to see one. A man like Ressl might have one, but even then he wouldn't flash it around. In the hierarchy, first came permits for automobiles, then the ones that authorized a person to be out at night, finally those that allowed the bearer to go into certain forbidden zones.

The green card, with photograph and fingerprints, the signatures of the commandant of the armed forces and the chief of the political police, required all authorities to give the bearer free passage to "accomplish his mission without hindrance."

In other words, no one had the right to search you. At the sight of a green card, patrols stood at attention, apologized profusely, and were vaguely uneasy.

And the astonishing thing about it was that it had never crossed Frank's mind until his talk with Kromer. The idea came to him all of a sudden while they were discussing percentages, and he had started wondering what other exorbitant demands he could make.

And even more astonishingly, Kromer, after a moment of stupefaction, didn't burst out laughing or protest.

"I can try."

"Your general can take it or leave it. If he wants his watches, he knows what to do."

He would have his card, he was certain.

"The little girl?"

"Nothing new. It's all right."

"Have you touched her again?"

"No."

"Will you let me have her?"

"Maybe."

"She's not too thin, is she? Is she clean?"

Frank was almost sure now that the story about the strangled girl in the barn was just make-believe. It was all the same to him. He despised Kromer. And it was amusing to think that a man like Kromer was going to pull every string to get him a green card that he would never dare to ask for himself.

"Tell me, who is this Carl Adler?"

"The driver of the car? I think he's a radio engineer."

"What does he do?"

"He works for them, locating underground transmitters in the telegraph office. You can trust him."

"I hope so."

And Kromer kept coming back to his obsession. "Why don't you ever bring her here?"

"Who?"

"The little girl."

"I told you, she lives with her father."

"What difference does it make?"

"We'll see. Maybe I'll get around to it."

People must think he was hard. Even his mother was afraid of him. Yet he was capable of great tenderness, lapsing into a daydream while staring at a splash of greenish color, as he was now. It was nothing—part of the background of a decorative wall panel at Leonard's. It showed a meadow, and each blade of grass was distinct, the daisies had all their petals.

"What are you thinking about?"

"I'm not thinking about anything."

It was a question his wet-nurse used to ask him long ago. So had his mother, when she came to see him on Sundays.

"What's my little Frank thinking about?"

"Nothing." He answered angrily because he hated being called "my little Frank."

"Say, Frank! If I get that green card for you . . ."

"You'll get it."

"All right. Supposing. Then we could really pull something off, right?"

"Maybe."

That night he knew his mother had understood. He came home early because he was coming down with a bad cold, and he had always been afraid of being sick. They were sitting in the front room, the one they always called the salon. There was fat Bertha darning stockings, Minna with a hot-water bottle on her belly, and Lotte reading the paper.

They were all three so still and silent in the sleeping house that they looked like a painting. It was surprising to see their lips move.

"Home so soon?"

The paper must have reported what had happened to Mademoiselle Vilmos. There was no longer much fuss made over attacks of that sort, since they happened every day. But even if there had been only three lines on the last page, Lotte wouldn't have missed them. She never missed information about people she had known.

She must have understood part of the truth and guessed the rest. Even the noise he had made with Minna the night before must have come back to her. Knowing men the way she did, she would have found a special significance in a detail like that.

"Have you had dinner?"

"Yes."

"Would you like a cup of coffee?"

"No, thanks."

She was afraid of him. She walked on eggshells around him. It had always been like that, though not as flagrant or obvious.

"You're sniffling."

"I have a cold."

"Why not have some hot rum and let me cup you?"

He agreed to the rum but not the cupping. He had a horror of those little glasses that his mother had a perfect mania for putting on her girls at the slightest sign of a cough, leaving round pink or brown spots on their skin.

"Bertha!"

"I'll go," Minna said quickly, a sudden pain twisting her face as she rose.

It was warm and peaceful, Frank's cigarette smoke gathered around the light, the fire roared—there were four fires roaring in the apartment—while a very fine snow had once again started to drift lazily through the darkness outside the windows.

"You really don't want anything to eat? There's some liver sausage."

In the end, words meant nothing. They served only as a means of contact. He understood that Lotte simply needed to hear his voice, to see if anything about it had changed.

Because of the old Vilmos woman!

He smoked his cigarette, leaning back in a deep red-velvet armchair, legs stretched out toward the fire. The oddest thing was that he sensed guilt in his mother. If she had recognized his footsteps in time, would she have hidden the newspaper? Had he intentionally come up the last steps on tiptoe?

The truth is, he hadn't been thinking of Lotte, but of Sissy, afraid that she might open her door a crack.

This time of night she was alone with her saucers. Did she go to bed while waiting for her father to come home? Or stay up, all alone, till midnight?

He had been afraid, he admitted to himself, of seeing the door open and of being forced to go in, of being alone with her in the dimly lit kitchen with, perhaps, the remains of her supper on the table.

At night she must fold out the cot. And the door to her bedroom would be left open for the heat.

It was all really too lousy. Too sad, too ugly.

"Why don't you take off your shoes? Bertha!"

Bertha came to take them off. Sissy, too, would have taken them off, going down on her knees without hesitation.

"You look tired."

"It's my cold."

"You ought to get a good night's rest."

Again he understood. It was like automatically translating from a foreign language. Lotte was advising him to sleep alone, not to have sex. There was one thing she didn't know yet and that he was only beginning to realize himself: he didn't want Minna or Bertha or even Sissy.

A little later she saw to it that his bed was properly made up.

"Will you be warm enough?"

"Yes."

He wasn't going to sleep there. Tonight he would sleep in anybody's bed, even an old woman's. He needed to feel someone next to him.

And Minna, who hadn't had any experience at all when she first arrived and whose thighs still curved on the inside like a little girl's—Minna seemed to have learned everything in three days. She made a place for his head in the hollow of her arm. She was careful not to talk. She stroked him gently, like a woman nursing her child.

———

His mother knew. There was no longer any doubt. The proof was that the next morning the newspaper had disappeared. And there was a little thing he noticed that she would have refused to admit. When she kissed him, as she did every morning, she recoiled slightly. She checked herself instantly and all of a sudden was more affectionate than usual.

He would get his green card, he was sure. For someone else, that would represent an extraordinary success, a goal you hardly dreamed of attaining, since it made you equal to a section chief on the other side.

He could have been a section chief.

He had tried to enlist in the beginning, when they were still fighting with tanks and cannons, and they had sent him back to school.

For a long time he had hung around the sixth-floor tenant, a bachelor of about forty with a huge brown mustache and mysterious ways. He turned out to be the first to be shot.

Had the violinist been shot already, or deported? Had they tortured him? No one would ever know, probably, and his mother would be at wit's end from then on, like so many others. She would keep at it for a while, waiting in lines, knocking on office doors and being sent on her way, then no one would see her anymore, everyone would stop thinking about her, and, one fine day, the concierge would decide to call in a locksmith.

They would find her in her room, dead for the past week or two.

He didn't feel pity, not for anyone. Not even for himself. He didn't ask for pity, didn't accept it, and that was what irritated him about Lotte, whose eyes brooded over him, anxious and tender at the same time.

What interested him was talking to Holst, just once, at

length and alone. That desire had been gnawing at him for a long time, even when he was still unconscious of it.

Why Holst? He didn't know. Maybe he would never know. He refused to think that it was because he had never had a father.

Sissy was stupid. That morning while she was cleaning, Bertha had found an envelope addressed to Frank slipped under the salon door. In the envelope was a sheet of paper with a question mark in pencil and the signature: "Sissy."

Because she hadn't heard from him yesterday! She had wept. She had believed her life was over. Just for that, just because of her insistence, he decided not to see her, to go alone to the movies, if he had to, while waiting for his appointment with Kromer.

But she was even more determined than he thought. He was hardly on the stairs—and he had been careful not to make any noise—when she came out, with her coat and hat on, which showed she had been waiting for hours behind the door, ready to leave the whole time.

He couldn't do anything. He waited for her on the sidewalk, where the falling snowflakes melted on his lips.

"Don't you want to see me anymore?"

"Of course I do."

"You've been avoiding me for two days."

"I never avoid anyone. I've been busy."

"Frank!"

Was she thinking about the old Vilmos woman, too? Was she smart enough to have connected him with the story in the paper?

"Why don't you trust me?" she reproached him.

"I do trust you."

"You don't tell me about the things you do."

"Because it's not a woman's business."

"I'm frightened, Frank."

"Of what?"

"Frightened for you."

"What good could that do you?"

"Don't you understand?"

"Yes."

It was beginning to get dark. A fine snow was falling, and when a fine snow like that kept coming down for days you found yourself desperately waiting for a blizzard—big flakes that would purge the sky and let the sun through, if only for a moment. Like after a summer thunderstorm.

"Come with me."

They walked along arm in arm. Girls always liked that.

"Your father hasn't said anything to you?"

"Why?"

"He doesn't suspect anything?"

"It would be terrible if he suspected."

"You think?" Frank's skepticism shocked her.

"Frank!"

"He's a man like any other, isn't he? He's made love, too, hasn't he?"

"Be quiet!"

"Is your mother dead?"

She hesitated, awkward. "No."

"They're divorced?"

"She left him."

"Who for?"

"A dentist. Let's not talk about it, Frank."

They had passed the tannery. They reached the Old Basin, which—before the dam was built—had once been an anchorage. There was very little water in it now and the old boats that had been left there, God knows why, were slowly rotting away, some of them upside down. In summer, where they were walking was a grass-covered embankment where the neighborhood children came to play.

"Was he good-looking, this dentist?"

"I don't know. I was too young."

"Did your father try to get her back?"

"I don't know, Frank. Let's not talk about Papa."

"Why?"

"Because!"

"What did he do, before?"

"He wrote books and magazine articles."

"Books about what?"

"He was an art critic."

"Did he go to museums?"

"He knew all the museums in the world."

"And you?"

"A few."

"Paris?"

"Yes."

"Rome?"

"Yes. And London, Berlin, Amsterdam, Berne . . ."

"Did you stay at good hotels?"

"Yes. Why do you ask?"

"What do you do when you're together, the two of you?"

"Where?"

"At home, when your father has finished driving his streetcar."

"He reads."

"And you?"

"He reads aloud. He explains what he reads."

"What does he read?"

"All kinds of books. Poetry, often."

"You like that?"

How she wanted to talk about something else! She sensed him stiffen, that he detested her. There was no use in her leaning more heavily on his arm, twining her fingers around his. He pretended not to understand.

"Come on!" he suddenly decided.

"Where are you taking me?"

"Nearby. To Timo's. You'll see."

It wasn't yet the hour for Timo's. There was no music. The people you saw there now were making deals with Timo or with one another. There were no women. And the colors of the walls and the lampshades seemed garish. It was like going into a theater in the middle of the day while a rehearsal was going on. It was almost as if such a place couldn't exist at this time of day.

"Frank . . ."

"Sit down."

"I wish you'd taken me to the movies."

Because of the darkness, right? But that was just what he didn't want at the moment. Not the sour taste of her saliva. Not running his fingers along her garter.

"He doesn't mind not seeing anyone?"

It took her a moment to understand that he was still talking about her father.

"No. Why should he mind?"

"I don't know. Were you rich, before?"

"I think so. I had a governess for a long time."

"Does it pay well, driving a streetcar?"

She groped for his hand under the table, begging, "Frank!"

Ignoring her, he called out, "Timo! Come here. We'd like something especially good. Appetizers to start with. Then lamb chops with french fries. And you can begin by bringing us a bottle of Hungarian wine, you know the one."

He leaned toward her. He was going to talk about her father again. The telephone rang. Timo, wiping his hands on his white apron, answered it, looking at Frank.

"Yes . . . Yes . . . I can find that . . . Not too much, no, but not cheap . . . Who? I haven't seen him today . . . But your friend Frank is here . . ."

He put his hand over the receiver and said to Frank, "It's Kromer. Do you want to speak to him?"

Frank got up and went to the telephone.

"Is that you? Did you make out all right? Good...
Yes...I'll get them to you tonight. Where are you now?
... At home? You're dressed? Alone? You'd better drop by our
friend Timo's...I can't explain...What?...Something like
that...No, not today! You'll have to be satisfied with just
looking... From a distance...No, I tell you! If you make a
fool of yourself, you'll spoil everything..."

When he sat down again, Sissy asked, "Who was that?"

"A friend."

"Is he coming here?"

"Of course not."

"I thought you asked him to come."

"Not now...Tonight."

"Listen, Frank..."

"What now?"

"I want to go."

"Why?"

Thick lamb chops with fries were brought to them on a
silver dish. It must have been months, years since she had
eaten fries, to say nothing of breaded chops trimmed with
frilled paper.

"I'm not hungry."

"Too bad."

She didn't dare tell him she was frightened, but he sensed
she was.

"What is this place?"

"A restaurant. A bar. A nightclub. It's anything you like.
It's heaven. It's Timo's."

"Do you come here often?"

"Every day."

She tried to chew the meat, couldn't, put down her fork,
and sighed as though from weariness. "I love you, Frank."

"Is that such a catastrophe?"

"Why do you say that?"

"Because you say it with such a tragic air, like it was a catastrophe."

Looking straight ahead of her, she repeated, "I love you."

And he wanted to say, *Well, I don't love you.*

Then he forgot about it, since Kromer had come in, with his fur-lined coat, his big cigar, his air of being—here as everywhere—the principal actor. Without seeming to recognize Frank, he went to the bar and lifted himself onto one of the stools with a sigh of contentment.

"Who's that?" Sissy asked.

"What difference does it make?"

Why was she instinctively afraid of Kromer? He looked at them, looked at her, especially at her, through the smoke of his cigar, and when she bent her head over her plate he took the opportunity to wink at Frank.

She started eating mechanically, perhaps out of embarrassment, so as not to meet Kromer's eyes, and she ate so conscientiously that she left nothing on her plate but the bones. She even ate the fat. She wiped her plate clean with her bread.

"How old is your father?"

"Forty-five. Why?"

"He looks sixty."

He sensed the tears coming to her eyes, which she tried to hold back. He sensed the anger in her struggling with another sentiment, and her desire to leave without a word, to walk out of the restaurant alone, without looking back. Would she even be able to find the exit?

Kromer, very excited, kept casting glances at Frank that grew more and more significant.

Then Frank gave a little affirmative nod of his head.

The agreement was made.

So that was that. Too bad!

"There's cake with mocha icing."

"I'm not hungry anymore."

"Bring two mochas, Timo."

At that moment, Holst was driving his streetcar. The big headlamps could have been part of him, shining out of his belly, as the car pushed forward, casting a puddle of light on the snow and on the two gleaming black tracks ahead. His little tin lunch box was there near the controls. Perhaps he took an occasional bite out of his sandwich, chewing slowly, his feet in the felt boots tied around his legs with string.

"Eat."

———

"You really believe you love me?"

"How can you ask such a question?"

"If I asked you to go away with me, would you do it?"

She looked straight into his eyes. He had taken her home and now they were in her apartment. She was still wearing her hat and coat. The old man next door must be listening behind the transom. He would come. They didn't have much time.

"Would you like to go away, Frank?"

He shook his head, no.

"If I asked you to sleep with me?"

He had intentionally used an expression that would shock her.

She still looked at him steadily. It was as though she wanted him to see down to the very depths of her blue eyes.

"You want to?" she said slowly.

"Not today."

"Anytime you want."

"Why do you love me?"

"I don't know." There was a catch in her voice, and her glance wavered. What had she been about to reply? There had been different words on the tip of her tongue.

He wanted to know, yet he was afraid to insist. He was a

little scared of what she might say. Maybe he was wrong. He would have sworn—it was stupid, since there was nothing to make him think so—he would have sworn that she had been on the point of saying, "Because you're unhappy."

And it wasn't true. He wouldn't let her or anyone think that. Besides, why should she care?

Their neighbor had stirred. They could hear him breathing outside the door. He hesitated, then knocked.

"Excuse me, Mademoiselle Sissy. It's me again . . ."

She couldn't help smiling. Frank left, growling a vague good night. He didn't go to his apartment. Instead he went down the stairs two at a time and headed toward Timo's.

"Tonight?" asked Kromer, his mouth watering.

Frank gave him a stony look. "No."

"What's the matter?"

"Nothing."

"Have you changed your mind?"

"No." He ordered a drink, but he wasn't thirsty.

"When?"

"Before Sunday night, in any case, because Monday her father's on the morning shift and he'll be home in the late afternoon."

"Have you spoken to her about it?"

"She doesn't need to know."

"I don't understand." Kromer was a little uneasy. "You want . . . ?"

"Of course not. But I have an idea. I'll explain when the time comes."

His eyes had narrowed. His head ached. His skin was clammy, and every now and then he shivered, like someone coming down with the flu.

"Have you got the green card?"

"You'll have to come to the department with me tomorrow to get it."

And then the conversation turned to watches.

What possessed him later on, a little before midnight, to loiter around in the street just to see Holst come home?

He had no intention of sleeping at Lotte's. Without letting her know, he went to Kromer's, where he sank down on the couch.

## PART TWO
## SISSY'S FATHER

# PART TWO
# SISSY'S FATHER

# 1

MINNA was ill. They had put her on the cot usually reserved for Frank, and they shifted her from place to place, depending on the time of day, because there wasn't much room for a sick person in the house. They couldn't very well let her go home to her parents in the state she was in, and they couldn't call a doctor.

"It was that Otto again!" Lotte told her son.

His real name was Schonberg. And his first name wasn't Otto. Almost all the clients had a nickname, especially if they were very well known, like Schonberg. He was a grandfather. Thousands of families depended on him, and people bowed in fear to him on the street.

"He always promises me to be careful, and then he goes and does it again."

Minna was there with her red rubber hot-water bottle, being pushed from room to room, spending most of her time in the kitchen, looking ashamed, as though it was all her fault.

Then there was the matter of the green card, which had involved a lot of running back and forth, since at the last moment quantities of documents were needed and five photographs instead of the three Frank had taken with him.

"Why is your name Friedmaier, like your mother's? You should use your father's name."

The redheaded official with coarse orange skin seemed to think that was suspicious. He, too, was afraid of responsibility. Kromer had to telephone the general from the poor man's own office.

Frank got his card at last, but it had taken hours. He still looked feverish, but he wasn't running a temperature. Lotte kept glancing at him surreptitiously. She wondered why he had become so animated all of a sudden.

"You'd better rest in bed for a day or two."

He had also found a girl to take Minna's place on Saturday, the busiest day of the week at Lotte's. He knew where to go. He knew several places.

All that had taken time. He had been constantly busy and yet, during those two days, time had seemed to drag.

There was still the dirty snow, piles of it that looked like they were rotting, stained black, peppered with garbage. The white powder that loosed itself from the sky in small handfuls, like plaster falling from a ceiling, never managed to cover up the filth.

He had gone to the movies with Sissy again. By that time everything had been decided, all arrangements made between him and Kromer. Sissy, of course, knew nothing.

The same day he had asked his mother, "Are you going out on Sunday?"

"Probably. Why?"

She went out every Sunday. She went to the movies, then to eat pastry and listen to music.

"Will Bertha be going to her parents'?"

The house was usually closed on Sundays. Bertha would go see her parents, who lived in the country and thought she worked as a housemaid for a nice family.

Only Minna would be in the apartment. Nothing could be done about that.

As soon as they were seated at the movies—it was Friday—Sissy had asked, like a little girl begging for something, "Is it all right if I do this?"

She shifted in her seat a little, pushed Frank's arm out of the way, took off her hat, and buried her head in the hollow of his shoulder.

She almost purred, there was such an innocent satisfaction in her first little sigh.

"You're not uncomfortable? I'm not bothering you?"

He said nothing. Maybe she kept her eyes closed the whole time while he, this time, watched the film.

He hadn't touched her that afternoon. The idea of kissing her troubled him. She had suddenly pressed her lips against his, just once, a little before they reached their building. Then, just as she was leaving, when they were a step apart, she said very quickly, "Thank you, Frank."

It was too late. Everything had in a way already begun. On Saturday the military police had come to search the apartment of the violinist and his mother. Frank had just stepped out when they arrived. When he came home, he could sense even from outside that there was something wrong with the building, though exactly what he couldn't tell. At the entrance a plainclothesman was talking to the concierge, who was trying to act natural.

When Frank reached the first landing—he had gone out to telephone Kromer—he found several men in uniform, three or four of them, who were keeping the housewives from going up to their apartments while preventing the other tenants from leaving.

Everyone was silent. It was deathly quiet. Other uniforms could be seen in the hall. The violinist's door was open—had they brought him back to be present at the search? There were noises of furniture being smashed and, at times, an old woman's pleading voice, beyond tears.

Frank had calmly taken out his green card, which he hadn't used yet, and everyone saw it, everyone knew what it meant. The soldiers stood back to let him pass. The silence behind him had grown even more oppressive.

He had done it on purpose. And the day before, he had brought Minna a dressing gown. He hadn't bought it in a shop; it was a long time since the shops had had any quilted satin dressing gowns. In any case, he couldn't be bothered to actually go into a shop.

His pockets had been stuffed with the money—he didn't know what to do with it all—that he had received as his share for the watches, enough large bills to feed an ordinary family, even two or three families, for years. At Timo's, as often happened, someone had been unpacking merchandise in one corner, and Frank had bought the dressing gown.

He half-believed he was buying it for Sissy. Not exactly, of course, since everything had been decided down to the smallest detail already. It was something he couldn't explain. He would give it to Minna, that was understood, but it wouldn't stop him from thinking about Sissy. Lotte would be furious. She would insist it looked like they were apologizing to Minna for her accident with that brute Otto.

It was the first time he had ever bought anything for a woman, something personal, and, crazy or not, the fact remained that he had Sissy partially in mind.

There was all that. Then there had been the replacement for Saturday—she had arrived already and was ill-tempered. What else had happened?

Nothing . . . Always this touch of a cold lingering, not getting any worse, this persistent headache, a vague discomfort in every part of his body that couldn't actually be called illness. The sky white as a sheet, whiter and purer than the snow, which looked as though it had hardened and on which there fell only a little icy dust.

Sunday morning he had tried to read. Then he had gone over to the window and stood looking out through the frosted panes at the empty street for so long, remaining so motionless, that Lotte, more and more uneasy about him, had grumbled, "You'd better take your bath while there's still hot water. Bertha is waiting her turn. If she goes first, the water will be lukewarm."

Since the rooms wouldn't be used that day, Lotte wanted

to install Minna in the bed in the little room, so she was surprised when her son said brusquely, "No. Put her in the big bedroom."

Lotte sensed something. She knew he was expecting someone. She must have guessed it was Sissy. That was why she wanted the big bedroom free, thinking it would please him. She gave up.

"Whatever you want! You're planning on staying in?"

"I don't know. In any case, I'd prefer it if you didn't come home too early."

As for Minna, she was idiotically grateful for the dressing gown, which she insisted on wearing in bed that day. She mistook it for a gesture of affection on his part. And for that very reason, before his bath, Frank seized Bertha, pushed her down across the foot of the bed, and took her. As usual in the morning she had nothing on over her big babyish body but a nightgown.

It didn't last more than three minutes. He did it angrily, as if seeking revenge. His cheek never brushed the girl's cheek. Their heads never touched. When it was over, he left her without a word.

During all this time an appetizing smell of cooking floated through the apartment. At last everybody was washed and dressed. They ate. Lotte was dressed almost like she used to be when she came to see him in the country; she had barely aged a day. He suspected she had started her so-called nail salon, and given up receiving men herself, for his sake.

She didn't need to be ashamed on his account.

Bertha, who had to make connecting trains, was the first to leave. Then Lotte powdered her face, looked at herself in the mirror, and hung around a while longer for no reason, still anxious.

"I think I'll have dinner in town."

"I'd prefer that."

She kissed him once on each cheek, then a second time on

the first cheek, a thing that he detested because it reminded him of his wet-nurse. It was a mania with some people. Mechanically he counted, "Two . . . three!"

She went out and also waited for the streetcar at the corner. He knew that Minna, troubled about spending the whole day in the double bed in the big bedroom—at night it was Lotte's—couldn't keep her mind on the Zola novel he had loaned her.

She was waiting, without quite daring to expect it, for him to come to her, talk to her. She too had heard him knock on the door of the Holsts' apartment.

She wouldn't allow herself to be jealous, or at least to show it. She knew she wasn't a virgin, that she had come to Lotte's of her own free will, that she had nothing to hope for.

Nevertheless, after an hour, she tried a little ruse. She began by breathing hard, then she let out a little groan and allowed her book to fall to the floor.

"What's the matter?" he came in to ask.

"It hurts."

He took the hot-water bottle and filled it in the kitchen, put it back on her belly, and, to show her that he didn't want to talk, picked up the book and laid it on the quilt beside her.

She didn't dare call him back. She couldn't hear him moving around. She wondered what he was doing. He wasn't reading, since all the doors were open and she would have heard him turning the pages. He wasn't drinking. He wasn't sleeping. Only from time to time he would go to the window and stand there for a minute.

She was frightened for him, and she knew that was the best way to repel him. He was old enough to know what he was doing. He was doing what he wanted to do. And he was doing it coldly. Once he had even gone over to the mirror to look at himself furtively, wanting to make sure his face was perfectly composed.

Hadn't he attracted Holst's attention, in the blind alley, when it wasn't necessary, when otherwise there would have been no witness to his act?

And, with the old Vilmos woman, had he used any tricks or ruses?

He wouldn't accept pity from anyone. Or anything that resembled pity. He never wanted to be the sort of coward who feels pity for himself.

That was what they would never understand, none of them, neither Lotte nor Minna nor Sissy. And in a little while Sissy would be out of the picture.

What had she been thinking, with her head on his shoulder all through the movie? Sometimes she lifted her head a little and asked, "I'm not bothering you, am I?"

His arm had fallen asleep, but nothing could have induced him to admit it.

Kromer wouldn't understand either. He didn't understand even now. Deep down Kromer was worried, although he wasn't going to say so. Worried about everything and nothing. Frank troubled him. Frank had his green card in his pocket and they were barely out of the offices of the military police when Kromer had asked him, "What are you going to do with it?"

And Frank had taken malicious pleasure in replying, "Nothing."

Kromer didn't believe him. He tried to guess what Frank was scheming. He was no more reassured about the situation with Sissy. "You really haven't touched her?"

"Only enough to know she's a virgin."

"That doesn't do anything for you?" Then Kromer pretended to laugh, adding with a wink, "You're still too young!"

Kromer had seemed so ill at ease that Frank spent a good part of the afternoon wondering if he would show up. He was excited about Sissy. He must have tossed and turned all night thinking about her. But he was liable to panic at the last moment and go to Leonard's or somewhere and get drunk instead of keeping the appointment.

"Why didn't you tell her the truth?"

"Because she wouldn't have agreed."

"You think she's in love with you? That's what you mean?"

"Maybe."

"And when she finds out?"

"I guess it will be too late."

In reality they were all a little bit afraid of Frank because he was willing to do what had to be done.

"What if her father shows up?"

"He can't leave his streetcar and it runs on Sunday."

"If the neighbors . . . ?"

Frank preferred not to mention Monsieur Wimmer, who knew too much and might decide to interfere.

"The neighbors are always out on Sunday. If necessary the sight of my card will shut them up."

That was true, broadly speaking. But there were fools who had let themselves be arrested for less than that, for the pleasure of shouting an insult in front of their friends at soldiers going by. And they were almost always people like Monsieur Wimmer.

Wimmer hadn't said anything to Holst so far. Perhaps because he didn't want to worry him, or because he thought he was clever enough to look out for Sissy himself. Or again, perhaps because he was convinced that she was a good enough girl not to get herself in trouble. Old people were like that. Including the ones who had had a child before they were married. Later on they forgot.

Minna let out another sigh. It was dark now. Frank thoughtfully went in to turn on her light, draw the curtains, and fill her hot-water bottle for the last time.

He would have preferred that she wasn't there. He didn't want any witnesses. So what? Wasn't it better, in fact, that someone should know, someone who would say nothing?

"Is she coming?" Minna asked.

He didn't reply. If he had picked the back room it was, first of all, because it had a door that opened right into the hall. And you could get to it from the kitchen.

"Is she coming, Frank?"

That was in bad taste. In front of his mother she called him "Monsieur Frank." It annoyed him that she should be less formal when they were alone, and he replied impatiently, "It's none of your business."

She seemed contrite, but then almost immediately she asked, "Will it be her first time?"

No, not that, of all things! No sentimentality, please! He had a horror of girls who felt sorry for other girls who hadn't gone through the things they had. Was she going to ask him, in another minute, to promise not to hurt Sissy?

Luckily, Kromer rang just then. He had come after all. He was even ten minutes early, which was irritating because Frank didn't want to talk. Kromer had just had a bath. His skin, too pink, too smooth, smelled like a whore's.

"Are you alone?"

"No."

"Your mother?"

"No." And out loud, on purpose, "There's a girl in the next room who got her plumbing wrecked by some bastard."

It wouldn't have taken much for Kromer to run away, but Frank was careful to shut the door behind him.

"Come in. Don't be frightened. Take off your coat."

He noted scornfully that Kromer wasn't smoking his usual cigar but sucking a mint instead.

"What'll you have?"

Kromer was afraid of drinking, which might affect his performance.

"Come into the kitchen. That's where you'll wait. In our house it's the holy of holies."

Frank sniggered like a drunk, and yet the glass of brandy

he clinked against Kromer's was the first drink he'd had today. Happily his companion didn't know it. He would probably have been really terrified if he did.

"There it is. It'll happen the way I told you."

"What if she turns on the light?"

"Have you ever known a girl who wanted the lights on?"

"What if she speaks to me and I don't answer?"

"She won't speak."

Even those ten minutes were long. He followed their slow passage on the face of the alarm clock over the stove.

"Make sure you can find your way in the dark. Follow me. The bed's to the right there, just as you come in the door."

"I see."

Frank had to make him another drink, otherwise Kromer would lose his nerve. And he mustn't lose his nerve at any cost. Frank had arranged the whole thing like clockwork, with the minute care of a child.

There were things that couldn't be explained, that it was useless to try to ask someone else to understand. It was absolutely necessary for this to happen. Afterward he would be all right.

"Got it?"

"Yes."

"To the right, as soon as you go in."

"Yes."

"I'll turn out the light."

"What about you? Where will you be?"

"Here."

"You swear you won't leave?"

And to think that just ten days ago he had regarded Kromer as an older, stronger man, in short, as a man, while he himself was nothing but a child.

"It's really no big deal," he said contemptuously, to bolster Kromer's flagging courage.

"Of course it isn't, Frank . . . It's for your sake. I don't know the house. I don't want to . . ."

"Hush!"

———

She had come. Like a mouse. And Frank had such keen ears that he heard Minna get up and, barefoot, noiselessly, in her pretty dressing gown, go listen at the door. So from her bed Minna had heard the Holsts' door open and close. What had made her go look, probably, was that this time there hadn't been any footsteps going downstairs.

Who knew? Anything was possible. Maybe Minna had seen another door, one that wasn't quite closed, move a bit, maybe old Wimmer's. Frank was sure old Wimmer was on the lookout.

But Minna didn't know that. On second thought, Frank was sure she didn't, because if she had she would have been so frightened for him that she would have come running to tell him.

Sissy slipped along the hall, her feet hardly touching the uneven floor. She knocked, or rather scratched, at the door of the little bedroom.

He had turned out the light. If they spoke, Kromer could hear from the kitchen.

She said, "I'm here."

He felt her rigid in his arms.

"You asked me to, Frank."

"Yes."

He shut the door behind her, but there was still the one into the kitchen that she couldn't see because of the darkness. It was ajar.

"You still want to?"

They could see nothing except the dull reflection, through the curtains, of the gaslight on the corner lamppost.

"Yes."

He didn't have to undress her. He began to, and she continued on her own, standing beside the bed, not saying a thing.

Perhaps she hated him without being able to keep from loving him. He didn't know. He didn't want to know. Kromer could hear them. Frank said, and the words he forced out with such difficulty sounded stupid, "Tomorrow it would have been too late. Your father is on the morning shift."

She must be naked. She was naked. He could feel the soft heap of her clothes under his feet. She was waiting. Now came the hardest part: laying her down on the bed.

She groped for his hand in the dark. She murmured, and it was the first time her voice uttered his name with that intonation. Fortunately, Kromer was waiting behind the door.

"Frank!"

Then he said, very quickly, very softly, "I'll be right back."

He brushed against Kromer as he passed. He almost had to shove him into the room. He closed the door at once with a haste he would have been at pains to explain. He stood there, motionless.

There was no more town, there was no more Lotte, no more Minna, no more anyone, no more streetcars on the corner, no more theaters, and no more universe. There was nothing but an emptiness rising around him, an anxiety that made beads of sweat stand out on his temples and forced him to put his hand to the left side of his chest.

Someone touched him and he almost screamed. It took all his strength not to. He knew it was Minna, who had left the door of the big bedroom ajar, from which a bit of light filtered.

Could she see him? Had she been able to see him when she came in, before waking him with her touch, the way one wakes a sleepwalker?

He kept his mouth shut. He hated her, he loathed her for

not having uttered one of the stupid expressions they all knew so well how to use.

But no! She just stood there beside him, as stiff and pale as he was, in a halo of dim light that made it impossible to distinguish any features, and not until much later did he realize she had put her hand on his wrist.

It was as though she were taking his pulse. Did he look ill? He wouldn't allow her to look at him as though he were ill, to look at him at all, to see what no one had the right to see.

"*Frank!*"

Someone shrieked his name. Sissy had shrieked it. Sissy had shrieked his name to him; Sissy was running in her bare feet, shaking the handle of the hall door, crying for help, trying to escape.

It was perhaps because the other girl, whom Frank didn't like, whom he despised, who was nothing but a prostitute, less than nothing—it was perhaps because Minna kept stupidly holding his wrist that he didn't budge.

Now there was an uproar in the room, like the day the military police had searched the violinist's place. The two of them were running around in bare feet, chasing each other, struggling, and Kromer's voice was on the edge of panic.

"At least put something on," he begged. "Please, you must! I swear I won't touch you again . . ."

"The key . . ."

It would all come back to him later. Now he didn't think. He didn't move. He was going to see it through to the end.

Kromer, in spite of everything, had had enough presence of mind to take the key out of the lock. There was a light on in there, yes. A thin rosy line of it showed under the door. Had Sissy turned it on? Had she, by chance, found the electric switch hanging from its cord at the head of the bed?

What were they doing? They were banging around. It was as though they were fighting. There were inexplicable dull thuds. Kromer kept repeating, like a skipping phonograph record, "Not before you put something on . . ."

She didn't say Frank's name again. She had spoken his name only once, had shouted it with all her strength.

If any of the tenants were home, they'd hear. It was Minna who thought of that. Frank still hadn't moved. There was just one question he wanted to ask somebody, it didn't matter who, on his knees if necessary, so vital had it suddenly become, "Had Kromer . . . ?"

Something snapped in him.

She was gone. The door had slammed. They heard footsteps in the hall. Minna let go of his wrist and dashed into the front room, since she thought of everything, even of opening the door to the hall a crack to peer out.

Kromer didn't come out immediately. Frank knew him well enough. He was careful to pull himself together first. At last he opened the door.

"Well, there you are, Frank . . ."

Frank didn't move a muscle.

"What's the matter with you?"

"Nothing."

"If you'd only told me there was an electric switch at the head of the bed, everything would have been all right."

Frank didn't move, wouldn't move.

"I was very careful not to say anything to her. I felt her hand groping in the dark, but I didn't think she was going to turn on the light."

Frank hadn't asked the question. His eyes were pinpoints, his glance hard, so hard that Kromer was a little frightened, even wondering for a moment if it wasn't some sort of a trap.

It didn't make sense. There was no rhyme or reason to it.

"At any rate, you can boast . . ."

Minna came back and turned on the light switch in the kitchen, flooding the room with white light that made them blink.

"She ran downstairs like a madwoman. She went right past her own door. One of the neighbors, Monsieur Wimmer, tried to stop her in the hall. I bet she didn't even see him."

So! It was done!

Kromer could go. But he was in a state. Leaving didn't cross his mind. He was furious.

"When will I see you?"

"I don't know."

"Are you coming to Timo's tonight?"

"Maybe."

She had gone, and Monsieur Wimmer had tried to stop her. She had run down the stairs.

"Look here, my little Frank, it seems to me that you . . ." Kromer hesitated, which was just as well. He was no longer anybody's "little Frank." He had never been. They might think anything they pleased.

Now he had paid for his seat.

He asked, with the absent look of someone who hadn't been listening, "What?"

"What do you mean?"

"Nothing. I asked you: What?"

"And I asked you if you were coming to Timo's tonight."

"And I answered you: What?"

He couldn't stand much more. The sensation in his chest, on the left side, was getting unbearable, as though he were going to die.

"Well, in that case . . ."

"Yes, go!"

He had to sit down, lie down, quickly. Why didn't Kromer go? Why didn't he go tell Timo and his friends whatever he pleased?

Frank had done what he wanted to do. He had rounded the cape. He had looked at the other side. He hadn't seen what he expected to see. Who cared?

Why didn't he go? In God's name, why didn't he go?

"What are you waiting for?"

"But . . ."

Minna, who had gone into the little bedroom, who should never have done so, who was incapable of understanding such things, came back with a black stocking in each hand.

She had left without her stockings, her feet bare in her shoes.

And Kromer didn't understand either. If they continued, the two of them, he would go mad, roll on the floor, start chewing on something, anything.

"Get out, for the love of God! Get out!"

Didn't anyone see that he was on the other side, that he had nothing in common with them anymore?

# 2

In the garden belonging to Madame Porse, his wet-nurse, there was only one tree, a big linden. One day, just as it was beginning to get dark and a low sky seemed to weigh down on the earth, absorbing everything into itself, little by little, like blotting paper, the dog started to bark, and they discovered a stray cat in the tree.

It was winter. The barrel of rainwater under the gutter was frozen. From the back of the house you could see the windows in the village lighting up one after another.

The cat crouched on the first branch, about ten or fifteen feet from the ground, staring fixedly down at the earth. It was black-and-white and didn't belong to anyone in the area. Madame Porse, the wet-nurse, knew all the local cats.

When the dog started to bark, they had just filled a tub with hot water for Frank's bath and placed it on the tile floor of the kitchen. It wasn't a real tub, in fact, but half of a barrel that had been sawed in two. The windows were covered with steam. From the garden came the voice of Monsieur Porse, who was the road repairer, saying with the same conviction he brought to bear upon everything, especially when he had had a glass or two, which was most of the time, "I'll get him with my rifle."

Frank was struck by the word "rifle." The shotgun was hanging on the white wall over the hearth. Already half undressed, Frank put on his coat and pants again.

"First try to catch him. He may not be badly hurt."

It was still light enough to make out flecks of red on

the cat's white fur, and one of its eyes was hanging out of its socket.

Frank couldn't recall just how it all happened. Very soon there were five people, ten, their noses in the air, not counting the children. Then someone came with a lantern.

They tried to lure the cat down by putting a saucer of warm milk in plain sight under the tree. Naturally, they had first chained the dog to its kennel. Everybody had shifted a little distance away and tried not to make any sudden movements. But the cat didn't budge. From time to time it would meow plaintively.

"You see! It's calling."

"It may be calling, but not to us!"

The proof was that as soon as someone stood on a chair and tried to take hold of it, the cat would leap to a higher branch.

This went on for some time, at least an hour. More and more neighbors kept arriving. They could be recognized by their voices. A young man climbed up the tree, but every time he stretched out his hand the cat climbed even higher. At last, nothing could be seen but a dark ball.

"To the left, Helmut . . . At the tip of the big branch . . ."

The most surprising thing was that as soon as they gave up the chase, the cat started meowing louder than ever. It seemed to resent being abandoned.

Then they went to get ladders. Everybody helped, and there was a lot of excitement. The road repairer kept talking about getting out his rifle, until they made him stop.

They didn't catch the black-and-white cat that night. Everyone went home. They left some milk and scraps of meat for it on the ground.

"Since he knew how to get up, he'll know how to get down."

The next day the cat was still in the linden tree, almost at the top, and it meowed all day long. They tried again to catch it. They kept Frank from going to look at it because of the eye hanging out of its head. Even Madame Porse was almost sick.

He never learned how the story turned out. On the third day they told him that the cat had gone away. Was that true? Had they said it so he wouldn't be upset?

It was almost exactly what had happened now, except that this time, instead of a cat, it was Sissy.

Frank at last went into the back room, alone, carefully closing the doors behind him with a kind of solemnity, as though he were going into a room where a dead person had been laid out.

Carefully avoiding glancing at the sheets, he pulled up the cover. Perhaps he intended to lie down on the bed. Then he noticed something on the bedside table.

A few minutes before, he had held Sissy's stockings in his hand. Black wool stockings with the toes neatly darned, the way young girls were taught in convents.

It wasn't out of curiosity that he had picked up the bag on the bedside table. He just wanted to touch it. He could do that, since he was alone. And then the thought occurred to him. He remembered how Lotte, who almost always rang the bell when she came home, would excuse herself and say, "I must have forgotten my key in my other bag."

Sissy, too, must have had a key, the key to the apartment across the hall. And where would she have put that key but in her handbag? She hadn't remembered it when she fled. At that moment she had no thought of going home. She hadn't even seen Monsieur Wimmer when he tried to stop her as she flew by.

So the key must be here, in her bag, with a handkerchief and ration cards, a few banknotes, some small change, and a pencil.

"Where are you going, Monsieur Frank?"

It wasn't even six o'clock yet. He saw distinctly the black hands on the face of the alarm clock in the kitchen. Minna hadn't gone back to bed. She was sitting beside the stove. She was calling him "Monsieur Frank" again and she followed his movements with an expression of fear in her eyes.

He didn't realize he was holding the little black bag, which was made of oilcloth, that he was without hat or overcoat, and that he was going outside like that.

"At least put on your overcoat, if you're going out."

A sick person no longer feels sick when there's someone even worse off to look after. Minna no longer felt the pains in her stomach. If she hadn't been so certain of a refusal, she would have offered to go with him.

"You'll come back right away, won't you? You're not well."

The door opposite was closed, without the strip of rosy light showing underneath. Frank went down the stairs with an air of determination. You would have thought he knew where to find her.

At the foot of the rue Verte there was a street to the right, Timo's street, with the Old Basin beyond. By following that street you reached the one leading over the bridge, and that was practically the center of town, with lights, shops, people.

If, instead, you turned left, as he had done once with Sissy, there was nothing to see but vacant lots and the backs of houses. Some parts of the Old Basin had embankments, others did not. They had begun to build a high school, but the war had kept them from finishing it; it was nothing but an immense roofless skeleton with steel beams and exposed walls. Two rows of trees, small and spindly and protected by iron grills, marked what would one day be a boulevard, but it was cut by deep gullies and ended abruptly in a sandpit.

Night had fallen. In that whole corner of the universe there was only one single streetlight. On the other side of the water, where the streetcars passed in front of the houses, the lights formed an almost continuous garland.

He knew he'd find her, but he didn't want to frighten her. He didn't intend to speak to her. Just to give back her key.

Because Holst wouldn't return until midnight, because she couldn't stay outside, her feet bare in her shoes, her legs bare, with no money.

He passed close to someone, a man standing on the corner of the street, and he was certain it was Monsieur Wimmer. He hesitated for a moment, afraid that if the man took it into his head to strike him he wouldn't defend himself.

Monsieur Wimmer must have been looking for Sissy, too. Had he been following her, then lost track of her in the vacant lots?

For the space of a second the two men almost touched each other. That particular spot was dimly illuminated. The moon couldn't be seen behind its bank of clouds, but the outlines of objects were visible.

Had Monsieur Wimmer seen the bag Frank was still holding in his hand? Had he also thought about the key? Did he realize what the young man was doing?

Whatever the case, he let Frank pass. Frank began quickly walking among the vacant lots, stumbling over piles of hardened snow, then suddenly stopping to listen and look around.

He was tempted to call out Sissy's name, but that would probably be the surest way to scare her off, making her plunge deeper into the darkness of the vacant lots, or hole up somewhere, like the black-and-white cat in the village.

Sometimes something could be heard moving. He'd rush toward the sound and find nothing, then, hearing footsteps, he'd run in the opposite direction and realize it was Monsieur Wimmer, tracing a route parallel to his own.

Several times his feet had broken through the hard icy crust, and his legs had sunk in up to his knees.

There she was. He had seen her. He recognized her silhouette and he didn't dare rush toward her, to speak or shout. He had simply held out the bag at arm's length, the way they had showed the saucer of milk to the cat.

She was gone again. She had disappeared into the darkness

and only then, ashamed of the sound of his own voice in that desert of silence, did he risk shouting, "The key!"

He caught sight of her again as she crossed a patch of whiteness, ran toward her, stumbled, repeated, "The key!"

He wouldn't utter her name for fear of frightening her. He should have given the bag to Monsieur Wimmer, who had a better chance of catching her than he did. He hadn't thought of that. Nor had Monsieur Wimmer. Did the old neighbor really have a better chance than he did? Frank could no longer either see or hear him. He was too old to be bumbling about on this broken ground. She wasn't far away, a hundred yards at most. But the tree climber in Madame Porse's garden had several times had his hand within a few inches of the cat. Everybody had thought it would let itself be taken. Perhaps the cat hesitated between alternatives, but at the last moment it always leaped to a higher branch.

The river was frozen, but the sewer wasn't far off, and the water there stayed free of ice.

He tried again, once, twice. He was so discouraged he was almost in tears.

It became an obsession: the key. This little shiny black bag, worn, with a handkerchief, ration cards, a little money, and a key.

Then, since she wasn't far away, since she must be able to see him, he chose the best-lit spot he could find and stopped there, stood motionless, very straight, the bag held out at arm's length, and shouted once more, as loud as he could, not caring if he sounded ridiculous, "The key!"

He waved the bag around. He wanted to be sure she saw him and understood. Then, as conspicuously as he could, he placed the bag on the snow, in plain sight, repeating, "The key! I'm leaving it here!"

For her sake, he had to leave. She would be wary as long as he stuck around. Disgusted, he floundered back. He literally tore himself out of the vacant lot, forced himself back onto the track, onto the black path between the banks of snow that now constituted the sidewalk of his street.

He didn't go to Timo's, which was just around the corner. He passed by the dark alley of the tannery without noticing it. When he entered his building, the concierge, who must have known by then, watched him from behind the curtain. Tonight, tomorrow, the whole place would know.

He went upstairs. There was no light in Monsieur Wimmer's apartment, so he hadn't returned.

All this had begun to merge into a gray, incoherent, monotonous chaos. Hours piled on hours. They were certainly the longest hours he had ever lived. Sometimes it got to the point where he wanted to scream, looking at the alarm clock and seeing the hands still in the same place.

Out of all those hours nothing would be left—just a few charred sticks poking out of the ashes in the fireplace.

His mother came home and her perfume immediately took possession of the room. She glanced at him once, quickly. She turned to Minna next; she gestured for Minna to follow her into the big bedroom. Did they think he couldn't hear them whispering? Let Minna tell her everything! Of course, she hadn't waited for his permission. She must have thought it was her duty, for his own good. From now on they would all be protecting him!

That didn't matter.

"I wish you'd eat, Frank, just a bite."

Lotte expected him to say no. Yet he had eaten. He didn't know what, but he had. His mother went to make up the bed in the back room. Minna hadn't returned to bed. She had assumed an air of innocence. She was sitting in one of the armchairs in the salon, as near to the door as possible, waiting.

Was it Holst they were afraid of? The police? Old Wimmer? He smiled scornfully.

"You can go to bed, Frank. Your room is ready. Unless you'd rather sleep in the big bedroom tonight?"

He didn't go to bed. He would have been incapable of saying what he did, what he thought. At times—and it was the only thing he remembered—objects came to life before his eyes as they had when he was a child: for instance, a copper ashtray with reflections like rays of light, a fabric-covered footstool placed in front of the stove on which his mother always put her feet when, rarely, she was sewing.

He had the feeling the hours would never pass, and yet they did after all. They made him drink something alcoholic with lemon in it. They changed his socks for him and he let them put on his slippers. They talked about Bertha, who wouldn't return until the following morning and who would try to bring some pork and sausages back from the country.

Monsieur Wimmer returned, alone, around eight o'clock. Other tenants on the different floors came home, and the concierge must have told them, one by one, as they came in.

Maybe Sissy was already dead.

The road repairer had kept saying it would be better to finish the cat off with one good blast from his rifle. Some people in the building might think the same thing about Sissy. Others, if they dared, would shoot Frank with pleasure.

He didn't care.

"Why don't you go to bed?"

And, since they both knew what he was waiting for, Lotte added, "We'll be listening. I promise to wake you if there's any news."

Had he burst out laughing? In any case, he had wanted to.

It had to end one way or another, and for the cat it had lasted at least two days. Had the black-and-white beast really gone away by itself, its eye dangling?

It was more likely that the road repairer had finally used the rifle while Frank was at school, and they had found it better to lie to him.

There were endless minutes just before midnight, even

longer than those just before five o'clock. Those were already so far away they belonged to another world.

The two women were the first to start when footsteps sounded on the stairs, but they pretended to press on, Lotte with her work, Minna with her Zola, although she certainly couldn't have remembered much of what she was reading.

The door downstairs slammed. It was him. It must be, and the concierge would waylay him with the news. How was it that footsteps could be heard so soon on the stairs? They were still far off. Up to the first landing the sound was hardly perceptible. After the second landing, Frank recognized the soft sound of the felt boots, and, at the same time, the rhythm of another step.

He held his breath. Minna was on the point of rising and going to the door to look out, but Lotte made a little sign for her not to move. All three of them listened. The other step was that of a woman; the sound of her high heels could be heard, then a key turning in the lock. And Holst's voice saying simply and gently, "Go on in."

Frank would learn only much later that she had been waiting for her father at the corner of the blind alley, where he himself had stood one night with his back flat against the wall. He would learn, too, that she had been on the point of letting Holst go by, that he was already out of sight of the corner where she was crouching when, with the last of her strength, she had called, "Father!"

They had gone in. The door had closed.

"You go to bed now, Frank. Be sensible."

He understood. His mother was afraid that as soon as his daughter was in bed, Holst would come and knock on their door. She would much rather receive him herself. If she dared—but Frank's stony expression intimidated her—she would have advised Frank to go to the country for a few days, or to a friend's.

But God knows it was all simple enough. Old Wimmer

hadn't stirred from his lair. He must still have been up, too. He could hear everything through the transom.

Did Holst go to bed that night? There were noises in the apartment for a long time. They must have had a little coal or wood left, since he lit the fire. There was the sound of the poker, and then of water being put on to boil.

The light was still on. Twice Frank had looked out, the first time at one-thirty in the morning, the second time a little after three, and there was still the rosy line under the door across the hall.

He didn't sleep, either. He remained in the salon, where the women had insisted on setting up his bed. They had tried to knock him out with hot grog, but didn't succeed. He drank everything they gave him and his head remained clear. He had never been so lucid in his life. It almost frightened him, as though there were something supernatural about it.

They undressed. His mother tended to Minna. He could hear their whole technical conversation, all about the female organs, and Otto's name was mentioned again.

They must have thought he was asleep. When Lotte came in to turn off the light, she was astonished to hear her son's wide-awake voice saying categorically, "No."

"All right. But try to get some rest."

It was about five o'clock when Holst opened his door and went to knock on Monsieur Wimmer's. He had to knock several times. They whispered together in the hall, then Monsieur Wimmer probably went in to get dressed. After a while he, in turn, knocked on Holst's door and was admitted immediately.

Holst left. It wasn't difficult for Frank to understand what was happening. He had gone for a doctor. It wasn't yet the hour when people were permitted to be out on the streets, but Holst didn't care. He could have telephoned from downstairs. But Frank would have done just what he had done. Doctors hated to be disturbed, especially by phone.

Holst had to go a long way off. There were no doctors left in the neighborhood, except one old bearded fellow who was always drunk and couldn't be trusted. His only patients were referred to him by the Welfare Bureau.

Holst had to cross the bridges. In the end he had found someone, since a car stopped in front of the house at six. Was it an ambulance? What if they were going to take her somewhere? Frank ran to the window to try to see. He couldn't make out anything apart from the two headlights.

Only two men came up the stairs. If they were going to take Sissy away, there would be orderlies with a stretcher.

He turned out the light so Holst wouldn't know he was up. Perhaps out of decency, because it might look like a challenge. It wasn't out of fear, at any rate. He wasn't afraid of Holst. On the contrary, he would do nothing to avoid him.

The doctor was there a long time. They had replenished the stove, stoked up the fire, and must have put more water on to boil. Had Sissy gone to get her bag where he'd left it? Had she understood his gesture? If not, her father would have to make endless applications to get new ration cards, and even then they might not get them.

The doctor left after half an hour. Monsieur Wimmer should have left, too. He stayed. He was still there. It wasn't until ten minutes to seven that he returned to his apartment.

So much for all those hours. After that, Frank slept. He slept so soundly he never noticed that they had moved his bed, with him in it, into the kitchen, by the stove, and had put a hot-water bottle at his feet.

The kitchen didn't look directly onto the street. The only daylight came from the transom. Yet as soon as he opened his eyes, he knew that something was different. The stove was purring within reach of his hand. He had to raise himself up to see the alarm clock, which showed eleven. He recognized Bertha's peasant voice in the next room.

"You'd better stay in bed, Frank!" said his mother, hurrying into the room. "We didn't want to wake you to put you in a real bed, but I'm sure you're running a fever."

He didn't have a fever, he knew that. It would be too easy to be sick. They could stick as many thermometers as they pleased in his mouth and rear end.

The snow was falling, thick, silent, so thick that you could hardly make out the windows across the street. Even in the kitchen the quality of the air was different.

"Why won't you ever let people take care of you?"

He didn't even answer.

"Come here, Frank."

Since he was up and had put on his robe, she led him into the salon, where the rug was rolled up—they had been cleaning—and closed all the doors.

"I'm not going to warn you. You know I never have. I'm only asking you to listen to me. Believe me, Frank, it would be better if you didn't show yourself today, in fact for several days. I sent Bertha to the market this morning. They almost refused to serve her."

He wasn't listening, and she understood the look he threw in the direction of the Holsts' apartment. She hastened to reassure him. "It probably isn't serious."

Did she think he was in love, or feeling remorse?

"The doctor came this morning. He had an oxygen tank sent. She caught cold. Her father . . ."

Well? What was she waiting for? "Her father . . . ?"

"He won't leave her. The tenants have got together to give them a little coal."

They, of course, had two tons of it in the cellar, but nobody was going to touch their coal.

"When she's better again, people will forget all about it. Even if it's pneumonia, as they're saying, it never lasts more than three weeks. Listen, Frank. Listen to me seriously for once. I'm your mother."

"Oh, God!"

"This evening, or better still, tonight, since you have papers you've preferred not to tell me about but that everybody has seen . . ."

The green card! That worried her, too. She procured barely pubescent girls for the officers of the Occupation, but she was shocked because her son had this famous green card! But, since he had it, he might as well take advantage of it.

"It would be best if you went away for a few days and didn't show yourself in the neighborhood. You've done that before. You have friends. You have money. If you need more, I can give you some."

Why did she say that, since Minna must have told her about the roll of bills in his pocket? She had probably even looked at it when he was sleeping. That must also have terrified her. There was too much. You had to do something pretty dangerous to get that much.

"If you'd rather, I can find a quiet room for you. The friend I went out with yesterday keeps one for me to use, and she'd like nothing better than to have you there. I'll come see you and take care of you. You need rest."

"No!"

He wouldn't leave the house. He knew exactly what was on his mother's mind. He had gone too far, and she was panicking. As long as she quietly went about trafficking in girls, even for the officers, people despised her but didn't dare say anything. They were satisfied with keeping their distance, turning their heads the other way when she came upstairs, leaving a space when she happened to stand next to them in line.

But this was more serious. There was a sentimental aspect that had excited the tenants: a little girl was sick, she might die, and worse still, she was poor.

Lotte was scared, pure and simple.

And Lotte, who was always so charming to someone like Otto, to officers who perhaps had had dozens of people shot

117

or tortured, resented the fact he had gotten that green card, which she had never dreamed of for herself.

If only he hadn't shown it to anyone!

The whole building was against them. Their victim was at their door, right at their door. Emotions had already been stirred by the search at the violinist's the day before. People were already saying they had pistol-whipped the mother to keep her quiet.

Even if no one connected them with that business, tongues were wagging. The building wouldn't be likely to forget anytime soon that Frank, a mere boy, had calmly passed through the police lines—one that housewives with children stuck in their unheated apartments weren't allowed to pass—with a flash of his green card.

Lotte was afraid of Holst, too.

"Frank, I'm begging you to listen to me!"

"No."

Too bad for her and the girls. He was going to stay. He wouldn't run away in the night the way they were trying to make him do. He wouldn't hole up with Kromer or a friend of his mother's.

"You do as you please."

"Yes."

And now more than ever. From now on he'd do as he pleased, not bothering about anybody, and Lotte was going to find it out, and the others, too.

"Well, in any case, go get dressed. Someone may come."

It wasn't a client who rang the bell a little later, just before noon. It was Chief Inspector Kurt Hamling, always cold and courteous, with that air of having dropped by for a neighborly visit. Frank was taking a shower when he arrived, but, as usual in the morning, all the doors were open and you could hear everything that was said in the apartment.

Among these was his mother's stock phrase, "Don't you want to take off your galoshes?"

Today it wasn't an idle question. It was snowing heavily, and later on there would be a puddle of mud on the carpet in front of the armchair where the policeman sat.

"Thank you, but I just dropped in for a moment."

"A little drink?"

He never said yes, but tacitly accepted. He remarked, "It's getting milder. In a day or two the sky will clear up."

You couldn't be sure what sky he was talking about, but Frank wasn't afraid of him; he slipped on his bathrobe and, almost defiantly, made his appearance in the salon.

"Well! I didn't hope to find your Frank at home."

"Why?" the latter asked aggressively.

"I was told you went to the country."

"Me?"

"People talk, you know . . . And we have to listen to them, because that's our job. Fortunately we only listen with one ear, otherwise we'd end up arresting everyone."

"Too bad."

"What?"

"That you only listen with one ear."

"Why?"

"Because I'd like to be arrested. Especially by you."

Lotte protested, "Frank, you know very well you can't be arrested."

She was really frightened, since she added, with a look of defiance at the chief inspector, "With the papers you have!"

"Exactly," he insisted.

"What are you saying, then?"

"Just what I said."

He poured himself a drink, touched glasses with Kurt Hamling. They both seemed to be thinking about the door across the hall.

"To your health, Inspector."

"To yours, young man."

Why did he keep coming back to the same issue?

"I really did think you were in the country."

"I never meant to go."

"That's a pity. Your mother is a good woman, at heart."

"You think so?"

"I know what I'm talking about. Your mother is a good woman, and you'd make a great mistake to doubt it."

Frank snickered, "I doubt so many things, you see!"

Poor Lotte, who was futilely signaling for him to shut up. It was all beyond her. It was as though they were wrestling over her head. She didn't get it, but she had enough intuition to realize that this was something like a declaration of war.

"How old are you, my boy?"

"I'm not your boy, but I'll tell you I'm eighteen, almost nineteen. Allow me a question. You are, if I'm not mistaken, chief inspector?"

"That's my official title."

"How long have you been chief inspector?"

"I was appointed six years ago."

"How long have you been with the police?"

"Twenty-eight years next June."

"I could be your son, couldn't I? I owe you respect. Twenty-eight years doing the same job, that's a long time, Monsieur Hamling."

Lotte was about to speak, to order her son to be quiet, since he was going too far and there was bound to be trouble. But Frank amiably filled the glasses, handing one to the inspector.

"To your health."

"To yours."

"To your twenty-eight years of good and loyal service."

They had gone pretty far. It would be hard to go on any longer like this, but even harder to turn back.

"*Prosit!*"

"*Prosit!*"

It was Kurt Hamling who beat a retreat.

"My dear Lotte, it's time for me to go. Many people must be waiting for me at my office. Take care of this young man."

He left, his back wide, his shoulders square, his big galoshes leaving a wet footprint on every stair.

He didn't realize that he had just rendered Frank the greatest service he could: for several minutes, Frank hadn't thought about the cat.

# 3

THE SCENE with Bertha took place on Thursday. It was almost noon and Frank was still asleep, since he had come home around four in the morning. That was the third time since Sunday. And the fact that he slept so late that it interfered with the housework may have contributed to the dispute. After it was over he never bothered to ask.

He had had a lot to drink. He had taken it into his head to steer two couples whom he had never met before around to all the nightspots, paying their way, each time taking the fat roll of bills out of his pocket. When the patrol arrested them as they were walking along the street singing, he had displayed his green card and the officers had let them go.

There was a new girl in the house who had arrived out of the blue, turning up alone with calm assurance. Her first name was Anny.

"Have you worked before?" Lotte asked her, examining her from head to foot.

"Do you mean have I slept with men? Don't worry, I've had more than my share."

And when Lotte asked her about her family, she replied, "What would you like me to say? That I'm the daughter of a general or a judge? Anyway, if I do have a family somewhere, they're not going to give you any trouble, I promise."

Compared to the others, all the others they had ever had, she seemed like a thoroughbred. She was very small, slender, and yet plump at the same time, with brown hair and golden skin without the slightest blemish. She made you think of a fine piece of goldsmith's work. She was hardly eighteen but already a thorough bitch.

When she saw the others washing dishes, for instance, she immediately went to the salon and started reading one of the magazines she had brought with her. She did the same thing after dinner that evening. The following morning she said to Lotte, "I don't suppose you expect me to be a house-maid in the bargain?"

Minna was beginning to work again, though it still caused her pain. But the clients almost always chose the new girl. Which was strange, in a way. Frank had climbed onto the table out of curiosity. She maintained a surprising dignity. It was the men who seemed degraded, to appear in a ridiculous or odious light. Frank could guess what she said, speaking without a smile, patiently, with absolute indifference.

"You want me to turn over? Higher? Lower? Is that right? And now?"

While they worked her, she would stare at the ceiling with her beautiful eyes, like those of an untamed animal. At one point her glance met Frank's—she could see him in outline through the glass of the transom. For a long time he wondered if she really had seen him, since she hadn't given a start or a sign of surprise. She just kept on, waiting, thinking of other things, until the man was satisfied.

"Does the boss make you spy on us?" she asked him a little later.

"No."

"You just like to watch?"

"Not that either."

She shrugged her shoulders. Because of her, Minna and Bertha had to sleep in the same bed, and Frank had once more taken possession of his cot in the kitchen. Tuesday evening he had gone into Anny's room and she had said to him, "If you just want to get off, make it quick, since I suppose I have to do that for the boss's son. But don't think you can stay in my bed all night. I hate sleeping with people."

Minna tried to make friends with her, but Anny spent all her time reading. As for Bertha, she was increasingly relegated to the role of maid, and she never said a word to the new girl, serving her sullenly, since Anny expected to be waited on. She even got them to help her wash and dry her hair.

Frank was asleep when the argument started. Like every morning, they had pushed his bed—with him in it—into the back room. Much later he heard an outburst of loud voices and recognized Bertha's accent. He had never seen her angry before. And the words she was screaming were not part of her ordinary vocabulary, which was timid and polite.

"I'm fed up with this dump and I'm not going to stay another day. With all this dirty business, soon things are going to go wrong, and I don't want to be here when they do."

"Bertha!" Lotte said sharply. "Be quiet!"

"You can yell at me as loud as you want, but I wouldn't if I were you. There are enough people in this building who have it in for you already who'd settle your hash if they dared."

"Bertha, I order you . . ."

"Order me! Order me! Yesterday at the market a kid no bigger than that spit right in my face yet again, and it wasn't for me, it was for you. I don't know what's keeping me from doing the same thing to you now!"

Would she have done it? Probably not. She was a girl who had kept her resentments bottled up for a long time, but now they were flooding out. She hadn't heard Frank come into the kitchen behind her in his bare feet and pajamas. So she was shocked into silence, while she was glaring at Lotte and threatening to spit in her face, when she got slapped. The slap seemed to come out of nowhere.

When she saw Frank, she set her jaw.

"You snot-nosed brat, why don't you just try that again?"

Lotte didn't have time to interfere before two fresh slaps resounded, loud and distinct as at the circus. Suddenly Bertha threw herself at him, purple in the face, grabbing at him any which way, while he tried to hold her off.

"Bertha! Frank!"

Minna had fled into the salon while Anny, smoking a cigarette in a long ivory holder, leaned against the doorjamb, watching.

"A snot-nosed little bastard, that's what you are, a little louse who thinks he can get away with anything because his mother runs a whorehouse! Dirty, filthy things that would make a whore blush . . . Let me go! Let go of me or I'll yell loud enough to rouse the whole building! You won't get rid of them with your gun or your damn papers once they're after you!"

"Frank!"

He let her go. His cheek, where she had scratched him, was bleeding a little.

"Just wait till they get you cornered, that won't be long. There won't always be foreign soldiers in the country to protect you, you and everyone like you . . ."

"Come here, Bertha. I'll settle up."

"I'll come when I'm good and ready! Let's see what you do tomorrow morning with no one to make your coffee and empty your piss pots! And to think that I even brought you pork from my parents!"

"Come here, Bertha."

She turned toward Frank again, her eyes shining, and spat at him by way of good-bye. "Coward! Dirty little coward! "

And yet it had been Bertha who was the most tender when he slept with her, with a tenderness that was almost motherly.

———

Bertha probably wouldn't say anything. Yet Lotte was worried. She should have remembered that it wasn't the first time. Dozens of scenes like this had taken place before, none of them with the least consequence. She listened when Bertha went downstairs with her bundle, trying to determine if she was speaking to other tenants or the concierge. It wasn't likely, since Bertha was just as badly thought of as they were. Hadn't the kid spit at her? If anything, it would be easier to take his anger out on her.

She could be seen waiting at the streetcar stop on the corner, perhaps already regretting what she'd done.

Lotte regretted the fallout even more. Though men were never very enthusiastic about Bertha, she still managed to get them off, and besides, the good thing about her was that she did practically all the housework.

Minna would begin doing that now, but she wasn't strong and her insides still hurt. As for Anny, the most you could hope for from her was that she'd make her bed in the morning.

And then there was the shopping, the standing in line, where you inevitably found yourself rubbing elbows with people from the neighborhood, sometimes other tenants in the building.

"You shouldn't have slapped her . . . Anyway, it's all over now."

She noticed how pale her son was, the dark circles under his eyes. Frank had never drunk so much. And he had never gone out as often without saying where he was going, his eyes hard, and always with his loaded pistol in his pocket.

"Do you think it's a good idea to walk around with that on you?"

He didn't bother answering or even shrugging his shoulders. He had acquired a new habit that quickly became automatic: he would look at people talking to him as though he didn't see them and hadn't heard a thing.

Not once had he met Holst on the stairs, though he went up and down them five or six times a day, much more than usual. Holst had probably asked the streetcar company for time off in order to nurse his daughter. Frank felt sure that Holst would have to go out, if only to buy medicines and food. But other arrangements had been made. First thing every morning, Monsieur Wimmer knocked on his neighbor's door. He did all the errands. Once, when the door had been left open, Frank caught sight of him in a woman's apron, doing the housework.

The doctor came at around two o'clock every day. Frank contrived to run into him. He was quite a young man, and he looked like an athlete. He didn't seem worried. True, it wasn't his daughter or wife. Could Holst be ill, too? That had occurred to Frank. Then Wednesday, just as he was getting into the streetcar, he happened to glance up at the window and saw him there through the curtains. Their eyes had met across the distance, Frank was sure of it. Nothing would come of it, of course, but Frank was completely shaken by that moment of contact. They remained calm and serious, both of them, without hatred, the only thing between them was something akin to a great void.

His mother would be even more anxious if she knew that every day, sometimes twice a day, he made a point of going to the little café near the streetcar stop, the one where you had to go down two steps. It was practically a provocation, since there was no reason to go. The regulars always stopped talking when he came in and immediately looked away. The owner, Monsieur Kamp, who usually sat with them—they played cards—would get up to serve him with obvious reluctance.

Monday, Frank paid for his drink with a very large bill pulled from his roll.

"I'm sorry," said Monsieur Kamp, handing it back, "I can't make change for this."

When he left, Frank put the bill on the bar saying casually, "Keep it."

On Tuesday he could have sworn the regulars were waiting for him, and he felt something like a cold shiver. It wasn't the first time. One fine day something was bound to happen, exactly when or what he couldn't tell. It could just as well be in this quiet, old-fashioned café. Why had the customers looked at Monsieur Kamp expectantly, with barely concealed smiles?

Monsieur Kamp served Frank without a word. Then, when he was about to pay, Kamp took an envelope that was lying in plain sight on the shelf, between two bottles, and held it out.

Frank could feel the notes and coins. It was change from the big bill he'd left the day before.

He said thank you and left. It didn't stop him from going back.

He almost had a fight with Timo. It was two o'clock in the morning. He had been drinking. He saw, sitting with a woman in a corner of the room, a man whose face he didn't like. Frank, who was standing at the bar, showed Timo his gun and said, "When that guy leaves, I'm going to take him down!"

Timo looked at him stonily, without a hint of friendliness. "You're crazy, right?"

"I'm not crazy. I don't like his face and I'm going to take him down."

"You'd better watch it or I'll take you down with my fist."

"What did you say?"

"I said I don't like the way you're acting lately. Go have your fun somewhere else if you want, not here. If you touch that guy I'll have you arrested immediately—that's number one. And from now on you'll leave your little toy somewhere else; if you don't, you won't set foot in here again—that's number two. And now I'll give you some advice. Don't drink so much. It makes you cocky, and at your age that won't do."

But Timo came over a little later to apologize. This time he talked in earnest.

"I laid it on a bit heavy just now, but it's for your own good. Even your friend Kromer says you're getting dangerous. I don't want to know anything about what you do. But for some time now you've been acting like you think you're a big shot. You think it's smart to flash your roll of bills at anybody who comes along? You think people don't know how that kind of money is made?"

Frank showed him his green card. Timo didn't seem impressed. Embarrassed, rather. He made him put it back in his pocket.

"That, too, it's better not to wave it around too much."

He returned to the attack a third time. Conversations with Timo took place in snatches, since customers were always calling him from every direction.

"Listen here, my friend. I know you'll think it's envy on my part, but I'm just telling you the way it is. I'm not saying that card's not valuable. Only there's a right way to use it. And then things get more complicated . . ."

He wasn't anxious to explain.

"Like what?"

"What's the use talking about it? People always end up saying too much. I'm in fine with them. They leave me alone. Some of them bring me merchandise and they've always been straight with me, business-wise. Maybe it's because I see a lot of them, all kinds, but there are other things I can figure out."

"What?"

"I'll give you an example. About a month ago, over there, at that third table, there was an officer, a colonel, a good-looking guy, still young, in good shape, medals all over his chest. He was with two women, and I don't know what he was telling them—I was busy somewhere else. Anyway they were laughing loudly. And at one point he took his wallet out of his pocket, I guess to pay the check. The women grabbed it and began having fun with it. They were all drunk, the three of them. The women kept passing his papers and photographs back and forth. I was at the bar. And just then I saw a guy get up, someone I hadn't even noticed, just an ordinary-looking guy, a civilian, like anybody you'd see in the street. He wasn't even well dressed. He went over to the table and the colonel looked at him sort of startled, but still trying to smile. The other man said just one word, and I tell you, that officer got right up and stood at attention. He took his wallet from the women. He paid his check. You could see the starch go right out of him. He left the women there, without a word of explanation, and went out with the civilian."

"What's that got to do with me?" Frank mumbled.

"The next day he was seen at the station, headed for an unknown destination. That's what I mean. Some of them seem powerful, and maybe for the moment they are. But they're never—and don't forget it—as powerful as they pretend, because no matter how powerful they are, there are always others who are more powerful still. And they're the ones you never hear about.

"You work with one department where everybody shakes hands with you and you think you're safe. Only, at the same moment, in another department, there's a paper being drawn up with your name on it.

"If you want to know what I think, well, they have several sections. And no matter how good you're in with one, you shouldn't mess with another one."

Frank remembered that the next morning, and it bothered him, all the more because he had a hangover. It was getting to be a habit. Every morning he promised himself to be more careful, but then he'd start drinking again because he needed to calm himself.

What struck him was the connection in his mind between Timo's talk and something Lotte had said that he hadn't paid any attention to at the time.

"You can feel that Christmas is coming. The faces are beginning to change."

That meant her clientele was changing, at least as far as the occupiers were concerned. For her it was always an unpleasant period, since it kept her in a constant state of uneasiness. Every three months, or every six months—it usually happened around the big holidays, but that was probably a coincidence—there were personnel changes, both civil and military. Some went back to their country, others arrived who had different ways and whose characters were still an unknown quantity. Everything had to start all over again. Whenever a new client rang, Lotte believed she had to put on the manicure act again, and she never relaxed until the man pronounced the name of the friend who had sent him.

Without knowing exactly why, Frank didn't want his general to leave. He called him his general, but he didn't know him, in fact had never seen him. It was Kromer who knew him. His passion for watches had something innocent and reassuring about it. Frank was like his mother. He felt more comfortable with people who had a passion. For example, when you knew about Otto's vices, you couldn't be afraid of him. He was someone Frank could probably make use of one day. Otto would pay a good deal to avoid having certain of his peculiarities made known.

The sun had come out and there was a fine frost in the air. The last snowfall hadn't had time to get dirty yet, and in certain areas gangs of unemployed men hired by the city were still busy shoveling the snow into dazzling piles on either side of the walkways.

He had the impression Kromer was avoiding him. True, he was also avoiding Kromer. So what was worrying him? And why say he was worried when he was perfectly calm, when it was he, of his own free will and in full awareness, who was doing everything to bring about his own destruction?

Going to Kamp's, for example. There were surely, among

the customers of the little café, people from the underground and the patriots' leagues. There must be some, too, in the lines he passed every day, and he knew that his clothes and his shoes alone constituted a provocation.

Twice he had run into Carl Adler, the driver of the little truck that had taken him to the village the night of the Mademoiselle Vilmos business. It was odd: twice in four days, and both times by chance in unexpected places—the first time on the sidewalk opposite the Lido, the other time in a tobacco shop in the Upper Town.

Yet he had never met him before. Or rather, since he didn't know him then, he might have brushed by him a hundred times without noticing.

That's how ideas get into your head.

Was it on purpose, out of caution or a sort of decency, that Adler pretended not to recognize him?

But that didn't matter. Even if it did, if there was treachery behind it, Frank would be delighted. One little detail, however, troubled him. Adler hadn't been alone across from the theater. He had been with a man who lived in their building.

It was someone he had only caught a glimpse of on the stairs. Frank knew he lived on the third floor to the left and had a wife and a little girl. He must have been twenty-eight or thirty. He was thin and unhealthy looking, with a beard that was too blond and too sparse. He didn't work in a factory. In an office, perhaps? No, not that, since Frank ran into him at all hours, and he didn't look like a traveling salesman.

He was probably a technician like Adler, and in that case it was only natural that they should know each other.

One never knew who belonged to the underground or to a patriots' league. They were often the most inoffensive-looking people, and the young blond man, with the wife and little girl, on the third floor was just the kind of tenant you never noticed.

Why should those people want to eliminate him? He hadn't

done anything to them. Mostly they killed their own members who betrayed them, and Frank couldn't possibly do that, since he didn't know them. That they despised him he was certain. But, like his mother, he had much more to fear from the animosity of their neighbors, which was based on envy and was only a matter of coal, warm clothes, and food.

And Lotte, too, only worried about the neighborhood. Since the authorities had left him alone so far about the Mademoiselle Vilmos affair, she realized he would never be asked about it. Even Kurt Hamling's attitude, the little remarks he had let fall, implied nothing more than a local danger. Otherwise there would have been no sense in advising Frank to go to the country for a few days or to friends somewhere else in town.

He hadn't succeeded in meeting Holst, as he would have liked, but they had seen each other at a distance. Holst, who must be as familiar with his footstep as Frank was with his, heard him coming in and out ten times a day, and could have accosted him on the landing.

Frank wasn't afraid. It wasn't a question of fear. It was much more subtle than that. It was a game he had invented, like the games he used to make up as a child, which he alone understood. It had usually been in his bed in the morning, while Madame Porse was preparing breakfast, and preferably when it was sunny outside. His eyes closed, he would think, for example, "Fly!"

Then he would half open his eyes, looking at a certain spot on the wallpaper. If there was a fly there, he won.

Now he might have said, "Destiny!"

Because he wanted destiny to pay attention to him, he had done everything to force it to, and he continued to defy it from morning to night. The day before, he had said in an offhand way to Kromer, "Ask your general if there's anything else besides watches that he'd like to have."

He didn't need the money. Even at the rate he was going, he still had enough for months. There was nothing he needed.

He had bought himself another overcoat—even flashier than the one he already had—light beige, of pure camel's hair, a coat like maybe only five others in the whole town. It wasn't quite warm enough for the season, but he wore it out of bravado. Likewise, he always carried his automatic in his pocket, although it was uncomfortably heavy and might one day, in spite of his green card, put him in a bad spot.

He didn't want to be a martyr. He didn't want to be a mere victim. But it did him good to think, as he walked around the neighborhood, especially at night, that a shot might suddenly come out of the shadows.

No one took any notice of him. Even Holst didn't seem to, and yet Frank had done enough to attract his attention.

Sissy must hate him. Anybody else, after what he'd done, would have moved out of the building.

Destiny was lying in ambush somewhere. But where? Instead of waiting for it to appear in its own good time, Frank went out looking for it, poking around everywhere in his search. He was calling out to it just as he had done when he held out the bag with the key at arm's length in the vacant lot. "Here I am. What are you waiting for?"

He didn't have enough enemies so he had to make new ones. Wasn't that why he had slapped Bertha? And now, whenever Minna was even a little affectionate, or slightly attentive, he would say, to wound her, "I hate bellyachers."

He would bring chocolates to Anny, who never shared them with the others and never thanked him. He liked to look at her. He could have looked at her body for hours, but there was no satisfaction in taking her to bed. It bored her, too. The second time he came to her room, she had sulked, "Again?"

Though her body was a work of art, it was all she had. And it seemed lifeless, without animation. She placed it wherever or however you wanted it, as though to say, "Look at it, touch it, do whatever you want with it, only hurry up."

Bertha left on Thursday. At three o'clock in the afternoon

on Friday, he was on the street when he noticed the tenant from the third floor standing in front of a shop window. Only later did it occur to him that the man had been looking at a display of corsets. It must have been an hour later. Frank had gone with an acquaintance named Kropetzki to eat pastry at Taste's. Ressl, the editor in chief, was there. At Taste's Frank felt at home. It had the refined atmosphere he liked, and he had seldom seen a woman as well dressed, as pedigreed, as the one with Ressl.

Ressl did him the honor of greeting him with a little wave of his hand. Frank and his companion listened to the chamber music—Taste's was one of the few places left in town where you could still hear it after five o'clock in the afternoon. He thought of the violinist, because the one playing was tall and thin.

Had they shot him? People were always in a panic about being shot, but more often than not, one fine day, those who were said to have been killed came home again. Only a few of them spoke of torture. Unless the ones who said nothing were too frightened to talk.

The thought of torture made his heart skip a beat, and yet he wasn't really afraid. Would he be able to hold up under torture? He was sure he would. It was a question he often thought about. He had been familiar with it even before torture became a subject of general concern. When he was little, he had hurt himself for fun, sticking a pin into his skin in front of a mirror and watching for the spasm of pain to cross his face.

They wouldn't torture him. They wouldn't dare. The others used torture, too. At least that was what people said.

Why should they torture him when he had nothing to reveal?

In a few days it would be Christmas. Another sham Christmas. He had never known, except as a small child, anything but sham Christmases. Once, when he was seven or eight years old, he had come to town at this season of the year, when the streets were all lighted up like a ballroom. Men in heavy coats and women in furs hurried through the streets. Merchandise was piled up in the shop windows, which looked like they were about to overflow.

They would put up a little tree in Lotte's salon, as they did every year. It was mostly for the clients. Who would be there? Minna must have a family. Even if the girls never thought about their families during the rest of the year, they remembered them at Christmas. As for Anny, no one knew where she had come from. Maybe she'd stay. She'd probably be happy to stuff herself and then bury her nose in magazines.

Even Kromer was going home, about twenty miles away, for the holidays.

Sissy would still be in her bed. Holst would spend his last pennies, if he had any, or sell some of his books to decorate a tree for her. They would have old Wimmer with them, who had discovered his vocation and become their housemaid.

"What are you thinking about?" his friend asked him.

He gave a start. "Me?"

"I didn't mean the pope."

"Nothing. Sorry."

"You looked like you wanted to strangle the musicians."

He hadn't been looking at the musicians. He had forgotten about them.

"Listen, Frank, I wanted to ask you a favor, but I don't dare."

"How much?"

"It's not what you think. It's not for me. It's my sister. She's needed an operation for a long time. They told me you have lots of money."

"What's the matter with your sister?"

And Frank thought ironically that she, at least, hadn't done time at Lotte's.

"It's her eyes. If she isn't operated on she'll go blind."

Kropetzki was a young man about his own age, but soft and timid, born to be pushed around. There were tears in his eyes already.

"How much do you need?"

"I don't know exactly, but I think if you could lend me . . ."

Frank handled his roll of bills like a magician. It had become a game.

"If you say thanks, you're a bigger fool than I thought."

"Frank, I . . ."

"What did I say? Come on, let's go."

And then, by chance, there was the blond guy from the third floor only a few steps away again, this time standing in front of a shop window full of dolls. He had a little daughter. Christmas was coming. Maybe it was only natural for him to look at window displays.

What if Frank went up to him and asked him straight out what he wanted, if necessary sticking his green card or automatic under his nose?

Timo's talk had had an effect on him. He kept on walking, then turned to look back. The man wasn't following him. It was Kropetzki who stuck to him, and Frank had a world of trouble shaking him.

If destiny awaited, it wasn't apparent that night, since he was able to have dinner in town, meet Kromer—who was preoccupied, almost distant—have drinks in three different places, and engage in a long conversation with some stranger at a bar, without anything happening.

Between Timo's and his house, passing by the blind alley that led to the tannery, nothing happened either. It would be funny if destiny should choose just that spot to lie in wait. It was the sort of idea you got at three o'clock in the morning when you'd been drinking.

There was a light in Holst's window. Perhaps it was the

hour for compresses, or drops, or God knows what. He listened at the door. They had heard his footsteps. Holst knew he was on the landing, and Frank intentionally lingered for some time, his ear glued to the door.

Holst didn't open the door, didn't make a movement.

Idiot!

There was nothing to do but go to bed, and if he hadn't been so tired he would have screwed Anny first, just to annoy her. As for Minna, she disgusted him. She was stupidly in love. She sometimes cried, probably when she thought about him. Maybe she prayed, too. And she was ashamed of her belly.

He went to bed alone. There was a little fire left in the stove and for a long time he lay staring at the red circle where you stuck in the poker.

Idiot!

It was in the morning, when he had a hangover again, that it happened. He had searched for destiny in every corner and it was in none of the places he'd looked.

It was pure chance again: there was no more wine in the house, the two carafes were empty. For several days, Lotte had forgotten to tell him that their stock was exhausted.

He had to go to Timo's. It was better to see him in the morning about things like that. Timo didn't like to sell, even at a stiff price. He insisted that he always lost out that way, that a good bottle was worth more than bad money.

Frank was thirsty. Lotte's hair was in curlers. She had put on a loose smock to do the cleaning with Minna, while Anny didn't even move as they swept around her legs. She was imperturbable as a goddess, plunged not in reverie or contemplation but in one of her magazines, and flicking her cigarette ashes on the floor.

"Don't buy too much at once, Frank."

Strange. He was on the point of leaving his gun in the apartment, but he didn't—not because of what Timo had said, but because to do so would seem like cheating.

He didn't want to cheat.

He met Monsieur Wimmer coming upstairs with provisions, a shopping bag in which there was a cabbage and some turnips, but Monsieur Wimmer didn't do anything, just went past him without a word.

Idiot!

He remembered stopping on the second landing to light his cigarette—it had tasted rotten, as always after he'd been drinking the night before—and glancing mechanically down the hall to the left. He saw no one. The hall was empty except for a baby carriage at one end. Somewhere a baby was crying.

He was downstairs in the hall and about to pass the concierge's apartment. At that moment the door opened.

He had never thought it would happen like this. To tell the truth, he didn't even realize it was happening.

The concierge was the same as usual, the same face, the same cap. Beside him stood a commonplace-looking man with a vaguely foreign air who was wearing an overcoat that was too long for him.

As Frank went by, the stranger touched the brim of his hat, as though thanking the concierge. He followed Frank out and overtook him before he reached the middle of the sidewalk.

"You will kindly follow me."

That was all. He showed Frank something he was holding in the palm of his hand, a cellophane-covered card with a photograph and seals. What kind of card? Frank had no idea.

Very calm, a bit stiffly, Frank said, "Okay."

"Hand it over."

He hadn't time to wonder what he was meant to give him. The man had already plunged his hand into the correct pocket and appropriated the automatic, which he slipped into his overcoat.

If people were watching—Frank didn't know if they were —they couldn't have understood what was going on.

There wasn't a car waiting at the curb. They walked side by side toward the streetcar stop and waited for the streetcar like anybody else, not even looking at each other.

# 4

IT WAS the eighteenth day. He was holding out. He would keep on holding out. He had discovered that everything depended on holding out, and that if he did he would get the better of them. Was it really a question of getting the better of them? That was another problem he would have to solve eventually. He had thought a great deal—too much. Thinking, too, was dangerous. He must stick to a strict discipline. When he thought he'd get the better of them, it simply meant that he'd get out. And the term "get out" wasn't limited to the place he was in now.

It was amazing how, outside, words were used without anyone paying any attention to what they meant. He certainly wasn't well educated, but then there were lots like him—in fact, most poeple were like him—and now he realized that he had always been satisfied with words that were just approximations.

This question of the meaning of words had lasted him two days. Maybe it would come back to him later.

In any case, it was the eighteenth day, that was an absolute certainty. He made sure this certainty was absolute. He had chosen an almost untouched piece of wall where he scratched a line with his thumbnail every morning. It was harder than you'd think. Not to draw the line, even though the nail was already worn down. But to draw only one. To be sure you had drawn it. The wall was covered with plaster, which made the operation easier. But it hadn't been easy to find a clean spot, because of all the others who'd been there before him.

And it was impossible to be too careful—this was another of his discoveries—because here you tended to doubt, and he realized that anyone who doubted was lost.

He would solve the problem all alone, provided he observed his rules and kept from dreaming. You became very strict about certain matters. For example, the last morning he had spent outside, he hadn't known the date. He'd known it without knowing it. He wasn't sure. The result was, though he knew for certain he had spent eighteen days here, he couldn't swear to the exact date of his arrival.

That was how you lived.

Today was probably the seventh of January. Maybe the eighth. Before that he lacked clear points of reference. As to the time he had been here, there were his scratches.

If he held out, if he didn't let himself go, if he concentrated enough—without, however, concentrating too hard—it wouldn't be long before he understood, and everything would be over. That reminded him of a dream he'd had several times. There were many dreams, but the one that mattered most was the flying one. He would rise into the air. Not outside, in a garden or on the street, but always in a room, always in the presence of witnesses who didn't know how to fly. He would say to them, "Look how easy it is!"

He would put his two hands flat against the air and press. The takeoff was slow and painful. He had to use a lot of willpower. Once in the air, he had only to move slightly to make it happen, sometimes with his hands, sometimes with his feet. His head almost touched the ceiling. He never understood why the others were so amazed. He would smile at them condescendingly.

"I'm telling you, it's easy! It's simply a question of wanting to!"

Well, here it was the same thing, and if he only wanted to

badly enough, he would understand. Conditions were difficult. He had realized from the first that he'd have to be careful about adjusting.

One little example: his arrival. Those last hours, his last minutes *outside*. Or *before*. He used the two terms interchangeably. He had to preserve the memory of those moments with almost mathematical precision. He did. He guarded them carefully. But it required constant effort. Every day he risked changing certain details, he was tempted to, he would force himself to go over the events again, one by one, to link each image with the one that followed.

Thus it wasn't true that Kamp had come and stood in the doorway, nor had there been a burst of laughter from the regulars inside the little café. He had been on the point of putting that in. He almost believed it. The truth was that he'd seen nobody, absolutely nobody until the streetcar, rattling along as usual, came to a stop in front of them. They hadn't looked at each other to decide whether to get in up front or in back. It was as though the man knew Frank's habits and wanted to please him. They got in front.

Frank had been smoking a cigarette; the other man had about a quarter of a cigar in his mouth. He might have preferred to toss it away and sit inside. Except when he had been little and forced to, Frank had never sat down in a streetcar. For no reason, it made him feel panicky.

The man had stayed with him on the front platform.

After crossing the bridges, the streetcar ran almost the entire length of the Upper Town, ending up in a working-class neighborhood not far from open country. They had passed quite close to some military administration offices, and yet they had stayed on the streetcar. Three blocks farther, he signaled to Frank, and they got off and waited for another streetcar at a yellow sign.

The sky had been dazzling that morning. It seemed that the whole town was glittering, all its windowpanes, all its snow, all its white roofs. Was he misremembering things? There was one detail, at least, that wasn't a delusion. While waiting for the second streetcar, he had dropped his cigarette butt on the snow. Ordinarily, the snow was hard and crusted. The cigarette should have continued burning. But it had gone out, doused by the wetness of the melting snow. If he were less disciplined, he would have said that it had stuck in the snow and sputtered out.

That was the sort of detail he tried to look out for, since it was a point of reference. Without details like that, you could start to think anything at all and believe it.

The second streetcar they took followed a sort of circular boulevard through neighborhoods that were no longer actually in town, but not quite in the suburbs either. Several times, women with shopping bags climbed onto the streetcar for short stretches. Frank helped them once or twice and the man didn't object.

For a moment, Frank had almost wondered if it weren't all some sort of joke. On Kromer's part? Or Timo's? Revenge on the part of Chief Inspector Kurt Hamling?

He'd been right not to show anything. Overall he was pleased with himself, even now that he'd had time to go over the details carefully. Others would have probably asked questions, gotten angry, or even made stupid jokes. He had been simple but dignified, modeling his behavior on that of the man he was with, who must have been a minor official, a mere inspector without special instructions.

They must have ordered him, "Bring us that young man." Adding, "Be careful. He's armed."

It was out of habit that he had known right away which pocket Frank carried his pistol in. What Frank was even prouder of, with respect to his own behavior, was that he hadn't nervously smoked one cigarette after another. When he threw one away, he would say to himself, "Not another one for two more stops."

They got out of the streetcar in a bright, newly built district that people in town would barely have known about, where the bricks were still pink and the paint fresh. Just opposite the stop was a group of large buildings with a courtyard in front, surrounded by a high iron fence.

It was a school. Most likely a high school. There was a sentry box at the gate with a guard in it, but there was nothing sinister about the place. Directly opposite, Frank noticed a little café, the same sort of café as Monsieur Kamp's, but newer.

"We may have to wait a bit. We're ahead of schedule."

Those were the first words the man had spoken since accosting Frank. He said them guardedly, as though afraid of being proved wrong. It occurred to Frank that ordinarily he never went out so early, and that he had gone out that morning only because there was no more wine in the house.

Did Lotte know yet? And Holst? And Sissy?

He was calm. He had been calm the whole time. Even now, reviewing his actions over and over again, he was satisfied with himself. It wasn't too daunting to enter a school courtyard, even one with a sentry box and guard at its gate.

They headed to the right and up a few steps. The man walked ahead of him to a glass door that he opened, standing aside to let Frank enter first.

It was hard to say what this little building had been before. Maybe the concierge's apartment?. There was a bench, and the room was cut in half by a high desk, like a counter. The woodwork and furniture were painted a light gray. The man went toward an adjoining room, said a few words, came back, and sat down beside Frank.

He didn't look any happier than Frank. On the contrary. He was sad and conscientious. He did his duty without pleasure, maybe even against his principles. He kept his cigar butt, soggy with saliva, in his mouth and it was starting to smell. He made no objection when Frank stamped his cigarette out on the floor and lit another.

He was what Frank called a "nothing," someone like Kropetzki, born to be pushed around. There must have been more important people in the adjoining room. The door to that room was open, but only the upper half of it was visible since the counter blocked the view. Frank and his companion must have arrived at a slow hour. He had hardly lit his cigarette before he heard the dull sound of a blow against a face, but without any groan after, just the voice of the person who had landed the blow, or someone else, asking: "Well?"

Frank was sorry he couldn't see, but he didn't dare stand up. He waited for the blows that followed one another in quick succession, but only once was a feeble groan exacted from the man they were beating.

"Well, you swine?"

Frank had remained calm. He was sure of that. He had had eighteen days to think about it, and they only had made him more honest with himself.

What stirred in him was curiosity. First he asked himself, "Do they really make you strip naked?"

Very soon, probably, it would be his turn. Why was he suddenly thinking about Minna's belly? Because it was said they hit you in the genitals with their feet or knees. That had made him turn pale. But the man in the next room didn't break. In the intervals of silence you could hear his wheezy breathing.

"You still say it wasn't you?"

A blow. With a little practice, you should to be able to tell what part of the body had been hit.

An avalanche of blows now. Then a dull groan. Then nothing.

Nothing but a few words spoken in a foreign language in a tone of reproach.

Had it all been arranged simply for his benefit? He had to find out. It was hard to believe, of course. He no longer thought like people outside, but he wasn't thinking like his neighbors in the classrooms yet either. He tried to keep his mind clear, to find a balance. He was convinced he would succeed. They wouldn't get him.

*Especially if this was only a test.* He couldn't speak like this to Lotte, to Kromer, even to Timo. Frank had come a long way since he had seen them. They hadn't. Their little lives were going on, they continued to think in the same way, they wouldn't make any progress.

He felt like smiling when he remembered what Timo had said about the green card and the different sections.

Was Frank now in one of those sections?

Was it a serious section?

Timo could walk by in the street, see the gate with the guard, and not suspect anything. Things had to be seen from inside, and Frank was inside. But was he actually inside?

He was willing to admit that there was some truth in what Timo said. Timo hadn't known it, he had just been talking, the way people talked outside. The green card existed. If they had created it, it had its importance. If it was important, it was no less important that it shouldn't fall into the wrong hands.

Once, just to become a Freemason, as all functionaries were, you had to go through the ordeal of initiation.

That was what Timo didn't understand, what neither Timo, nor the others, and not even Frank had understood. This thought didn't contribute to his calm—he despised himself all the same—but he liked to contemplate it for a while every day, turning it around, considering it from various angles.

Why, in the office where he had first arrived, hadn't they dealt with him the way they had with his predecessor? Two men had carried him out, one at his head, the other at his feet. He'd had enough, perhaps more than enough. They must have been a bit too quick and too rough. The chief hadn't been pleased. The word he'd uttered in a flat voice, rapping on the table with a letter opener, must have meant, "Next!"

Frank's companion stood up and slipped the end of his cigar into his vest pocket. Frank, too, stood up, very composed.

Had he been confident, at that moment, that in a few minutes he would be free to walk out and take the streetcar in the opposite direction?

He was no longer sure. There were some questions he had asked himself too often, which became more complicated every day. Some he reserved for the morning, others for the afternoon, for sunrise or sunset, for before or after the soup. It was another rule he observed very strictly.

"Come along!"

Had the man told him to come along? Probably not. He hadn't said anything. He had simply motioned to Frank to go around the counter, or else he had gone in front of him to show him the way.

After that it had been almost ridiculous. The chief official before whom he appeared didn't look like a chief official at all, any more than Monsieur Wimmer did. He wasn't in uniform. He was dressed in a gray suit with a coat that was too tight. His collar was too high, his tie carelessly knotted. He couldn't have been any stiffer or more awkward in his clothes.

He was a little man, middle-aged or more, like the ones who gave out ration cards and coal stamps—just another petty official. He wore glasses with thick lenses, like a jeweler's loupe, and he seemed to be waiting impatiently for lunch.

Here was another crucial question, one that went to the base of the problem: *Had they or hadn't they made a mistake?*

Timo seemed to think they were like anybody else, that one of their departments might be altogether ignorant of what was going on in another. With rationing, for instance, people would receive two cards by mistake when they had only asked for one, while others who lost their cards could never get another.

It was serious. He mustn't fool himself, but he had to take

this possibility into account as carefully as all the others. He mustn't forget, either, that it was lunch hour, that the chief was hungry and had just shown signs of annoyance when the preceding man passed out.

But it was impossible to draw any definite conclusions from his behavior. Had he deigned to glance at Frank? Did he know him? Did he have his file in front of him?

When Frank had been waiting on the gray bench in the adjoining room, there must have been five of them in the office. Now there were three, with the chief seated at the desk and the other two standing, one of them very young, even younger than Frank, and badly dressed.

Two standing. One seated.

Frank immediately handed his card across the desk. He had been holding it ready for the last half-hour. He was fingering it in his pocket during the whole trip in the streetcar. If Timo was right, the older man would have shrugged at him or sneered.

The older man took the card without bothering to glance at it and placed it near him on a pile of papers on the desk. The two others methodically but politely searched his pockets.

No one said anything. They didn't ask questions. The man who had brought him stood in the doorway, watching without any particular interest.

The older man must have been thinking about something else, looking at another file, while waiting for the contents of Frank's pockets, including the roll of bills, to pile up on the corner of the desk.

When the search was over, he raised his head as if to ask, "All through?"

The man who had arrested Frank remembered a detail. He came over and laid the revolver down.

"That's it?"

And at last, with a sigh, he picked up a lengthy document, a printed form with blank spaces to fill out.

"Frank Friedmaier?" he asked in a monotone.

He wrote down the name in block letters, then—it took nearly a quarter of an hour—in a special column he listed all the things in Frank's pockets, including a box of matches and a pencil stub.

They hadn't roughed him up. No one paid him any attention. If he had suddenly made for the door and run away at top speed, probably only the sentry would have sent a shot after him—and missed.

Was it really so ridiculous to think it was a test? Why would they give a green card to someone they didn't know and weren't sure of?

Why hadn't they hit him, like the other guy? Had they really hit the other guy? There was no way things like that could happen in an office where anybody could walk right in.

He had thought about it for eighteen days. He had thought about it at enormous length. And not only about that. He'd had time to think about Christmas, about New Year's, about Minna, Anny, and Bertha. And all of them, including Lotte, would have been very surprised to know what he found out.

Yet because of his neighbors it was hard to think. There were neighbors here as there were on the rue Verte. Yes, indeed, Monsieur Holst! Yes, indeed, Monsieur Wimmer! The difference was you didn't see them, and because of that you were less sure of them here than elsewhere.

They had been trying to get him since the first day, but he had been suspicious. He was suspicious of everything. He was about to become the most suspicious man in the world. If his mother showed up to see him, he would have wanted to know if she'd been sent by them.

His neighbors knocked on the walls, on the water pipes, the radiators. There was no heat, but the old radiators were still in place.

Of course, he wasn't in a real prison but in a school, a high school that, from what he had seen, must have been pretty classy.

Right away his neighbors had started sending messages. Why?

He hadn't been so preoccupied that he didn't notice the general layout of the place, and he realized that he was privileged. How many people were there to his right? At least ten, as far as he could tell. He caught a few words as they passed down the hall, and from their way of speaking, they must be workers or country people.

Probably what the papers called "saboteurs." Real or false? Or false ones mixed in with the real ones?

He wasn't going to let himself be fooled.

They hadn't hit him. They'd been polite. They had searched him, but with perfect civility. They had taken everything: cigarettes, lighter, wallet, papers. They had made him take off his tie, belt, and shoelaces. All that time, the older man kept absentmindedly filling out the form, and when he was done he handed it with a pen to Frank, pointing to the dotted line and saying, almost without an accent, "Sign there."

Frank had signed. He hadn't stopped to think. He had signed mechanically. He didn't know what he'd signed. Was that a mistake? Or, on the contrary, did it prove to them that there was nothing on his conscience? It wasn't because he was afraid of being hit that he had signed it. He simply understood it was an indispensable formality and that it would be entirely pointless to refuse.

He had thought a great deal about all that, too, and he had no regrets. If he regretted anything, it was opening his mouth to say, "I'd like—"

There wasn't time to say more. The old gentleman made a sign with his hand, and they led him off across a second courtyard, paved with brick, so far as he could tell from the paths that had been carved out in the snow. What had he been about to say? What would he have wanted? A lawyer?

No—he wasn't that naïve. To communicate with his mother? To reveal the general's name? To contact Kromer, or Timo, or Ressl, who had remembered him at Taste's and waved to him?

It was lucky he hadn't finished his sentence. He had to get out of the habit of speaking pointless words.

He didn't know yet that everything he saw had its importance, and became a little more important with each day. You think "school." And you have a ready-made image of it in your mind. But in some cases, the tiniest detail might one day become so precious that you would never forgive yourself for not having looked at it more carefully.

A large closed courtyard, which at first seemed even larger than it was, since just then it was flooded with sunlight. A building, two stories high, red brick, ran all along one side of it. Probably there were no stairs within since on the outside, like on a boat, there were iron ones with walkways between them connecting the various classrooms.

How many classrooms? He had no idea. He had an impression of vastness. On the other side of the courtyard was another building, the assembly hall or gym, lighted by tall windows like the windows of a church. It reminded him of the tannery. Then there was the covered playground he had been looking at from his window for the last eighteen days, with dark wooden school benches, desks, classroom furniture piled up to the roof.

Despite the bars on the windows, it wasn't a real prison. There were practically no guards to be seen. At night he'd caught a glimpse, as he passed through, of two soldiers armed with machine guns.

Only at night, when the searchlights played over the buildings, did it seem more daunting.

Since there were no shutters on the windows, the light kept him from sleeping—or woke him with a start.

In short, if there weren't any guards, it was because there

was a watchtower on the roof with searchlights, machine guns, and grenades. He heard footsteps, sometimes, on an iron stairway that couldn't possibly lead anywhere else.

In any case and whatever the reason, it was obvious he wasn't being treated like an ordinary prisoner. He hadn't been wrong when he'd made a note of the politeness of the old gentleman with the glasses—a chilly politeness, but politeness all the same.

So to the right of him there were at least ten men, sometimes more, you never knew because there was always a lot of coming and going. To his left there were three, maybe four, and one was sick or insane.

It wasn't a cell, it was a classroom. What had it been used for when the building was a school? Courses in which only a few pupils enrolled, third- and fourth-year courses, most likely. For a classroom it was small, but for a cell it was huge, much too big for one person. It bothered him, since he didn't know what to do with himself. His bed seemed tiny. It was an iron bed, an old army cot, with boards instead of springs. They hadn't given him a mattress. All he had was a rough gray blanket that smelled of disinfectant.

That was a lot more disgusting than the smell of sweat, more disgusting than if the blanket had reeked with human odors. The chemical scent made him think of a corpse. They probably only disinfected blankets after the people who'd been using them died. And men must have died in this room. Certain inscriptions had been carefully erased. But you could still see hearts with initials in them—like the ones on trees in the country—flags that were impossible to identify, and everywhere the vertical scratches that marked the days, with a crossbar for each week.

It had been difficult for him to find a clean spot of his own. Now he was on his third crossbar.

He didn't reply to the messages. He had decided not to, not even to try to understand. During the day a soldier paced up and down the walkway, looking through the windows at the prisoners from time to time. At night they relied on the searchlights, and the tread of boots was seldom heard.

Night fell early, and the racket soon broke out. The walls and pipes rang. He didn't understand any of it. It wouldn't have required much effort, only a little patience. Probably it was some sort of simplified Morse code.

He decided, once and for all, not to pay attention. He was alone. So much the better. They had done him the favor of putting him by himself, and that must mean something. So much the worse if it meant that his case was more serious. He had enough experience to doubt it.

From the room on the right, where new prisoners were brought all the time, they took them out to be shot, not every day but several times a week. It was the holding cell. They seemed to select them at random, like fish out of a pond.

It always happened just before daybreak. How did they manage to sleep? Some moaned or cried out in the middle of the night. Probably the young ones.

Two soldiers would come from the courtyard, always two, boots clanging up the iron stairs and down the walkway. At first, Frank had wondered each time if it was his turn. Now he remained unmoved. The steps always stopped outside the classroom next door. Had some of the people shut up inside once studied there?

Then everybody started shouting a patriotic song, and you saw vague forms passing in the dim light, two or three prisoners followed by a couple of soldiers.

If they did it like that on purpose, it was a stroke of genius. The hour was so well chosen that Frank was never able to distinguish anyone's features. Only silhouettes. Men walking, hands behind their backs, without hats or overcoats in spite of the cold. And invariably with their collars turned up.

They must take them into an office one last time, because there was a wait and the sun was already coming up when footsteps crossed the courtyard. It took place near the covered playground. A few yards nearer and Frank would have been able to see it from his window. As it was, all he ever saw was the upper part of the body of the commanding officer of the firing squad.

Afterward he slept. Because they let him sleep. He didn't know what happened in the other classrooms. Something else, since there was always a lot of noise early in the morning. As for him, they didn't bother him until they brought his breakfast, a gruel made out of acorns without any sugar in it together with a little piece of gluey bread.

It would have been all right for Bertha, that cow. But he managed. He sucked down the gruel to the last drop. He ate the bread. He wasn't going to give in. He had set up a routine on the very first day.

He wouldn't permit himself to think about a particular subject other than at its appointed time. He had a complete schedule in his head. Sometimes it was difficult to keep to it. His thoughts had a way of getting mixed up. Then, to relax, he would stare at a black spot on the wall, high up, where the crucifix must have hung when this had been a classroom.

"Bertha is a stupid bitch . . . but it wasn't her."

But since it wasn't the right time, since it wasn't the moment to think about the rue Verte, he went back to the point where he'd left off speculating the day before.

Often Sissy or Holst interrupted him. Sissy, for example, coming to pick up her bag with the key in it, when in fact he didn't know whether she had ever picked it up, or even if she'd seen it. It wasn't important, but it was forbidden by his rules. As for Holst, he had become, you could say, Public Enemy Number One. He kept cropping up all the time, in his gray felt boots, his overcoat, with his tin lunch box and his droopy frame. Oddly, Frank never could see his face. It was just a blur. Or, more exactly, an expression.

What expression? If he wasn't careful, he'd go on thinking

about it for minutes and minutes—too long, at any rate, since there was no way to keep track of the time. If necessary, he'd have to measure it by his pulse.

How would you describe the look they had exchanged when Holst was at the window and Frank was waiting for the streetcar?

There was no word for it.

And there wasn't a word for Holst's expression, either. It was a mystery, an enigma. And when you were in Frank's position, you didn't have the right to puzzle over enigmas, even if for the moment it seemed to do you good.

The questions had to be taken up one after another, with determination. You had to force yourself to keep calm, to be lucid, not to let yourself fall into the mentality of a prisoner.

There was this.

That happened.

So-and-so, so-and-so, and so-and-so might have acted like that.

Without overlooking anything, neither the details nor the people.

All day long he kept his coat on, his collar turned up, hat on his head. He spent most of his time sitting on the edge of his bed. They only emptied his bucket once a day and the bucket didn't even have a cover.

Why was it a prisoner who always came to empty it? Why hadn't Frank been taken down to the courtyard for exercise, while three of his neighbors to the left always went?

He didn't want to walk the courtyard. He couldn't see them. He could hear them. He didn't want anything. He didn't complain. He never tried to talk to his guards, who changed almost every day, and he never whined, as others must have done, in the hope of getting a cigarette or even a drag off one from a soldier.

There was this.

There was Frank.

Then there was this and that.

The neighbors from the rue Verte, Kromer, Timo, Bertha, Holst, Sissy, old man Kamp, old Wimmer, others too, including the violinist, Carl Adler, the blond man from the third floor, even Ressl, even Kropetzki. No one must be omitted. He didn't have paper or pencil, but he kept his list up-to-date in his head, tirelessly, with, in the margin, anything that was of interest, no matter how small.

There was Frank . . .

He wasn't going to let Holst's face, or expression, interfere with the task he'd undertaken.

Sissy was probably better now.

Or dead.

What mattered was the list, thinking, not forgetting anything, while at the same time being careful not to add extra importance to the things that meant nothing.

There was Frank, son of Lotte . . .

That reminded him of the Bible. He smiled with disdain— it was like a joke. He hadn't come to prison to joke.

Besides, they hadn't put him in a prison, but in a school, and that had to mean something.

# 5

THE NINETEENTH day.

*They hadn't put him in a prison, but in a school.*

Automatically he picked up where he'd left off the day before. It was an exercise. You got used to it quickly. It started by itself, and then the wheels kept going round, like a watch. You did this and that. You made the same movements at the same times, and, as long as you took some care, your thoughts went on ticking.

There was nothing annoying about the school itself, but if there really were sections, as Timo claimed, Frank was certainly in a serious one, since they shot prisoners almost every day. If they kept on paying no attention to him, or pretending not to, it might become more disturbing.

They hadn't questioned him before and he still wasn't being questioned. They didn't spy on him. If they had been watching all the time he would have noticed. They simply left him alone. They'd done nothing about his clothes, which he'd been wearing for nineteen days. He hadn't been able to wash properly once, since he was never given enough water.

But he wasn't angry at them. As long as it didn't imply contempt, he didn't mind. He hadn't shaved. Other young men his age didn't have real beards, but he had started shaving just for fun when he was very young. Before, he shaved every day. His beard was almost an inch long now. At first it was bristly, but it was starting to feel soft.

In town there was a real prison. Naturally, they'd taken it

over, and it must be full. It didn't follow that they put the most interesting cases there.

Nothing proved they were making fun of him. He had come to the conclusion that if the guards never spoke to him it was because they couldn't speak his language. The prisoners who brought him his pitcher of water and emptied his pail also avoided speaking. They could roam freely about the buildings. Some of them were shaved and had their hair cut, which showed that there was a barber in the school. If they didn't take him to the barber, did that mean they'd forgotten about him? Was he being kept in solitary?

Someone was at the bottom of all this, an informer, something of that sort. He reviewed the names and the actions of everyone, studied all the possibilities. It always embarrassed him to sit on his pail with that big window through which everything could be seen from the walkway. Yet he wasn't ashamed of being unshaven anymore, of his dirty underwear and clothes, all wrinkled because he slept in them.

The others went down for exercise at nine o'clock. Probably, they made them go out that early on purpose, so they would feel the cold even more, especially the ones without overcoats. Why didn't they wait until eleven or noon, after the sun had warmed things up a little?

That wasn't his problem, since he never went out. If he had, he would have missed the scene at the window a little later.

The wheels kept going around, his thoughts had started to whir again, which didn't stop him, after nine o'clock, from waiting. It was nothing, less than nothing, in fact. It would have been impossible in a real prison, where they're careful to prevent contact with the outside, even for an instant. It seemed that no one had thought of the window. And it had been careless of them not to take adequate precautions, because it could turn out to be important.

Beyond the assembly hall or gym, on the other side of the courtyard, there seemed to be an empty space, perhaps a street, perhaps a row of low single-family houses like most of the others in this neighborhood. Far away, much farther, rose the back of a building at least four stories high and almost entirely hidden by the gym. Because of the slope of the roof one window was visible, only one, probably on the top floor, suggesting the tenants there were poor.

Every morning, a little before nine-thirty, a woman opened the window. She wore a dressing gown—like Lotte—with a light-colored scarf around her head, while she shook out the rugs and blankets over the emptiness below.

From so far away you couldn't make out her features. But from her brisk movements and from what she was doing, he guessed she had to be young. In spite of the cold, she left the window open for a long time while she came and went, tending to things inside, her cooking or her baby. He knew she had a baby, since the clothes she hung out to dry on the line stretched across the window were always tiny.

Who knows? Maybe she was singing. She must be happy. He was fairly sure she was happy. After she closed the window she would be in her own home, with all the familiar household smells taking possession again.

That day, his nineteenth, he was furious because they came to get him at a quarter past nine, or at least before she had appeared at the window. Ever since his arrival he had been waiting for them to come. He thought about it all day long. And now that it had happened, he was furious because they had disturbed him a quarter of an hour too early.

A civilian, accompanied by a soldier, stopped on the walkway outside his door. He had a brown mustache. He made Frank think of a school principal. Immediately Frank said to himself it must be one of the two men who had been beating the man ahead of him while he was waiting on the day of his arrival. He was a man who beat prisoners when he was ordered to—beat them calmly, without hate or enthusiasm, just as he might add up columns of figures in an office.

Were they taking Frank down for that? Neither the civilian nor the soldier took the trouble to glance around the room. They said nothing. They simply motioned for him to come. The civilian went ahead and he followed, unthinking, without looking into the other classrooms, though he'd intended to. There were other things to see. It was the hour when the prisoners were taking their exercise in the large courtyard. He saw them from the walkway and also as he came down the stairs outside.

He forgot to observe them closely. Later he could only remember a sort of long, dark snake. They walked single file about a yard or so apart, and formed an almost closed oval, undulating a bit.

If they hit him, what would it mean? That they'd made a mistake, that they suspected him of things he hadn't done—because they couldn't care less about Mademoiselle Vilmos. Strangely, he never even thought about the noncommissioned officer. That seemed to him so minor he felt innocent.

They turned toward—they turned him toward—the little building where he'd been received the first morning, and he went up the same steps. This time they didn't keep him waiting. Without pausing, they took him into the office of the old gentleman, who was at his place behind the desk, and Frank, looking around the room, saw his mother.

His first reaction was to frown, and, before looking again, before speaking, he waited for instructions from the official. He seemed just as indifferent as before. He was busy writing, in a very small hand, and it was Lotte who spoke first. It was a moment or two before her voice sounded natural. It had been too flat, like a voice in a cave.

"You see, Frank, these gentlemen have permitted me to come see you and to bring you a few things. I didn't know where you were."

The last words were said quickly. They must have set

guidelines. There were certain subjects she could broach, others that were forbidden.

Why was he so glum? In truth, he felt uneasy. He didn't trust her. She came from somewhere else. She looked too much like herself. It was awful how much she looked like herself. He recognized the scent of her powder. She had put rouge on her cheeks, the way she always did when she went out. She was wearing her white hat with a tiny veil halfway over her eyes, out of vanity, because of the little wrinkles on her "onionskins," as she called her eyelids. She must have spent at least half an hour in front of her mirror in the big bedroom. He could see her putting on her kid gloves, fluffing out her hair to either side of her hat.

"I can't stay long."

They had told her how long she could stay. Why didn't she say so?

"You look well. You don't know how happy I am to see you looking so well."

That meant: "To see you alive."

Because she had thought he was dead.

"When did they tell you?"

She answered in a low voice, casting an anxious eye on the old gentleman. "Yesterday."

"Who?"

She didn't reply, but said with forced animation, "Guess what, they've let me bring you a few things. First, some clothes. At last, my poor Frank, you'll be able to change."

This failed to give him the pleasure he would have imagined. Two weeks before, he would have valued it more than anything.

He shocked her. His appearance shocked her. She looked at his rumpled clothes, the collar of his coat turned up to hide his filthy, tieless shirt, his unkempt hair, his nineteen-day-old beard, and his shoes with no laces. She was sorry for him, you could feel that. He didn't need anyone's pity, especially Lotte's. She was sickening, with her makeup and white hat.

Would the old gentleman like a taste of her? Had she tried? She had probably paid special attention to her underthings.

"I put everything in a suitcase. These gentlemen will give it to you."

He saw her eyes casting about, and he recognized his own suitcase standing against the wall.

"You mustn't, above all, let yourself go . . ."

Let himself go how?

"Everybody has been very kind. Everything is going well."

"What's going well?"

He was brusque, almost curt. He didn't like it, but he couldn't seem to help it.

"I've decided to close down the shop."

She held her handkerchief, rolled into a ball in the palm of her hand. She looked like she was ready to cry.

"Hamling advised me to. You're wrong not to trust him. He's done everything he could."

"Is Minna still there?"

"She doesn't want to leave me. She sends her best. If I could find an apartment somewhere else, we'd move, but it's practically impossible."

This time the look Frank gave her was pitiless, almost ferocious. "You'd leave the building?"

"You know how people are. Now that you're not there it's even worse."

He asked curtly, "Is Sissy dead?"

"Good Lord, no! Why on earth would you say that?"

She glanced at her little gold wristwatch. Time still counted for her. She knew how many minutes were left.

"Does she go out?"

"She doesn't go out. She's . . . Well, Frank, I really don't know how she is. I think she's depressed. She can't seem to get well."

"What's the matter?"

"I don't know. I haven't seen her myself. Nobody sees her except her father and Monsieur Wimmer. They say she's neurasthenic."

"Has Holst gone back to driving his streetcar?"

"No. He works at home."

"Doing what?"

"I'm not sure. Bookkeeping, I think. The little I know comes from Hamling."

"He sees them?"

Before, the chief inspector only knew the Holsts by name.

"He's been to see them a few times."

"Why?"

"Come on, Frank, what do you expect me to say? You ask me questions as though you didn't know the building. I don't see anyone. Anny left. It seems she's being kept by a . . ."

Here, you didn't have the right to talk about members of the Occupation forces.

"If Minna had left me, too, I don't know what would have become of me."

"Have you seen any of my friends?"

"No."

She was disconcerted, disappointed. She must have been excited and happy at first, the way people are when they visit a sick person in the hospital, bringing grapes or oranges, and he hadn't thanked her at all for her good intentions. Instead you would have sworn he blamed her, held her responsible for her own disappointment.

He pointed to a package beside her on the chair. "What's that?"

"Nothing. Things in the suitcase I wasn't allowed to leave."

"I don't want you to move to another building."

She sighed impatiently. Didn't he understand that she couldn't say what she wanted to? Yes, he knew. But he didn't care. The other tenants were making life impossible for Lotte? So what. He absolutely forbade her to leave the building. Was it for her or for him to decide? Who counted most?

"Has Holst spoken to you?"

She seem embarrassed when she replied: "Not directly."

"He sent you a message through Hamling?"

"No, Frank. Why bother about it? It's nothing to worry about. My time is up. If I'm to see you again, I mustn't overdo it the first time. I'd like to kiss you, but I guess I'd better not. They might think you're slipping me a message or whispering something in my ear."

He didn't want to kiss her anyway. She must have been there for some time before he had come down, since they'd had time to go through the suitcase.

"Don't give up. Take care of yourself. But mostly, don't worry."

"I'm not worried."

"You're acting so funny."

She, too, was eager to for it to be over. She would go wait for her streetcar opposite the gate and snivel all the way back home.

"Good-bye, Frank."

"Good-bye, Mother."

"Take care of yourself."

Of course! Of course! What did she think? That he was going to let himself fall to pieces?

The old gentleman raised his eyes to look from one to the other, then motioned Frank to take the suitcase. A civilian escorted Lotte across the courtyard, and you could hear the sound of her high heels tapping on the hard-packed snow and then fading away. The old gentleman spoke slowly, choosing his words. He insisted on finding just the right term, and was very careful about his pronunciation. He had taken lessons and was still trying to improve.

"You will now go and get yourself ready."

He enunciated each syllable. He didn't seem to be a bad sort. He just liked things done the right way. He hesitated before launching into a longer sentence, rehearsing it in his mind before he risked speaking out loud.

"If you desire to be shaved, they will take you."

Frank refused. A mistake. It would have given him a chance to see more of the buildings. He wasn't sure what had made him refuse. He wasn't particularly happy about being dirty or playing the bearded prisoner. The truth was—it would take him days to admit it—that when they mentioned his beard, he had automatically thought of Holst's felt boots.

There was no connection. He didn't want any sort of connection. He wanted to think about something else.

And there was no lack of things to think about now. They let him carry his suitcase. Again, on the way back to his classroom, a civilian went ahead of him and the soldier followed. He almost had the illusion of being escorted to a room in a hotel. They closed the door and left him alone.

Why had he been ordered to get ready? It was an order, no doubt about it. The moment had come. They were taking him somewhere. Would they make him bring his suitcase? Would he come back afterward? They must have removed the newspaper wrapping from the things in the suitcase— everything in it was disordered. There were little cakes of pink soap that reminded him of Bertha's skin, a smoked salami, a largish piece of salt pork, a pound of sugar, chocolate bars. And he found half a dozen shirts and several pairs of socks, as well as a new sweater his mother must have just bought. There was even, at the bottom, a pair of thick woolen gloves he would never think of wearing outside.

He changed clothes. He had missed the woman at the window. He was thinking too fast. Today didn't count. They were rushing him, and that made his mood worse. He even began to regret his solitude and all his little habits. When he came back, if he came back, he had to straighten it all out in his head. He munched on the chocolate without realizing that it had been nineteen days since he had done that, and what lingered after Lotte's visit was a sense of disappointment.

He didn't know how it had happened, but he was disappointed. There had been no point of contact between them. He had asked her questions, and it had seemed to him, it still seemed to him, that what she answered had nothing to do with what he asked.

Yet she had given him all the news as quickly and straightforwardly as possible. She couldn't have been hounded by the authorities because she had only been told where he was the day before. So he hadn't been in the newspaper. The local police had had nothing to do with his case, or she would have heard from Hamling.

Hamling continued to visit the apartment, but he had crossed the landing like someone fording a river. Now he was going to the Holsts'. Why? Holst no longer drove a streetcar. There was a very simple reason for that. Because of his job, Holst had had to come home in the middle of the night every other week, and while he was away Sissy was alone. He must have found some other job that kept him busy only during the day.

Sissy was never alone. He knew well enough how his mother and people like her talked about such things. If she used the word "neurasthenic," if she seemed embarrassed, it must be a lot more serious than that.

Was Sissy crazy?

He wasn't afraid of words. He made himself say it aloud: "Crazy!"

That was it! With the two men, her father and old Wimmer, taking turns staying with her, and the chief inspector coming from time to time, sitting in a chair in his overcoat and galoshes, which left wet marks on the floor.

They were going to take Frank somewhere. Otherwise

there was no sense telling him to get ready. Well, and now he was ready much too soon. There was nothing to do and no use thinking in the meantime. That would only lessen his power to resist. After the chocolate, he gnawed on the salami. It hadn't occurred to his mother that he wouldn't have a knife. And there wasn't any water left to wash his face with. He smelled of smoked meat.

Where were they? Why didn't they come for him? If only they'd take him! And, more than anything, bring him back as soon as possible and leave him alone.

The same civilian as before. In fact, apart from the soldiers, who kept changing all the time, there weren't that many civilians there. And they all bore a kind of family resemblance. If Timo was right, the section to which they belonged must be pretty important. Hadn't Timo told him that the man who had made the colonel shake in his boots looked like a minor functionary?

Here that's what they all looked like. Not one was light-hearted or showy. You couldn't imagine them in front of a really good dinner or chasing girls. From the way they looked, you'd say they were born to add up figures.

Since appearances were the opposite of the truth with these people—according, again, to Timo—they must be truly powerful.

The little office again. The old gentleman wasn't there. Had he gone out for lunch? Frank found his tie and shoelaces on the desk. They pointed to them and said in their terrible accent, "You are permitted!"

He sat down on a chair. He wasn't at all worried now. Had these people known his language a bit better, he would have talked about anything.

Two others were waiting with their hats on. Just before going out, one of them handed him a cigarette and then a match.

"Thank you."

A car was waiting in the courtyard, not a police van or

a military car, but one of those long shiny black cars that rich people who could afford a chauffeur used to own. It glided smoothly and noiselessly out of the gate and turned toward town, following the streetcar tracks. And although the windows were rolled up, the air tasted like the outdoors. He saw people on the sidewalks, shop windows, a little boy hopping on one leg kicking a brick along in front of him.

They hadn't made him take his suitcase. And he wasn't asked to sign anything. He'd come back. He was convinced that he'd come back, that he'd once more see the woman at the window, hanging up baby clothes. Hey! Had he only turned in time, he might have recognized the house. He should remember that on the way back.

It was faster in a car than in the trolley. They were already nearing the center of town. They circled an impressive building that housed most of the military offices. This must be where his general had his. There were guards at all the doors, and the sidewalks were barricaded to prevent civilians from using them.

They didn't stop at the monumental entrance but at a low door on a side street instead, where a police station had once been. They didn't have to tell him to get out. He knew. He lingered for a moment, very briefly, on the sidewalk. He saw people on the other side of the street. He didn't recognize anyone. No one recognized him, no one looked at him. He didn't stop long. That was certainly not permitted.

He went in first. He waited a second for them to lead the way through a labyrinth of dark and intricate corridors with mysterious signs on the doors. Occasionally secretaries, carrying files under their arms, passed by.

They wouldn't torture him here. There were too many stenographers in white blouses. They didn't look at him as they went by. There was nothing dramatic. There were simply offices, lots of offices, where papers piled up and officers and their subordinates smoked cigars while they worked. The mysterious signs on the doors, letters followed by numerals, evidently represented the different departments.

This was another section. Timo had been right. You could feel the difference right away. Was it less or more important? He wasn't able to tell yet. Here, for example, you heard bursts of chatter, whispering, laughter. Well-fed men stuck out their chests and buckled their belts before leaving. Women's breasts could be sensed under their blouses, the softness of their thighs under their skirts. Some of them surely made love on office desks.

Frank behaved differently. He looked around as he would have anywhere, and he was a little embarrassed because of his beard. He carried himself almost as before. He tried to catch a glimpse of himself in a glass door and his hand went instinctively to his tie.

They had arrived. It was almost at the top of the building. The ceilings were lower, the windows smaller, the hallways dusty. They led him into an empty office containing nothing but files and a large unpainted table covered with dirty blotters.

Was he wrong? It seemed that his two companions didn't feel at home, that their expressions had grown distant and at the same time humble, with a touch of irony perhaps, or contempt. They glanced questioningly at each other before one of them knocked on a side door. One man disappeared and returned almost immediately, followed by a fat officer in an unbuttoned tunic.

Standing in the doorway, the officer looked Frank over from head to foot, drawing on his cigar with an air of importance.

He seemed satisfied. At first glance he had appeared surprised to find that Frank was so young.

"Come in!"

He was gruff but hearty, placing his hand on Frank's shoulder as he guided him into the room. The two civilians didn't follow them in, and the officer closed the door. In one corner, near another door, a younger officer of a lower rank was working under an electric light, since that part of the room was almost dark.

"Friedmaier, isn't it?"

"That's my name."

The officer glanced at a typewritten sheet of paper that had been prepared for him.

"Frank Friedmaier. Very good. Sit down."

He motioned to a cane-seated chair on the other side of the desk and pushed forward a box of cigarettes and a lighter. That must be protocol. The cigarettes were there for visitors, since he himself was smoking an extraordinarily light-colored and aromatic cigar.

He leaned back in his armchair, his belly in evidence. He had sparse hair and the complexion of a heavy eater.

"Now then, my friend, what's the story?"

In spite of his accent he had a perfect command of the language, understood all its subtleties, and his familiar tone was intentional.

"I don't know," Frank replied.

"Ha! Ha! *I don't know!*"

He translated the reply for the benefit of the other officer, who seemed delighted.

"But it is most necessary that you should know, isn't it? You've been given plenty of time to think."

"To think about what?"

This time the officer frowned, stood up, went over to a cabinet, consulted a file. It was probably just for effect. He sat down again, resumed his former position, and flipped his cigar ash off with his little finger.

"I'm listening."

"I'd be glad to answer any questions you have."

"There you are! What questions? I bet you don't know, do you?"

"No."

"You don't know what you've done?"

"I don't know what I'm accused of having done."

"There you are! There you are!"

It was a verbal tic with him. He had a funny way of pronouncing the words.

"You'd like to know what we want to know. There you are. Is that it?"

"That's it."

"Because, maybe, you know other things, too?"

"I don't know anything."

"Nothing at all! You know nothing at all! And yet this was found in your pocket, wasn't it?"

For a moment Frank expected to see his hand come out of the desk drawer holding the automatic. He turned pale. He felt he was being scrutinized. Reluctantly he followed his questioner's hand with his eyes, and was astonished to recognize the roll of bills he had carried around in his pocket and flashed at every chance.

"There you are! And that's nothing, I suppose?"

"It's money."

"Money, yes. A lot of money."

"I earned it."

"You earned it, there you are! When you earn money, there's always someone, or some bank, that gives it to you. That is correct, isn't it? And all I want to know is who gave you the money. It's simple, it's easy. You only have to tell me the name. There you are!"

"I don't know."

"You don't know who gave you the money?"

"I got it from different places."

"Really?"

"I'm in business."

"You don't say!"

"You get paid here and there. Bills change hands. You don't pay attention . . ."

But suddenly the man's tone changed, he shut the drawer with a bang before pronouncing categorically, "No!"

He looked furious, menacing. For a moment, as he came around the desk and again put his hand on his shoulder, Frank thought he was going to slap him. Instead he pulled him to his feet. All the while the officer was talking, almost as if to himself.

"It's just money from wherever, isn't it? You're paid here and there and you stuff it in your pockets without bothering to take a look."

"Yes."

"No!"

Frank's throat tightened. He didn't know what his interlocutor was driving at. He felt a vague threat, a mystery. He had been racking his brains for eighteen, almost nineteen days. He had tried to foresee everything, and nothing was happening the way it should. All at once they confronted him with an entirely different situation. The school, the old gentleman with glasses, suddenly represented a world that was almost reassuring, and yet now he had a cigarette in his mouth, he could hear the clatter of typewriters in the next room, women walking down the corridor.

"Look carefully, Friedmaier, and tell me if it's still just money from somewhere or other."

He had taken one of the bills from the desk. He led Frank toward the window with his hand on his shoulder and held the money against the light.

"Closer! Don't be afraid! You needn't be afraid."

Why did those words seem more threatening than the sound of the blows he had heard the first day in the old gentleman's office?

"Look carefully. In the left-hand corner. Tiny little holes. Six little holes. There you are! And the little holes form a design. And there are little holes like these in all the bills that were found in your pocket as well as in the ones you spent."

Frank was struck dumb and couldn't think. It was as if a chasm had unexpectedly opened up in front of him, as if the wall around the window had suddenly ceased to exist, leaving the two men on the edge of the void over the street.

"I don't know."

"You don't know, do you?"

"No."

"And you also didn't know the significance of these little holes? There you are! You don't know!"

It was true. He had never heard of such a thing. He had the impression that merely knowing the meaning of what the officer called the little holes would be a more crushing indictment against him than any crime. He wanted someone to look into his eyes and read his good faith in them, his absolute sincerity.

"I swear I don't know."

"But I know."

"What do you mean?"

"I do know, yes. And that's why I also have to know where you got those bills."

"I told you . . ."

"No!"

"I swear to you . . ."

"Those bills were stolen."

"Not by me."

"No!"

How could he be so sure? And then he said, articulating and emphasizing each syllable: "They were stolen from *here.*"

As Frank looked around the room in terror, the officer corrected himself. "They were stolen here, *from this building.*"

Frank was afraid he was going to faint. From then on he understood the meaning of the phrase "cold sweat." He understood other things. Everything, it seemed.

The little holes in the bills were made by the Occupation authorities. Which bills? Of what issue?

No one knew, no one even suspected, and it was terrifying just to be in on the secret.

Damn it, they weren't accusing him! And not Kromer, either. They knew very well that they were only petty crooks and that people like them didn't have access to certain safes.

Did they already suspect the general? Had they arrested Kromer? Had they questioned him? Had he talked?

Frank had been groping in the dark for eighteen and a half days. Everything had been false, stupid. He had been concentrating on unimportant people, people like himself, as though destiny had any use for them.

Destiny had chosen a banknote, probably one he had spent at Timo's, or at the tailor's where he had bought his camel-hair coat. Perhaps one of the bills he had given to Kropetzki for his sister's eyes.

"We have to know, you see?" said the officer, sitting down.

Once again he pushed the box of cigarettes toward Frank.

"There you are, Friedmaier. There you have the whole business."

PART THREE
# THE WOMAN AT
# THE WINDOW

# 1

HE WAS lying on his stomach, asleep. He was conscious of being asleep. It was something he'd learned recently, along with a lot of other things. Before, it had been only toward morning, especially when the sun was coming up, that he had been conscious of being asleep. And since the feeling was stronger after getting drunk the night before, he often came home after drinking simply to relish that conscious sleep.

Still, it hadn't been quite the same as this new sleep. Before, he never slept flat on his stomach. Did all prisoners learn to sleep flat on their stomachs? He had no idea. He didn't care. And yet, if he'd had the patience and will to study it, he would have gladly used their complicated system of communication just to let them all know: "Sleep flat on your stomachs!"

But it wasn't just sleeping flat on your stomach. It was crushing yourself, like an animal, like a bug, onto the boards that he had for bedsprings. Hard as they were, he felt like he was leaving the imprint of his body on them, as if he was sleeping on a field of soft earth.

He was lying flat on his stomach, and it hurt. Lots of little bones and muscles hurt, not all at once, not all together, but in a regular sequence that he was beginning to recognize, and that he had learned to orchestrate like a symphony. There were deep, dark pains and there were much sharper ones, so sharp that you saw everything in pale yellow light. Some lasted only a few seconds, but were so voluptuous in their intensity that you regretted it when they were over; others formed a background, mingling and harmonizing so completely that it was impossible to tell where each pain came from.

His face was buried in his jacket, which he had rolled into a ball to make a pillow—a jacket, he was sorry to say, that had been almost new when he arrived. And he had been stupid, at first, to be so careful with it, to take it off at night, so that now it didn't smell as good as it might.

To get a good whiff of himself—to breathe in that smell of earth, of being alive, of sweat. Deliberately he sank his nose in where it stank most, under the arms. He wanted to stink, as people said outside, to stink as the earth stinks, because outside people think that men stink, that the earth stinks.

To feel his heart beat, everywhere, in his temples, his wrists, his big toes. To smell the smell of his breath, the warmth of it. To mix up the images in his mind, larger, bigger than life, things seen, heard, and lived, and others, too, that might have happened, to mix them all together, his eyes closed, his body still, while he listened for a certain footstep on the iron stairs.

He had gotten good at this game. But why call it a game? It was life. At school they had said, "He's good at math." Not him, but a schoolmate with an enormous head.

And now Frank was good at life. He knew how to sink into the boards, bury his face in his jacket, shut his eyes, sink in, throw ballast overboard, sink down and surface again at will, or almost. Somewhere there were still days, hours, minutes. Not here, not for him. Since arriving, when he really wanted to keep track of time, he counted it in so many "dives."

It sounded stupid. But he wasn't getting stupid. He hadn't lost his grip, and he was more determined than ever not to let himself go. Instead, he made progress. What was the use of bothering about hours, outside hours, in a building where nothing depended on them?

If you had a sweet tooth, and you cut a cake in quarters,

you'd keep an eye on the quarters. But what if you cut slices? What if you sliced the cake to bits?

Everything had to be learned, starting with sleep. To think that people believed they knew how to sleep! They all had too many hours to devote to it if they wanted. People complained about being slaves to alarm clocks, yet they set them themselves when they went to bed, they even checked, half asleep, to make sure it was on.

To wake up to an alarm clock you set yourself! To wake yourself up, in other words! They called that slavery!

Let them learn to sleep on their stomachs first, sleep anywhere, on the ground like worms, like bugs. And if they couldn't have the smell of the earth, let them be satisfied to stink.

Lotte sprayed perfume under her arms and probably between her legs. She made her girls do the same.

It was unthinkable!

To sleep flat on your stomach, to measure out, to be in wait for, to orchestrate your aches, to feel with your tongue the hole where two teeth were missing, to tell yourself that if everything went well, if it was a lucky day, you'd see the window beyond the courtyard, way over there, to sleep like that, to think like that—this was already getting closer to the truth. It wasn't the whole truth yet, he knew that very well. But it was a comfort to know you were on the right track.

There was a signal that meant that the others in the next classroom were going for recess. What else could he call it? Their steps were joyous. Whatever they said, their steps were joyous, even the ones who were going to be shot the very next day, maybe because they didn't know it yet.

They'd gone by. Very well! Now the question was whether the old gentleman had enough work or not. The old gentleman was more important than anyone else in the world. He wasn't married. Or if he was, his wife must have stayed in his country, which came to the same thing. Busy or not, all he had to do was raise his head and order, "Bring me Frank Friedmaier."

Luckily, he rarely summoned him at this hour. It was even luckier that no one knew—that was one of the reasons Frank slept on his stomach. Because if they knew what it was he was waiting for, if they suspected even for a moment how much joy it gave him, they would have been sure to change the school's whole schedule.

It was no longer winter. Well, not exactly. It was still, obviously, midwinter, with the worst of the cold yet to come. Generally it came in February or March, and the later it came the worse it was, sometimes lasting to the middle, even the end of April.

Let's say the darkest part of the tunnel was past. This year there was a false spring, not unusual at the end of January. At least, outside they called it a false spring. The air and the sky were limpid. The snow shone without melting, and yet it wasn't cold. The water was frozen every morning, and all day the sun was so bright that you would have sworn the birds were going to start building their nests. They must have been fooled, too, since you could see them flying around in pairs, chasing each other in a mating dance.

The window over there, beyond the gym or assembly hall, stayed open longer. One time he could make out from the woman's movements that she was ironing. And there had been another time that was wonderful, and completely unexpected. Probably because she was taking advantage of the warmer weather to do her spring-cleaning, the window had stayed open for more than two hours! Had she put the cradle in another room or covered the sleeping baby with extra blankets? She had shaken clothes out at the open window—some men's clothes, too. She had shaken them out and beaten them like rugs, and each of her movements not only hurt Frank horribly but did him good.

From that distance, she was no bigger than a doll. He wouldn't recognize her in the street—it didn't matter, that would never happen. She was just a doll. He couldn't make out her features. But it was a woman, and she was looking after her home. And he could sense her enthusiasm. He could feel it.

He watched for her every morning. Logically, at that hour, he should have been collapsed with exhaustion. At first he was afraid of missing her. It had happened only once, when he had been at the end of his rope. That was before he had learned how to orchestrate his sleep.

She didn't know. She would never know. It was a woman, not a rich one, a poor woman to judge by where she lived. She had a husband and a child. The man probably went to work early, since Frank never saw him. Did she put his lunch in a tin lunch box like the one Holst took with him on his street-car? Maybe. Probably. As soon as he left she began to work in her home, their home. She must sing with the baby and laugh with it a lot. Babies don't cry all the time—as his wet-nurse had tried to make him believe.

"When you used to cry . . ."

"The day you cried so hard . . ."

"The Sunday when you were so insufferable . . ."

She never said, "When you used to laugh . . ."

And the bed, the bed that smelled of the *two of them*. She didn't know. If she'd known, she wouldn't have hung the sheets and blankets to air in the window. She wouldn't even have opened the window. It was lucky for him that she was from the outside. In her place, he'd have shut everything, kept everything for himself. He wouldn't have allowed anything of their life to escape.

The spring-cleaning morning had seemed so extraordinary to him that he couldn't believe fate had reserved such joys for him. There she was celebrating the false spring in her own way, airing, cleaning, polishing. She shook everything, shifted everything. She was beautiful!

He hadn't really seen her, but it didn't matter: she was beautiful!

Somewhere in town there was a man who went to work every day knowing that in the evening she'd be waiting for him, with their child in its cradle, their bed that smelled of them.

It made no difference what he did or thought. It made no difference that the woman at the window was no bigger than a puppet. Frank was the one who lived their life the most. Even if, lying on his stomach, he only dared to use one eye, since if they noticed how fascinated he was, they would have altered his schedule.

He knew them. Hadn't Timo claimed he understood them? Timo only knew pieces of the truth—ready-made truths, like the ones you read in the papers.

When he was little, Madame Porse, his wet-nurse, used to make him angry by saying, "You've been fighting with Hans again *because* . . ."

And her *because* was always wrong. *Because* Hans was the son of a wealthy farmer. *Because* he was rich. *Because* he was stronger than Frank. *Because*. *Because*.

His whole life he'd seen people going wrong with their *becauses*. Lotte most of all! Lotte, who understood less than anybody.

There was no *because*. It was a word for fools. For people outside, at least. With their *becauses*, it wouldn't surprise him if, one day, they gave him a medal he didn't deserve or a posthumous decoration.

*Because* what?

Why hadn't he answered the officer who blew smoke in his face when he was being questioned at headquarters, up there on the top floor? He wasn't any more of a hero than anyone.

"You really have to know, Friedmaier."

That story of the banknotes with the little holes in them

had nothing to do with him. All he had to reply was, "Ask the general."

Stupid! A simple matter of watches. Since Frank didn't know the general personally, he would have had to add, "I gave the watches to Kromer, and Kromer gave me my share of the money."

He wasn't at all concerned for Kromer. He absolutely didn't want to risk his life for him. On the contrary. For some time, Kromer had been one of the few men, maybe the only one, he would like to have seen dead.

Then what had happened up there in the military building?

The officer stood in front of him, still friendly, with his light-colored cigar and his pink complexion. Frank had never seen the general. He had no reason to sacrifice himself for him. It would have been simpler to say, "Well, this is exactly how it happened, and you'll have to admit I had nothing to do with the banknotes."

Why hadn't he said that? No one would have known. Not even the general. He had thought of explanations two days, five days, ten days later, all of them different, all of them plausible.

The true reason, the only one, was perhaps that he didn't want to be set free, didn't want to return to everyone else's life.

He knew now. It made no difference whether he talked or not—not as far as the end result was concerned. There was no way he could answer someone who explained what he'd done by saying: "You knew very well you were going to jail no matter what!"

That was obvious. Not that he knew he was going back to jail but that he *had* to. But he had only admitted this after.

In reality, he had resisted just to resist. Almost physically. Maybe, deep down, it had been his way of countering the officer's insulting familiarity. Frank had replied, "I'm sorry."

"You're sorry for what you've done?"

"I'm sorry, that's all."

"Sorry for what?"

"I'm sorry for you that I have nothing to say."

And he knew. He was aware of everything, of the torture in store for him, of his death, everything. It was as though he did it on purpose.

He couldn't remember. It was all mixed up. He stood like a fighting cock, with this extraordinary figure of power planted there before him, and he acted like a little boy who wants to be slapped.

"You're sorry, aren't you, Friedmaier?"

"Yes."

He looked the officer straight in the eye. Had he been vaguely hoping that he'd get help from the other officer working under the light behind him? Was he counting on the stenographers hurrying up and down the hall, saying to himself that such things couldn't possibly happen here?

He held his ground, in any case. He didn't even blink. Again he said, "I'm sorry."

He swore to himself that he would never, not even under torture, pronounce the words "the general," or the name of that pig Kromer. No names. Nothing.

"I'm sorry."

"You really are sorry! Tell me exactly what you're sorry for, Friedmaier. Think before you answer."

His reply had been stupid, but he made up for it later.

"I don't know."

"You're sorry you didn't find out earlier that we made little holes in the banknotes, is that it?"

"I don't know."

"You're sorry you flashed the money around everywhere?"

"I don't know."

"And now you're sorry you know too much about it. There you are! You're sorry you know too much, Friedmaier!"

"I . . ."

"In a little while, you'll be sorry you refused to talk!"

It all took place in a sort of fog. Now neither of them was paying any attention to the meaning of their words. They were tossing them around like stones you pick up without even looking.

"You remember now, I bet. You're going to remember."

"No."

"Oh, yes. I'm sure'll you remember."

"No."

"Oh, yes. A big wad of bills like that!"

Sometimes the officer seemed to be joking. Other times his face assumed an expression of ferocity.

"You remember, Friedmaier."

"No."

"At your age, one always ends up remembering."

The cigar! Frank especially remembered the cigar coming close to his face, then receding again, the face going purple and blotchy, then suddenly the strange fixed pupils of those china-blue eyes, which looked nothing like any eyes he'd seen before.

"Friedmaier, you're a shit."

"I know."

"Friedmaier, you're going to talk."

"No."

"Friedmaier . . ."

It was funny how adults continued all their lives to act like children! The officer had behaved exactly like a schoolyard bully, or even a teacher dealing with an angry child. He had nearly had enough. He whispered, almost pleaded: "Friedmaier . . ."

Frank decided once and for all to say no.

"Friedmaier . . ."

There had been a ruler on the desk, a massive brass ruler.

The officer picked it up and repeated, barely able to restrain himself, "My dear Friedmaier, it's about time you understood."

"No."

Did Frank want to be hit in the face with the ruler? Possibly. In any case, it was what happened. Brutally. When he least expected it, when perhaps even the other wasn't expecting it, though the ruler was already in his hand.

"Friedmaier . . ."

"No."

He wasn't a martyr, he wasn't a hero. He was nothing at all. Four, perhaps five days later he understood that. What would have happened if he'd said yes instead of no?

Not much, actually, as far as the others were concerned. Kromer was on the run, he was almost sure of that. As for the general, first of all Frank didn't give a damn. Besides, the testimony of a nobody like himself wouldn't affect the fate of a general. He would drop out of circulation, if he hadn't already. No matter.

What counted, though Frank only discovered it later, was that his own fate would have been the same whether he talked or not, except for the ruler.

He knew too much now. They didn't let kids who knew as much as he did loose on the streets. If the general's suicide was announced tomorrow, there shouldn't be anyone around who could shout, "It's not true!"

If you said "Officer," there shouldn't be anyone to say, "They're all thieves."

At the time, when he was up there, he hadn't been thinking. He'd said, "No." And still he wasn't sure whether it was because he wanted to suffer. Because there was the actual attraction of torture of course, and of finding out whether he could take it or not. He had so often wondered about that.

Lotte used to say, "If he just nicks himself shaving, he puts the whole house in an uproar."

Lotte didn't matter. It had nothing to do with her or anything that concerned her. Only he'd been at stake when he said no. Only him. Not even Holst. Still less Sissy.

He didn't want to hear about his friendship with Kromer or about his obligations to the general. It had been for himself, for Frank, and not even Frank, for himself alone, that he'd said no.

To see.

And the big officer, just when he was about to lose control, had repeated, "Don't you see? Don't you see?"

Frank must have put on that stubborn expression of his, the one that always infuriated Lotte. It was his way of getting revenge for things—things that would have to be reckoned with later. In any case, he was consciously, almost scientifically, driving the officer to the edge.

"You'll have to . . ."

"No."

"You'll have to, don't you see?"

"No."

And bang! The ruler hit his face, straight across it. Frank had felt it coming. Until the last second he could have said yes, or dodged the blow. He didn't flinch. There was the sound of breaking bone.

He wanted it. He had been afraid of it, but he wanted it. He felt the shock throughout his body, from his head to his toes. He closed his eyes. He thought, he hoped, he'd be lying on the floor, but he was still standing up.

The hardest thing—in fact the only thing that was hard—was not lifting his hand to feel his face. It felt like his left eye had come out of its socket—like the cat at Madame Porse's, the cat that made him think of Sissy. When you had done what he had, did you have the right to flinch just because of an eye?

Blood had flowed everywhere, down his neck, over his chin, but he'd said nothing, he hadn't raised his hand to feel. Holding his head up, he continued to face the officer.

Was it then he realized he was lost no matter what, and that it didn't matter? If so, it was a fleeting thought. He had made the real discovery here, lying on his stomach, in his cell.

It didn't change anything.

He never imagined they did that kind of thing in an office building and he wasn't far off the mark. After striking him the officer seemed uneasy. He said a few words to his subordinate working under the light. Probably something like, "Do something about him."

It had been a mistake to hit him with the brass ruler. Frank knew that now. It shouldn't have happened there. Who knows if the officer hadn't been punished by now, or cashiered?

The sections, as Timo said.

Now there was a sigh from the officer under the light, a tall, thin man. It seemed this wasn't the first time his colleague had given way to violent impulses. And he opened a door, disclosing a washbasin and a towel.

Bones had cracked, or cartilage, Frank was sure. He didn't know which. When he opened his mouth, he spat out two teeth followed by a torrent of blood.

"Keep calm. It's nothing."

The second officer seemed upset. "When it bleeds, it's nothing," he said hesitantly.

He was deeply affected by the blood running on the floor. His superior clapped his cap on his head and left the office. The second officer seemed to be thinking, "He'll never change!"

Frank's eye hadn't come out, but it felt like it. He might have fainted. That would have been easy. The officer was somewhat afraid he would. But Frank wanted to stay tough.

"It's nothing. A scratch. You got him riled up. God, that was a stupid thing to do!"

Was the thin one any better than the other? Was he playing a game in order to get him to talk after all? He was tall and horsy, soft and slow in his movements. It upset him that the blood was still gushing out of Frank's nose, mouth, and cheek.

Finally, exasperated, he gave up and called in the two civilians waiting in the next room. They gave each other a quick look, and one of them headed downstairs.

They only took a few minutes. The man who'd left reappeared. They wrapped some kind of coarse dark scarf around Frank's face, and, each taking hold of an arm, they led him to the courtyard. The car was waiting in the side street.

Were they angry at each other, those two sets of men? Was there a real rivalry between them? The car started. Frank was all right, except that his head felt like it was slowly draining. It wasn't an unpleasant sensation. He remembered that he had to try to see the house where there was only one window that he knew, but at the last moment he didn't have the strength to open his eyes.

He was still bleeding. It was disgusting. There was blood everywhere. He hardly had time to glimpse the old gentleman, who gave a few brief orders. The old gentleman wasn't pleased, either.

That was how Frank got to know the infirmary just under the iron stairway, which he had never noticed before. It was a classroom, too, but they had fixed it up, put in some enameled furniture and a lot of instruments.

Was the man who treated him a doctor? At any rate he looked at the wound with an air of contempt, like the old gentleman with the glasses. Not contempt for the wound, but for the man who had inflicted it. He seemed to be saying: "Him again!"

Not Frank. The officer.

They treated him. They took out a third tooth that was loose. Now there were three teeth missing, two in the very front of his mouth, the other fairly far back. Sometimes when he went outside the raw sockets gave him an agreeable twinge.

They didn't take him back there. Was it because of the way the officer with the cigar had acted? No, definitely not. He remembered the blows he had heard right here, the morning of his arrival.

It was a question of tactics. Timo had been right, generally speaking, about some things. Timo didn't know everything, but he had a pretty good idea about the big picture.

Here, they treated him. They took him down to the infirmary several times. The painful thing was that they almost always came for him at the hour of the open window.

Maybe that was why he had recovered quickly.

He thought about it. The morning after his return from the city, he had deliberately not scratched a new line in the plaster to mark the day. For five whole days he left off doing it. Then he started trying to erase the marks he had already made.

From this point on they bothered him. They were the signs that an era was over. He hadn't known then. He thought life was outside. He kept thinking of the time when he would go back.

A funny thing: it was when he scratched his daily line in the plaster that he felt the most despair.

But not now. He'd learned to sleep. He'd learned to flatten his stomach against the boards of his bed and to breathe in the stink of the armpits of his coat.

He had also learned, above all, that you had to hold out as long as possible, and that that depended only on himself. He was holding out. He was holding out so well, he was so proud of it, that if he could have communicated with the outside, he would have written a treatise on how to hold out.

First of all, you had to make your corner, bury yourself deep in your corner. Did that mean anything to people who were free to wander the streets?

For ten days, at least, he was afraid of being called downstairs and finding himself face-to-face with Lotte. She had mentioned wanting to come again. They probably hadn't allowed her to because they didn't want her to see Frank in his present condition. Were they waiting for his face to get back to something like normal?

He liked it better that way. Lotte had come, or at least she had gone to one of their offices. She was doing everything she could. He knew that, since he had received two more packages of salami, salt pork, chocolate, soap, and clothes, just like the first time.

What did they think they'd find in the packages that made them rummage through them like that? Every evening in the room above the gym, a blind was pulled down, a light went on, and he could see nothing but a golden rectangle.

Was the man there, right then? Was there really a man? Probably, because of the child, but maybe he was a prisoner, too, or somewhere beyond the border.

What did he do, when he came home from outside, to absorb the house, the room, the peaceful warmth, the woman, the baby in its cradle, all of it at once? And the smell of cooking, his slippers waiting for him!

Lotte would have to come after all. He would do everything that was necessary. He would be docile for now. He would seem to be giving in.

Because he knew them. They had found out everything they wanted to know. Not the ones in the big building in the city, where officers smoked cigars and offered you cigarettes before hitting you with a brass ruler like a hysterical woman. Those fellows counted for nothing, Frank admitted.

The real ones were like the old gentleman with glasses.

With him, it was a different struggle. In the end, no matter what happened, no matter what the vicissitudes of the contest, it was over for Frank. The old gentleman would win. He couldn't help but win. All Frank could do was keep him from winning too soon. But if he made an effort, if he exercised enormous self-control, he might gain some time.

The old gentleman didn't hit him. And he didn't have others hit him. After two weeks of personal experience, Frank was inclined to conclude that if they had struck someone here the day of his arrival, it was because he deserved it.

The old gentleman didn't hit him and he was generous with his time. He was utterly patient. Apparently he knew nothing about the general and the banknotes, since he never alluded to them at all.

Was it really another section? Were the compartments between the sections airtight? Was there rivalry between them, or something worse? In any case, day after day the old gentleman looked with consternation at the gash on Frank's face.

His contempt was directed not at Frank but at the officer with the light-colored cigar. He never mentioned him. He acted as if he didn't exist. He never said a word outside the interrogations, which, no matter how disconnected or rambling they might appear, were following a terribly straight road.

Here no one offered him cigarettes. No one called him "Friedmaier" or patted him on the shoulder, no one bothered being friendly.

It was another world. In high school, Frank had never understood math. The word itself had always seemed a little mysterious.

Well, here they were using math. It was a world without boundaries, lit by a cold light in which it wasn't men that roamed but entities, names, numbers, signs that changed places and values every day.

The word "math" wasn't quite right. What was the space called where the stars went around? He couldn't recall the word. There were times when he was so tired! Not to mention that such precision didn't mean anything anymore. What counted was to understand, for him to understand.

Kromer, for a time, had figured as a star of the first magnitude. What Frank called "quite a time" was the interval between two interrogations. And nothing about them, not their length, not their rhythm, bore any resemblance to the officer's interrogation.

But Kromer was almost forgotten now, wandering among the anonymous stars, though brought in from time to time. An indifferent gesture would fish him out for a question or two before tossing him back in.

There was the logic of the one side and the logic of the other. The logic of the officer who thought of nothing but the banknotes and the general, maybe, and then the logic of the old gentleman who, you would swear, didn't give a damn about all that, if he even knew.

It all came to the same thing. They wouldn't free a man who knew what he knew.

For the officer, in short, he was already dead.

He had slapped him on the shoulder and Frank hadn't talked.

Dead!

But then the old gentleman showed up, sniffing around, deciding, "Not quite dead, not yet!"

Because even a dead man, even a man three-quarters dead, could be brought to account. And the old gentleman's job was to bring people to account.

What did the banknotes and the general matter, as long as there was *something*?

And there was definitely something, because Frank was there.

It could be Frank, it could be anybody at all. There would always be something.

What mattered, in order to stand up to the old gentleman, was sleep. The old gentleman didn't sleep. He didn't need to sleep. If he dozed off, he could wake himself up like an alarm clock. Every day, at the appointed hour, he found himself just as fit, just as cold, just as lucid as ever.

He was a fish, a man with a fish's blood. Fishes were cold-blooded. This one certainly didn't sniff his armpits, he didn't watch for a figure as small as a doll in a distant window.

He would win. The game was over. He had all the trumps, and in any case he was allowed to cheat. For Frank, it was a long time since there'd been a chance of winning.

And even if he could win, would he want to?

He wasn't sure. Probably not. It was holding out that counted, holding out for a long time, seeing the window each morning, the woman leaning out, the diapers drying in the sun on the line hanging over the void.

What mattered, each day, was to gain another day.

Which was why it was ridiculous now to go on scratching those meaningless marks in the plaster wall.

The point was not to give in, not on principle, not to save anyone, not out of honor, but because one day, without even knowing why, he had decided not to give in.

Did the old gentleman also sleep with one eye open?

A fish's eye, perfectly round, without eyelids, fixed, while Frank deliberately, voluptuously pressed his belly into the earth as he would into a woman.

# 2

HE DIDN'T blame them. It was their job to use every possible means to break down his resistance. They thought they'd get him by depriving him of sleep. They arranged it so he never had more than a couple of hours at a time, and they hadn't guessed—they had to be kept from guessing—that he'd learned how to sleep, and that they had taught him how.

Since the window across the way was closed, he knew it wouldn't be long before they summoned him. It was never at the same time two days running. Another of their little tricks. Otherwise it would be too easy. For the afternoon sessions, and especially the ones at night, the variation was considerable. For the morning sessions, it was more limited. The prisoners next door had come back from their exercise. They must hate him and think him a traitor. It wasn't only that he didn't listen to or answer their messages: he broke the chain. The messages were transmitted from classroom to classroom, from wall to wall, even if they weren't understood by everyone. There was always a chance they'd reach someone who would find them precious.

It wasn't his fault. He didn't have time. He didn't care. It seemed childish. Those men were interested in the outside, in their lives, in child's play. They were wrong to blame him. He was playing a game that was much more important than theirs, and he had to win it. It would be terrible to leave without having made it through to the very end.

He was asleep. He had gone to sleep as soon as the window closed. He plunged as deeply into sleep as he could, to recover. He could hear footsteps in the classroom next door, moaning in the room to the left, where someone very old or very young spent his whole time doing nothing but moaning.

As always, or almost always, they'd come just before a meal. Frank still had a little salt pork left as well as the last of the salami. In fact, he wondered why they had given him the two packages, since without them he would have been much weaker.

He was almost ready to credit the old gentleman with a certain honesty in the means he employed, a sort of fair play. Did he have a taste for difficult cases? Or did he, because of Frank's age, since he must think of him as just a kid, want to give him a better chance so he wouldn't have to be ashamed of his victory?

As far as dinner went, they played the same trick again today. What day it was didn't matter, since he no longer counted days or weeks. He had other points of reference. Principally he went by the subject of the interrogation, insofar as there was a subject, since the old man took pleasure in mixing everything up.

It was the day after Bertha, four days after the spring cleaning in the room with the open window. That was enough.

Besides, he was expecting it. He had noticed a rhythm, like the ebb and flow of the tides. One day they'd call for him very early; another, late; sometimes it was just before the soup, when the clatter of tin bowls could already be heard on the stairs.

In the beginning, he probably hadn't been able to eat all the soup. It was no good. It was nothing but hot water and some turnips, sometimes a few beans. Once in a while there was grease floating on top, like dishwater, and then you'd be lucky if you found a tiny piece of grayish meat at the bottom.

It shouldn't have mattered to someone who had salami and salt pork. But he liked to sit on the edge of his bed, tin bowl between his knees, feeling the warmth run down his throat to his stomach.

The old gentleman, who was never seen in the courtyard, and of course never on the walkway, must have guessed, since he always called for him just before the soup arrived.

Frank recognized the footsteps in his sleep, two different ones: the footsteps of the man in city shoes and those of a soldier in boots. They were coming for him. Those two always came. You'd think he was the only prisoner they ever questioned. He didn't lose a moment of sleep. He waited until the door opened. Even then he pretended to be snoring to gain a few seconds. They had to shake him. It had become a game, but they must never find that out.

He practically never washed now, just to gain a little more time. Whatever time he had to himself was consecrated to sleep. And what he meant by sleep was infinitely more important than what the rest of the world meant by it. Otherwise there would be no sense in scraping up all the crumbs of time the way he did.

He never smiled at them. They never said good morning. Everything happened without a word, with a grim indifference. He would take off his overcoat and put on his jacket. Downstairs it was very hot. The first few days he had suffered because he had worn his coat. It was better to risk catching cold on the walkway and stairs. His own body warmth ought to last for such a short distance.

He didn't have a mirror, but he felt that his eyelids were red like an insomniac's. They stung and burned. His skin was too tight, too sensitive.

He walked behind the civilian, in front of the soldier, and all the while he slept. He was still sleeping when he entered the little building where they would often make him wait a long time—an hour, perhaps?—on the bench in the first room, even when there was no one with the old gentleman.

He kept working on getting better. It was a habit. There

were noises, sometimes voices, and, at regular intervals, the rattle of the streetcar outside. Even children's shouts sometimes reached him, probably when a nearby school was letting out.

The children had a schoolteacher. At college there were professors, and there was always somebody who played the part of the old gentleman. For most grown-ups there was the boss, the head of the office or the factory foreman, or the owner.

Everyone had his old gentleman. He understood that, and it was why he bore him no grudge. He would hear pages being turned in the next room, papers rustling. Then a civilian would stand in the doorway and beckon, like at the doctor's or dentist's, and he would stand up.

Why were there always two civilians in the room? He thought about that. There were several plausible reasons, but they didn't satisfy him. Sometimes it was the ones who had taken him to the city on the day of the brass ruler, sometimes he recognized the one who had come to the rue Verte to arrest him, and sometimes it was others, but there weren't many of them: seven or eight in all, who took turns. They did nothing. They didn't sit at a desk. They never took part in the interrogation, perhaps because they didn't dare. They just stood there looking indifferent.

Was it to prevent him from escaping, or from strangling the old gentleman? Possibly. That was the first reason that came to mind. Yet there were armed soldiers in the courtyard. They could have stationed one at every door.

It was also possible that they didn't trust one another. He didn't dismiss out of hand the apparently absurd idea that they were there to watch the old gentleman and to record what he said. Who could tell? Might there be one among them who was even more powerful than he was? Perhaps the old gentleman didn't know which one it was, and trembled at the thought of the reports that might be sent to some higher-up.

But they seemed more like acolytes. They made him think of the choirboys who attended a priest during mass. They never sat down or smoked.

But the old gentleman smoked all the time. It was the only human thing about him. He smoked one cigarette after another. On the desk was a small ashtray, and it irritated Frank that nobody thought to replace it with a larger one. It was a green ashtray in the shape of a grape leaf. During the morning sessions it already overflowed with cigarette butts and ashes.

There was a stove in the room and a coal scuttle. All they had to do, every now and then, was empty the ashtray into the scuttle.

They never did. Perhaps he didn't want them to. The cigarette butts accumulated, and they were filthy. The old gentleman was a dirty smoker, never taking his cigarette out of his mouth. He would lick it, let it go out, light it again, wet the paper, chew the little grains of tobacco.

His fingertips were yellow. His teeth, too. And two little spots marked where he held his cigarettes between his lips.

The most unexpected thing about him was that he rolled his own cigarettes. He seemed to give no importance to the material side of life. You wondered when he ate, when he slept, when he shaved. Frank couldn't remember ever seeing him freshly shaved. And he would stop in the middle of an interrogation to pull his tobacco pouch out of his pocket. From his vest pocket would appear a packet of cigarette papers.

He was meticulous. The operation took quite a while. It was exasperating, since in the meantime life hung suspended. Was it a trick?

Night was nearing morning when, toward the end of the interrogation, he asked Frank about Bertha. As usual, whenever he threw out a new name, he did it in the way you least expected. He didn't use Bertha's last name. You might have thought the old gentleman was a regular at the house, a man like Chief Inspector Hamling, somebody who knew all about Lotte and her doings.

"Why did Bertha leave you?"

Frank had learned to gain time. Wasn't that the only reason he was there?

"She didn't leave me. She left my mother."

"It is the same thing."

"No. I never had anything to do with my mother's business."

"But you slept with Bertha."

They knew everything. God knows how many people they had questioned to find out all the things they knew! God knows how many hours it all represented, how much tireless activity!

"You did sleep with Bertha, did you not?"

"Sometimes."

"Often?"

"I don't know what you'd call often."

"Once, twice, three times a week?"

"It's difficult to say. It depended."

"Were you in love with her?"

"No."

"But you slept with her?"

"Occasionally."

"And you would talk to her?"

"No."

"You slept with her and you did not talk to her?"

He was always tempted, when they pressed him on subjects like this, to reply with an obscenity. Like in school. But you didn't use obscenities in front of your teacher. And not in front of the old gentleman, either. He wasn't looking for thrills.

"Let's say I spoke as little as possible."

"Which is to say?"

"I don't know."

"You never talked to her about what you had done during the day?"

"No."

"You did not ask her what she had done?"

"Never."

"You did not talk to her about the men she slept with?"

"I wasn't jealous."

That was the tone. But it had to be kept in mind that the old gentleman chose his words carefully, putting them through a sieve before he spoke, which took time. His desk was the monumental American kind, with pigeonholes and lots of drawers full of meaningless-looking scraps of paper that he would pull out at certain moments, glancing at them quickly.

Frank knew those scraps of paper. There was no stenographer. No one to record his replies. The two men who were always standing near the door were without fountain pen or pencil. Frank wouldn't have been surprised if they didn't know how to write.

It was the old gentleman who wrote, always on scraps of paper, old torn envelopes, on the bottoms of letters or circulars that he trimmed with care. His handwriting was unbelievably small and must have been illegible to anyone else.

If there was a scrap of paper that dealt with Bertha in his pigeonholes, that meant the big girl had been questioned. Was that right? When he entered the room, Frank would try to sniff it out, as if to detect the smell, some trace of whoever might have been brought there in his absence.

"Your mother entertained officers, government officials."

"That's possible."

"You were often in the apartment during those visits."

"I must have been sometimes."

"You are young and curious."

"I'm young but I'm not curious, and in any case I'm not a pervert."

"You have friends, connections. It is interesting to know what officers do and say."

"Not to me."

"Your girlfriend Bertha . . ."

"She wasn't my girlfriend."

"She is not any longer, not since she left you, you and your mother. I also wonder why on that day there was the sound of loud voices in your apartment, so loud that the other tenants were alarmed."

Which tenants? Who had they spoken to? He thought of old Monsieur Wimmer, but he didn't believe it was him who had talked.

"It is curious that Bertha, who according to your mother was almost one of the family, should have left you just then."

Was it on purpose that he let slip that Lotte had been questioned? Frank wasn't worried. He had heard worse.

"Bertha was very useful to your mama."

He didn't know that Frank had never called his mother that, that no one would call Lotte "mama."

"I forget who said"—he pretended to look through his scraps of paper—"that she was as strong as a stallion."

"As a mare."

"As a mare, yes. We must speak of this again."

At first, Frank thought that such remarks were shots in the dark, meant to intimidate him. He hadn't supposed that his actions could be so important in the eyes of the old gentleman that they would call for all the complicated machinery that was now at work.

The most extraordinary thing about it was that the old gentleman, from his point of view, wasn't wrong. He knew where he was going. He knew it better than Frank, who was only just beginning to perceive hidden depths that he had never suspected before.

In this building, there were no empty words, no bluffs. If the old man said, "We need to talk about this again," well, it was because he was going to do a lot more than just talk. Poor fat stupid Bertha!

Yet he didn't feel sorry for her or anybody. He'd rounded that cape. He bore no grudge. He didn't despise her. He didn't hate her. He was beginning to see certain people with the old gentleman's fish eyes, as through the glass of an aquarium.

The proof that the old gentleman didn't waste his time shooting in the dark was that he had got the better of Frank on the subject of Kromer. It was in the beginning, when Frank still didn't understand. He had supposed, as with the officer with the ruler, that all he had to do was deny everything.

"You knew a certain Fred Kromer?"

"No."

"You have never met anyone with this name?"

"I don't remember it."

"He goes to the same places you do, the same restaurants, the same bars."

"It's possible."

"You are sure you never drank champagne with him at Timo's?"

They were baiting the hook.

"I've drunk with a lot of people at Timo's, even drunk champagne."

A blunder. He realized it at once, too late. The old gentleman was gathering nonsense on his scraps of paper. It didn't seem a very appropriate occupation for a man of his age and position. Yet not one of those scraps of paper ever got lost, or failed to reappear at the right time.

"You don't know him by his first name, Fred, either? Certain people, in certain circumstances, are only known by their first names. For example, many people who used to meet you daily, so to speak, do not know that your name is Friedmaier."

"It's not the same thing."

"It is not the same thing with Kromer?"

Everything counted. Everything carried weight. Everything was recorded. He spent two exhausting hours denying any connection with Kromer, for no other reason than because that was the line of conduct he had adopted. The next day, and the days following, there was no further mention of his friend. He thought they had forgotten him. Then, in the very middle of a night interrogation, when he was literally swaying on his feet—they kept him standing on purpose—his eyes burning, he was handed a photograph of himself, together with Kromer and two women, on the bank of a river in the middle of summer. They had taken off their jackets. It was a typical summer snapshot. Kromer, natu-rally, had his hand on the breast of the blond girl he was with.

"You do not know him?"

"I don't remember his name."

"Nor that of the girls?"

"As if I could remember the names of all the girls I've gone canoeing with!"

"This one, the brunette, is named Lili."

"I'll take your word for it."

"Her father works at the mayor's office."

"Possibly."

"And your companion, that is Kromer."

"Hmm."

He didn't remember the snapshot, which he'd never seen before. What he remembered was that there had been five of them that day, three men and two women, never a very happy arrangement. Fortunately, the third man had been busy taking photographs. He himself had paddled the canoe. Even if Frank had wanted to, he couldn't have told the old gentleman the third man's name.

All this proved how thorough their investigations were. God knows where they'd dug up that photograph. Had they searched Kromer's place? If it was there, it was odd that Frank had never seen it. Had they found it at the third guy's place? Did they get it from the place that had developed the film?

That was the good thing about the old gentleman, what encouraged Frank, what gave him hope. The officer would probably have had Frank shot at once just to get it over, to keep things simple. With the old gentleman, he had plenty of time ahead.

To tell the truth, deep down he was convinced—no, it was faith rather than conviction—that it depended entirely on himself. He thought in pictures, in sensations, the way people who hardly sleep do, people who have to force themselves to sleep.

He would have to come back to his dream of flying. All he had to do was put out his palms and press against the empty air with all his might, *with all his willpower*, and then he'd rise, slowly at first, then with perfect ease, until his head touched the ceiling.

He couldn't talk about it. Even if Holst himself were there, he couldn't confess his secret hope. Not yet. It was just like his dream, it was marvelous that he'd had that dream several times, because now it helped him. Maybe he was living in a dream. There were times, because of the lack of sleep, when he was no longer sure. This time, again, it all depended on him, on his willpower.

If he had the energy, if he kept faith, it would last as long as it had to.

There was no question of returning to the outside. There was no question, for him, of entertaining hopes like the men in the next classroom. Such hopes didn't interest him; they even shocked him.

They did what they could. It wasn't their fault.

For him, there was simply a gap in time that he had to fill. If he had been asked to explain how important the gap was, to express it in days, weeks, or months, he wouldn't have been able to answer. And what if he had been asked what was waiting at the end of it?

Enough! Better to argue with the old gentleman. Everything had its appointed hour. All through the interrogation they kept him standing. He drew a distinction between seated interrogations and standing interrogations. It was a childish trick, really. They were always trying to wear him down. He didn't let on that he preferred standing. When they made him sit down, it was on a stool without a back. In the end that was even more exhausting.

The old gentleman never left his chair, never seemed to feel the need to walk around and stretch his legs. Never once, even during one five-hour interrogation, had he left the room to go to the toilet or get a drink of water. He drank nothing. There was nothing to drink on his desk. Cigarettes were enough for him, and he even let them go out two or three times before he was done with them.

He had all sorts of tricks. Like leaving Frank's automatic on the desk as though it had been forgotten, as though it were an anonymous object of no importance. He used it as a paperweight. Since the first day, after Frank had been searched, he had never alluded to it. But the weapon remained there, like a threat.

He had to reason coolly. Frank wasn't the only person in the old gentleman's section. Despite the time he devoted to him—a considerable time—a man of his importance must have other problems to solve, other prisoners to question. Was the automatic left there when he questioned them? Did they set the stage differently each time, replacing the automatic with something else, a dagger, a check, a letter, some other piece of evidence?

How could he explain that this man was a blessing from heaven? Others wouldn't understand him, would begin to hate him. If not for him, Frank wouldn't have this contstant sense of the time that he still had left. If not for him, if not for these tiring interrogations, he would never have known the lucidity he now enjoyed, which was so little like what he used to call by that name.

You had to keep on your toes, be careful not to give too much away all at once. There was the danger of going too quickly, of coming to the end too soon.

It mustn't end. Not yet. There were points Frank still needed to clear up. It was slow. Slow and fast at the same time.

It kept him from thinking about the men in the next class-room who were taken out at dawn to be shot. The most disturbing thing about it was the hour of the day, when the prisoners were only half awake, haggard, unwashed, ushaved, without a cup of coffee to warm their bellies. And then, be-cause of the cold, all of them, without exception, turned the collars of their jackets up. Why weren't they allowed to put on overcoats? It was a mystery. It wasn't as though the over-coats were worth much. And cloth, no matter how thick, wouldn't stop a bullet. Was it just to make it even more sinister?

Would Frank turn the collar of his jacket up, too? Possibly. He didn't think about it. He rarely thought about it. Besides, he was convinced they wouldn't shoot him in the courtyard, by the covered playground where all the desks were piled up.

Those men had been tried. They had committed crimes that could be judged and written down in the great ledgers of the law. With a little fudging if necessary.

If they had meant to try him, it was more than likely they would have taken him back to the officer with the brass ruler.

When everything was finally over, when the old gentle-man was satisfied in his soul and conscience that he had squeezed everything he possibly could out of Frank, they would dispose of him without ceremony. He didn't know where yet. He wasn't familiar enough with the building. They would shoot him from behind on the stairs or in some corridor. There must be a cellar for that somewhere.

And he wouldn't care. He wasn't afraid. His only fear, the one thing that haunted him, was that it would happen too soon, before he decided for himself, before he was done.

If they were set on it after that, he would be the first to say, "Do it!"

And if he got to make a last request, a last wish, he would ask them to perform their little operation while he was lying flat on his stomach in his bed.

Didn't this prove that the old gentleman was heaven-sent? He was sure to find out something new. Every day he found out something new. It was a question of staying on the alert on every front. He had to think of Timo as well as of the people he had met at Taste's, at the confectioner's, and all the anonymous tenants in his building. The old man with his eyeglasses mixed up everything on purpose.

What was his latest discovery? He wiped his glasses carefully with a huge colored handkerchief that was always sticking out of his pants pocket. He fiddled with his scraps of paper as usual. Anyone looking through the window would have thought they were lottery tickets or a hand of cards. He really seemed to be casting about at random. Then he rolled a cigarette with infuriating deliberation. He stuck his tongue out to lick the paper and looked around for matches.

He could never find his matches, which lay buried under oceans of paper. He didn't look at Frank. He rarely looked directly at him, and when he did it was with utter indifference. Who knows, perhaps the two others, the acolytes, were there to spy on Frank's reactions and to report on them afterward.

"Do you know Anna Loeb?"

Frank didn't blink. He never blinked anymore. He tried to think. It was a name he didn't know, but that meant nothing at the outset. More precisely, he knew the name Loeb like everyone else did. The Loeb brewery. He had drunk Loeb's beer ever since he had begun drinking. The name appeared in big letters on all the rooftops, in all the cafés and grocery stores, on calendars, even on streetcar windows.

"I know the beer."

"I am asking you if you know Anna Loeb."

"No."

"And yet she was one of your mother's lodgers."

So it was someone who used another name.

"You may be right. I don't know."

"Does this help you remember?"

He held out a photograph he had pulled from a drawer. He always had photographs in reserve.

Frank could hardly help exclaiming, "Anny!"

It was Anny, but a different Anny from the one he had known, perhaps because she was fashionably decked out in a sundress with a large straw hat, smiling, linking arms with someone the old gentleman masked with his thumb.

"Do you know her?"

"I'm not sure."

"She lived in the same apartment as you only recently."

"It's possible."

"She said she slept with you."

"That's possible, too."

"How many times?"

"I don't know."

Had Anny been arrested? With them, you never knew. It was often in their interests, in order to learn the truth, to tell lies. That was part of their job. Frank was never altogether fooled by the little scraps of paper.

"Why did you bring her to your mother's?"

"Me?"

"Yes."

"But I didn't!"

"Then who did?"

"I don't know."

"Do you mean to say that she came on her own?"

"There would be nothing strange about that."

"In that case, it must be supposed that someone gave her your address."

Frank didn't yet understand; he sensed a trap and didn't reply. Long silences like that made the interrogations last forever.

"Your mother's activities are illegal, but we don't need to go into that again."

That might very well mean that Lotte, too, had been arrested.

"For this reason, it would be in your mother's interest to let as few people know as possible. If Anna Loeb showed up at your mother's, it was because she knew she could find refuge there."

The word "refuge" warned Frank, who had to struggle against sleep and against vague thoughts that, if he let his attention stray even for an instant, would take possession of him, and that he only halfheartedly resisted because, in reality, they were his whole life now. Like a sleepwalker, he repeated, "A refuge?"

"You claim to know nothing about Anna Loeb's past?"

"I didn't even know her real name."

"What did she call herself?"

This was what he called giving ground. He had to do it.

"Anny."

"Who sent her to you?"

"No one."

"Your mother took her on without any references?"

"She was a beautiful girl and she was willing to sleep with the customers. My mother doesn't ask more than that."

"How many times did you sleep with her?"

"I don't remember."

"Were you in love?"

"No."

"Was she?"

"I don't think so."

"But you slept together."

Was he some sort of a puritan, or pervert, to attach so much importance to such questions? Was he impotent? He had gone on the same way about Bertha.

"What did she tell you?"

"She never said anything."

"What did she do with her time?"

"She read magazines."

"Magazines you brought her?"

"No."

"How did she get them? Did she go out?"

"No. I don't think she ever went out."

"Why?"

"I don't know. She only stayed a few days."

"Was she hiding from someone?"

"I didn't get that feeling."

"Where did the magazines come from?"

"She must have brought them with her."

"Who mailed her letters for her?"

"Nobody, I guess."

"Did she ever ask you to mail letters for her?"

"No."

"Nor to deliver messages for her?"

"No."

It all came so easily because it was true.

"She slept with clients?"

"Naturally."

"With whom?"

"I don't know. I wasn't always there."

"But when you were there?"

"I didn't pay any attention."

"You were not jealous?"

"Not at all."

"And yet she is pretty."

"I was used to that."

"Were there clients who came exclusively for her?"

"You ought to ask my mother."

"She has been asked."

"What did she say?"

And so, almost every day he was forced to relive life in the building. He spoke of it with a detachment that visibly surprised the old gentleman, all the more because he felt that Frank was sincere.

"No one ever called her on the telephone?"

"There's only one telephone that works in the building, the concierge's."

"I know."

So what was he hoping to find out?

"Have you ever seen this man?"

"No."

"This one?"

"No."

"This one?"

"No."

People he didn't know. Why was the old man always so careful to hide part of each photograph, letting him see only the face, not the clothes?

Because they were officers, of course! High-ranking ones, perhaps.

"Did you know that Anna Loeb was wanted?"

"I never heard that."

"Were you also not aware that her father had been shot?"

The brewer Loeb had been shot almost a year before, after a whole arsenal had been found hidden in the vats at his brewery.

"I didn't know he was her father. I never knew her last name."

"Yet she came to your place to hide."

It was extraordinary. He had slept two or three times

with the daughter of Loeb, the brewer, one of the richest and most important men in town, and he had never even known it. Every day, thanks to the old gentleman, he discovered new labyrinths.

"She left you?"

"I don't remember anymore. She was still there when I was arrested."

"You are sure?"

What should he say? What did they know? He had never liked Anny, who always seemed so contemptuous—so absent, which was worse—even in bed. None of that mattered now. Had she been arrested? Had they made a clean sweep of everyone since he'd been in prison?

"I think. I'd been drinking the night before."

"At Timo's?"

"Maybe. And other places."

"With Kromer?"

He didn't miss a trick, the old shark!

"With a lot of people."

"Before taking refuge with you, Anna Loeb had been successively the mistress of several officers, and she chose them carefully."

"Hmm."

"More for their rank than for their physique or their money."

Frank didn't reply. No question had been asked.

"She was in the pay of a foreign power, and she went to hide out at your place."

"It's not hard for a good-looking woman to be taken into a whorehouse."

"You admit it was a whorehouse?"

"Call it what you like. Women slept with clients."

"Including officers?"

"Perhaps. I wasn't on duty at the door."

"Not at the transom?"

He knew everything! He must have gone over the apartment himself with particular care.

"Did you know their names?"

"No."

Was, perhaps, the old gentleman's section working against the other section, the one where he had been hit with the brass ruler? The word "officer" recurred with a frequency that interested him.

"Would you recognize them?"

"No."

"Sometimes they stayed for a long time, no?"

"Long enough to do what they came for."

"Did they talk?"

"I wasn't in the room."

"They talked," affirmed the old gentleman. "*Men always talk.*"

You'd think he'd had as much experience as Lotte. He knew where he was going, and he went about it meticulously and patiently. He saw a long way ahead. He had plenty of time. He picked at a bit of thread and delicately teased it out.

The soup had been brought long before. Frank would find the liquid cold in his tin bowl, as he did almost every day.

"When women make men talk, it is in order to repeat what they say to someone else."

Frank shrugged.

"Anna Loeb slept with you, but you insist she said nothing. She did not go out, and yet she sent messages."

His head was swimming. He must hold out to the end, until bed, until he finally sank into the planks with all his weight, eyes closed, ears buzzing, listening to the blood circulating through his arteries, feeling the life in his body, thinking about things other than idiocies, things that made it possible for him to hang on, the window, the four walls, a room with a bed, a stove—he didn't dare add the cradle—a man who went away every morning knowing he'd come back to a woman who was always there and who knew that she'd never be alone, of the sun that always rose and set in the same place, of a tin lunch box you carried under your arm like a treasure, of gray felt boots, of a geranium in bloom, of things so simple that nobody really knew them, or that they despised, that they complained about when they were theirs.

There was so little time left!

# 3

THAT NIGHT he endured a particularly grueling interrogation. They must have woken him up in the middle of
the night, and he was still in the office when he heard the
noise of the firing squad in the courtyard, followed, as always, by single, fainter shots. He looked at the window. It
was dawn.

It was one of the few times he nearly lost his temper. He
was sure they were dragging out the session just for the sake
of it, that he was being asked questions of no importance
entirely at random. Ressl, the editor in chief, had been mentioned among others. Frank replied that he hardly knew him,
had spoken to him only once.

"Who introduced you?"

Kromer, again. It would be so much easier to put his
cards on the table, especially since, as far as Frank could tell,
Kromer was holed up somewhere out of reach.

He was asked about people he didn't know. He was shown
photographs. Either they meant to exhaust him completely,
driving him to the limit of his endurance, or else they imagined he knew a lot more than he really did.

When he left the office he could almost taste the dawn.
The air was full of the scent of the neighborhood wood fires.
Had the window been open? He couldn't recall. He'd seen
it, but he couldn't have sworn—that is, not in front of the
old gentleman, not in response to definite questions—that it
hadn't been a dream. But his eyes must have been open. He
was sure of that.

He couldn't recall. And now they were here, dragging him out of bed again. He walked, the civilian in front, the soldier behind, the noise of the two pairs of boots on each side. He was still asleep. He had plenty of time. They always kept him waiting on the gray painted bench. But this time they didn't. Without stopping they crossed the room, heading straight into the office.

Lotte and Minna were standing there.

Did he seem displeased when he caught sight of them? He hadn't realized it. His mother gave a start, he saw that. She opened her mouth as if to scream, but controlled herself. "Frank!" she stammered, with a pity in her voice he no longer understood.

She felt the urge to blow her nose in one of those lace handkerchiefs she always soaked in perfume. As for Minna, she hadn't moved. She hadn't said a thing. He saw her standing there, very straight and pale, with tears running down her cheeks.

It was because of his missing teeth, his beard, his reddened eyelids, his jacket that was now twisted hopelessly out of shape. Those things never crossed his mind anymore. He hadn't bothered to change shirts.

But they were deeply upset. He wasn't. He was almost as hardened as the old gentleman now. Instantly, he noticed that his mother had dressed in gray and white, an old habit she fell into whenever she wanted to appear distinguished. She used to dress up like that when she came to see him at school, his real school, and even then she had worn those same light little demi-veils to cover her eyes. They hadn't come back in fashion yet.

She smelled like a bath, like powder and scent. She must have come from home. In prison, she would never have had an opportunity to do herself up like that.

But why Minna? To look at them, you'd have thought it was a mother and some young relative who'd come to pay a visit. With her little tailored blue suit, white blouse, and hardly any makeup, Minna looked just like a young relative.

He looked around for the suitcase and the packages they must have brought, but there weren't any in the room, and he understood. And that Lotte was so embarrassed proved he was right. She didn't know where to begin. She looked at the old gentleman more than at her son. Perhaps she wanted Frank to understand that she hadn't come of her own accord.

"They have very kindly allowed me to visit you again, Frank. I inquired if I could bring Minna along, since she's always asking about you, and this gentleman was good enough to grant permission."

It wasn't true. It was the old gentleman's idea. Two weeks ago he had wanted to know about Bertha; a week ago it was all Anny. Now, in his unhurried way, he had gotten to Minna. He hadn't needed to rush things, since she was there right at hand. Minna turned away, embarrassed.

Pretty clever. Frank didn't believe in accidents. Finally, the old gentleman had understood that if there was any girl among those who had filed through Lotte's house that Frank might have felt even the slightest affection for, it was Minna.

Frank hadn't been in love with her, of course. He had been intentionally cruel to her. He no longer remembered exactly what he'd done. There were many things he had done when he was still outside that he had erased from memory. Toward Minna, though, he felt something like a pang of guilt. He knew he'd behaved disgustingly.

All three of them standing. Ridiculous. The old gentleman noticed it first and had chairs brought in for Lotte and Minna. He motioned for Frank to sit down on the stool, the stool from the seated interrogations.

He went back to looking preoccupied. You would have sworn that what was happening didn't concern him in the least. He appeared to be busy with his files, finding and classifying his little scraps of paper.

"Frank, I have to talk to you. Don't be afraid."

Why say that? Afraid of what?

"I've been thinking these last six weeks."

Six weeks already? Or only? He was struck by that. He would have liked to look at her less coldly, but he couldn't. She was afraid that she would burst into tears if she raised her eyes to his face. Was he so terrible to look at? Because of his missing two front teeth? Because he was dirty?

"Frank, I'm sure that if you did anything bad it was because you let yourself be led astray. You're too young. I know you. It was my fault letting you go out with friends who were so much older."

She lied badly. And yet Lotte knew how to lie. When she talked about her clients, about men in general, she always boasted that she could fool them as she pleased. Was she lying badly on purpose, to let him know she had come on their orders?

No automobile in the courtyard. They must have taken the streetcar.

"People of sound judgment have advised me, Frank."

"Who?"

"Well, Inspector Hamling, for one."

If she mentioned that name, it was because he had been permitted.

"I know you don't like him very much, but you're wrong. You'll understand later on. He's a very old friend of mine, perhaps my only friend. He knew me when I was a young girl, and if I hadn't been so stupid . . ."

Frank's eyes narrowed. He had a new thought, one that hadn't crossed his mind before. If the chief inspector came to see them so often, acting so friendly and familiar in spite of Lotte's more than dubious professional situation, if he appeared to take them under his protection and claimed the right to speak to Frank the way he had, well, wasn't there probably a very good reason for it?

He felt almost as tense as he used to. For a moment he assumed the expression he'd worn on the worst days in the rue Verte, and Lotte, who had been about to confide something, let the matter drop.

It was better that way. If Kurt Hamling happened to be his father, he didn't want to know.

"He has always taken an interest in us, in you—"

"All right!" He cut her short.

"He knows you better than you think. He's sure that you let yourself be led astray by others but that you refuse to admit it. It's false honor, Frank, that's what he says, and he's right."

"I have no honor."

"These gentlemen have been patient with you, I know."

What did she mean by that?

"They've allowed you to receive packages. They gave me permission to come see you today with Minna, who worries about you so much."

"Is she sick?"

"Who?"

"Minna."

Why did he break the train of Lotte's thoughts? There she was, not knowing what answer to give, casting a quick questioning look at the old gentleman.

"No, of course she isn't sick. Whatever made you think that? I had her examined again thoroughly last week. A young doctor who doesn't know anything wanted to operate, but it isn't necessary, the other doctor said. She's already doing much better."

He sensed something mysterious, something hidden. He said casually, "So now she'll have a chance to rest?"

His mother hesitated. Why? But the old gentleman didn't seem inclined to interfere, and she ventured, "We've reopened the house."

"With girls?"

"There are two new ones besides Minna."

"I thought your friend Hamling advised you to close."

"At the time, yes. He didn't know how much harm Anny could do."

Now Frank understood. He understood why they were here. He understood everything. The old gentleman didn't miss a trick.

"You were asked to stay open?"

"I was told it would be best from every point of view."

In other words, the apartment on the rue Verte had become a sort of mousetrap. Who looked through the transom and tried to overhear what was being said on these gentlemen's behalf?

That was why Lotte was so embarrassed.

"In short," he said quietly, without any sarcasm, "everything's okay at home."

"Very much so."

"Sissy's well?"

"I think so."

"You haven't seen her?"

"There's so much work, you know. I don't know whether it's the time . . ."

What more was there to say? They were worlds apart, separated by an unbridgeable gulf—by the scented handkerchief, even, which had become such an overwhelming presence in the room that Lotte herself noticed and stuck it back in her bag.

"Listen, Frank—"

"Yes."

"You're young—"

"You told me that."

"I know better than you that you're not bad. Don't look at me like that. Remember that I've never thought of anything but you. Everything I've done since you were born I've done for your sake, and now I'd gladly give the rest of my life for you to be happy."

It wasn't his fault he wasn't paying attention. He caught the drift of her words. He was looking at Minna's handbag. It was the very same bag as Sissy's, only red, not black, Sissy's bag with the key that he had brandished at arm's length in the empty lot and finally set down on a pile of snow. He had never learned whether she had found it or not.

"I told them that you knew Kromer, because it's true. He's your friend and I don't want you to deny it anymore. Nobody can make me believe it wasn't all his idea. He was cunning enough to wriggle out of it and leave you holding the bag."

Was that what she had come to tell him—that Kromer was safe? He was too near the stove. He was hot. Through the window—it was the first time he had sat facing this way—he could see the gate, the sentry box, the guard, a bit of street. It didn't affect him in the least to see the road again, with the streetcars going by.

"It's absolutely vital that you tell them the truth, everything you know, and they'll take that into consideration. I'm sure of it. I feel confident."

Never had the old gentleman seemed so distant.

"Tomorrow I may be allowed to leave a package for you. What would you like me to put in it?"

He was ashamed for her, for himself, for all of them. He was tired. He felt like replying, "Put shit in it!"

He would have said that at one time. Since then he'd learned patience. Unless it was weakness. He murmured, beneath his breath, "Anything you like."

"It isn't fair for you to take the fall for someone else, you see? Without meaning it, I've done a great deal of harm, too; I realize that now."

And she was paying for it by letting her whorehouse be used as a trap for perverts! The most astonishing thing was that four or five months ago it would have seemed perfectly natural to Frank. Even now, he didn't exactly feel indignant. He was thinking about something else. He had been thinking about something else all through the conversation, not realizing his eyes were glued to Minna's bag.

"Tell them honestly everything you know. Don't try to play tricks. You'll get out, you'll see. I'll take care of you and—"

He wasn't listening. It was all so far away. It was true that he was always sleepy, that at certain hours of the day, especially in the morning, he had dizzy spells. It was fatigue.

She rose. She smelled good. She was bright and crisp, with a fur around her neck.

"Promise me, Frank. Promise your mother. Minna, you tell him, too . . ."

Minna, who didn't dare look at him, struggled to say, "I'm so unhappy, Frank!"

And Lotte ran on: "You haven't told me what you want me to bring."

Then he said it. He was more surprised than anyone. He had thought it would happen much later, at the very end. But suddenly, he was too tired. He spoke without thinking. Without realizing it, he had made a decision.

Almost inaudibly, he said—and he was conscious of what the words meant, though only to him—"Could I see Holst?"

What happened then astonished him. It wasn't his mother who answered, and she couldn't have understood, anyway; she was quite lost. Minna choked back a sob that could just as well have been a hiccup. Minna knew a good deal more about it than Lotte.

It was the old gentleman who raised his head, looking at him. He asked, "You are speaking of Gerhardt Holst?"

"Yes."

"Curious."

He rummaged about among his scraps of paper, fished one out at last, and examined it closely. Frank held his breath.

"He has just asked for a visitor's permit."

"To see me?"

"Yes."

He wasn't going to leap with joy, to dance around the room in front of them. And yet his face was transfigured. Now he had tears in his eyes, like Minna. But he was afraid to believe it. It would be too wonderful. It would mean he hadn't made a mistake. It would mean . . .

"He asked to see me?"

"One minute . . . No."

Frank stood paralyzed. No doubt about it, the old gentleman was a sadist.

"It was not exactly that. A certain Gerhardt Holst sent in a request to the authorities for a visitor's permit. He addressed very high authorities indeed. But it is not for himself."

Hurry up, by God! And Lotte was listening to it all as though it were the radio!

"It is for his daughter."

No! No! No! He mustn't cry. He must do anything to keep from crying. Otherwise, he might spoil everything. It wasn't true! It wasn't possible! The old gentleman would pick up another scrap of paper and discover he was mistaken.

"You see, Frank," Lotte cried tremulously, with a beatific quaver in her voice, as if her radio had just played a sentimental tune, "you see, everyone believes you. I told you you'd get out. All you have to do is listen to these gentlemen."

She was a fool, an idiot! He wasn't even capable of hinting that, it was better that she never know the void that had opened between them.

And then she asked, with the air of a devout worshipper addressing a bishop, "And have you, sir, granted the permission?"

"Not yet. This request has only just reached me from another office. I have not had time to study it."

"I think you'll make her very happy. She's our neighbor across the hall from us. They've known each other for years."

It wasn't true. If only she'd keep quiet! Or rather, what difference did it make what she said? Even if everything fell through now, even if Sissy didn't come, the fact remained that Holst had asked.

They understood each other. Frank was right. It would be the same if Holst came or not. Not exactly the same, but it would mean the same thing.

God, if only they'd finish! If only they'd do him the favor of not questioning him any more that morning, let him go up to his own room. Strange— "his own room," he had thought. To throw himself on his bed, clutching to his breast his still-warm truth before it evaporated.

"She's a very well-bred young girl, believe me, a real young lady."

How could you be angry with anyone so stupid, even if she was your mother? And Minna, with her false cousinly air, who took advantage of their having risen now to sidle up and touch him when no one was looking!

"I thought," the old gentleman interrupted, "that you asked just now to see Gerhardt Holst."

"Either one."

"You have no preference?"

He hoped he wasn't making a mistake! "No."

A glance from under the glasses, and the two acolytes knew it was time to take him away. He didn't know how he left the room. His mother and Minna stayed. What more would Lotte have to say on the subject of Sissy?

He reached his room almost at the same time as his tin bowl, still nice and hot, and he simply held it between his knees, not eating, feeling its warmth spreading through him. The window was closed up there, beyond the gymnasium. It didn't matter. From now on, if necessary, he could get by without it. There was a lump in his throat. He wanted to talk. He wanted to talk to Holst, for Holst to come here.

He had just one question: "How did you come to understand?"

It seemed impossible, and if it was true, it was a miracle.

Frank had done everything so that no one would understand. He himself hardly understood. He had prowled around Holst and, at certain moments, he had compelled himself to believe that he hated him, that he despised him: he had laughed at the tin lunch box, at the badly fitting felt boots.

When had it happened?

Was it the night when Holst, coming back from the street-car station, saw him standing glued to the tannery wall with the knife in his hand?

He had to stop. It was too much for him. He had to keep calm, sit there sensibly on the edge of his bed. He wouldn't even lie down, because then it would be worse. He couldn't look at the window and scream, could he?

He wasn't going to go crazy. It wasn't the right time. Little by little he would regain his composure. If it had happened, it meant the end.

He had always known. It was one of those things you knew and didn't try to explain. In any case, he didn't have the strength to hold out much longer.

Holst had understood!

And Sissy?

Had she always known that it would happen this way, too? Frank had known. Holst had known. It was terrible to say it. It sounded like blasphemy. But it was true.

Holst should have come and killed him that Sunday, during the night, or the next day, but he hadn't.

It had to have happened this way. Frank couldn't have done anything else. He didn't know why, but he felt it.

If he wasn't afraid of torture, of the officer with the brass ruler or the old gentleman and his two acolytes, it was because no one could ever make him suffer the way he had made himself suffer when he pushed Kromer into that room.

Would the old gentleman say yes?

There had to be something to give him hope, so that he could believe that this was meant to serve some purpose.

Frank was eager for them to come. He wouldn't promise a thing—that would be stupid—but he'd let them think that he was going to be a good deal more talkative *afterward*. Let them come for him, quickly!

He would give ground. He'd give ground from now on, lots of it. On any subject they chose. Kromer, for instance, since it didn't matter now that Frank knew he was safe.

He wondered which he would really prefer: to talk to Holst or to Sissy. He didn't really have anything to say to Sissy. He only wanted to look. To have her look at him.

"Tell me, Monsieur Holst . . ."

*"How did you find out, Monsieur Holst, that a man, no matter what he was . . ."*

He couldn't find the words. None of them expressed what he wanted to say.

*"You can run a streetcar, can't you, or whatever? You can wear boots that make street urchins turn to stare at you and the well-dressed boys shrug their shoulders. You can . . . you can . . . I understand what you're going to say . . . That doesn't . . . It's enough to do what must be done, because everything is equally important . . . But I, Monsieur Holst, how could I have . . . ?"*

It was impossible that Holst had asked for a visitor's permit for Sissy. Frank began to weaken, to ask questions, to doubt. Perhaps it was some machination on the old gentleman's part? If that was true, Frank would hunt him all the way to the bottom of hell if he had to.

And how was it possible that Holst, who'd always avoided contact with the Occupation forces, who must have suffered because of them, had addressed himself to *very high authorities*, as the old gentleman had said. For that, he had to go through intermediaries, to compromise himself, to humiliate himself before them.

No one came for him. Time dragged on. He couldn't sleep. He didn't want to. He wanted the question settled now.

He found himself lying down. He didn't know if he had set his bowl of soup down on the floor or not. If he had spilled it, it would smell all night. It had happened to him once before. He wanted to cry. He wouldn't tell Holst he had cried. He wouldn't tell anyone. No one saw him. He stretched out his arm as though there was someone beside him, or as if someday someone might be there.

Perhaps, except everything would have had to be different!

He refused to accept that Chief Inspector Kurt Hamling was his father.

Why did he think of that?

He wasn't thinking about anything. He was crying like a baby. He was sleepy. His wet-nurse used to stick a pacifier in his mouth on such occasions. He would sniffle a few times, begin to suck, and then calm down.

It wouldn't be long now. And time didn't matter. How old was the woman in the window? Twenty-two? Twenty-five? Where would she be in ten years, in five? Perhaps her companion would be dead. Perhaps he was dead already. Perhaps at this very moment she was carrying in her body the germ of the disease that would kill her.

What would Holst say? How would he act?

Sissy would be silent, he knew. Or she would just say: "Frank!"

The old gentleman would be there. It didn't matter. He felt hot. Perhaps he had a fever. He hoped he wasn't getting sick, not now. The old gentleman wore glasses and had been dressed in black from head to foot. But why? He always wore gray. Frank was a Catholic. He had Protestant friends and sometimes he had gone to church with them. He had seen their clergymen.

He had to be careful, since the big American desk was changing shape, becoming a sort of altar. Lotte looked ridiculous dressed like that. She always dressed like that when she wanted to look distinguished. She overdid it with the grays and whites. He vaguely remembered a photograph of a queen dressed like that, only she was softer, more ethereal. But that was a queen. Lotte ran a whorehouse and she was ethereal, too. As for that poor Minna, she looked as though she had just come out of a convent. Cousin Minna.

Why was she crying? Lotte dropped her handkerchief, rolled into a ball, and Holst stooped to pick it up and handed it to her with his long arm. He said nothing because it was not the moment. The old gentleman was reading his little scraps of paper and was in danger of mixing them up. It was a very complicated prayer and of the utmost importance.

Sissy looked into Frank's eyes so intently that his pupils ached.

There was no longer a gun on the desk, but a key. They would be given a key instead of a ring. Not a bad idea. He had never heard of it being done, but it was a good idea. Who were they going to give it to? Evidently it was the key to a room with a window and a blind. It was dark. The blind should be closed and the lamp lighted.

He looked. His eyes were open. Someone turned on the light in his classroom. The civilian was standing beside his bed, the soldier waiting at the door.

"I'm coming . . ." he stammered. "I'm coming, I tell you."

He didn't move. He was forced to make a violent effort. His legs were stiff, his back ached. The man waited. The courtyard was dark. It was swept by the searchlight like a beam from a lighthouse. Frank had never seen the sea. He would never see it. He knew it only from the movies and there was always a lighthouse.

He'd gone to the movies with Sissy twice. Twice!

"Coming . . ."

He put on his jacket again. He felt like he was forgetting something. Ah, yes! He must be very nice to the old gentleman, encourage him.

The little room. The stove was purring. It was much too

hot. That was maybe on purpose, too. They didn't tell him to sit. It was going to be a standing session, though today, he didn't know why, he would have felt better sitting down.

"Perhaps you could tell me a little about Kromer?"

Nothing got by him, the old gentleman! He understood that this was the right moment!

"Gladly."

He would have preferred to talk about the gun, which he noticed on the desk. Then he would be done with the threat they were saving up for the end.

"Why did he give you money?"

"Because I procured certain merchandise for him."

"What kind of merchandise?"

"Watches."

"He was in the watch business?"

He wanted to beg: "You'll give permission?"

All through the session he had to keep swallowing that question.

"Someone had asked him for watches."

"Who?"

"I think it was an officer."

"You think so?"

"That's what he told me."

"Who was the officer?"

"I don't know his name. A high-ranking officer who collects watches."

"Where did you meet him?"

"I never saw him."

"How did he pay you?"

"He paid Kromer, who gave me my share."

"What was your share?"

"Half."

"Where did you buy the watches?"

"I didn't buy them."

"You stole them?"

"I took them."

"Where?"

"At a watchmaker's I used to know. He's dead now."

"You killed him?"

"No. He had been dead a year already."

It was going too fast. Normally it would have been enough for three or four sessions. He felt dizzy. Was he picking up the pace to get to the end more quickly?

"Who had the watches?"

The old gentleman consulted one of his scraps. They knew. Frank would have sworn they had known everything from the beginning. Then why all this pretense? What more did they want to know? What were they hoping for? After all, they were wasting their time more than they were wasting his.

"They were hidden at his sister's. I went. I took them and left."

"That is all?"

Sullenly, like a little boy caught doing mischief, he said, "I went back into the house again and killed her."

"Why?"

"Because she recognized me."

"Who was with you?"

"I was alone."

"Where did this take place?"

"In the country."

"Far from the city?"

"About five or ten miles."

"Did you go on foot?"

"Yes."

"No!"

"You're right. No."

"How did you get there?"

"By bike."

"You own a bicycle."

"I borrowed one."

"From whom?"

"I rented it."

"Where?"

"I don't remember. In a garage in the Upper Town."

"Would you recognize the garage if you were taken to the Upper Town?"

"I don't know."

"And if you were shown the truck you used, would you recognize that?" They knew that, too. It was depressing. "You will see it tomorrow morning in the courtyard."

He didn't reply. He was thirsty. His shirt was wet under his arms and his temples were beginning to throb.

"How do you know Carl Adler?"

"I don't know him."

"Yet it was he who drove the truck."

"It was dark."

"What do you know about him?"

"Nothing."

"Did you know that he did something with radios?"

"I didn't."

"He had a radio transmitter in the truck."

"I didn't see it. It was dark. I didn't look in the back."

"Who was sitting there?"

"I don't know."

"Was there someone?"

"Yes."

"Then someone must have introduced him to you. Who?"

"Kromer."

"Where?"

"In a bar across from the movie theater."

"Who was he with?"

"He was alone."

"What names did he use when he introduced you?"

"He didn't mention names."

"Would you recognize the one in the back?"

"I don't think so."

"Describe him."

"He was fairly big and had a mustache."

He was lying, but he'd gained some time.

"Go on."

"He was wearing overalls."

"In the bar?"

"Yes." They didn't know him. He felt sure of that. He wasn't risking anything, then. "Wait a minute. I think he had a scar."

"Where?"

He thought of the brass ruler. He improvised: "Across his face . . . the left cheek . . . Yes."

"You are lying, are you not?"

"No."

"I would be very sorry if you were, because that would prevent me, a priori, from giving the authorization I have been asked for."

"I swear I don't know him."

"And the scar?"

"I don't know."

"The description?"

"Again, I don't know. I'd certainly recognize him if I saw him, but I can't describe him."

"The bar?"

"That's true."

"Carl Adler?"

"I really don't know why I didn't tell you his name. I saw him again twice in the street. He didn't recognize me."

"The radio transmitter?"

"They never mentioned it to me."

Would he give permission? He anxiously studied the face of the old gentleman, who seemed to take a secret pleasure in being more inscrutable than ever. He rolled a cigarette. Then he began speaking slowly and softly.

"Carl Adler was shot yesterday by another service. He did not talk. It is necessary for us to find his accomplices."

Suddenly Frank flushed. Were they going to make him the kind of offer Lotte had accepted?

He knew nothing, it was true. They would end up convinced of that. But he might know. They would use him to try to find out.

He found it hard to breathe. He didn't know where to look. Once again, he was ashamed. What would he do if they asked him outright, if they made him a deal? What would Holst do?

He closed his eyes and stiffened. It was too easy. He shouldn't count on it. It would never happen. He wasn't crying. He wouldn't start crying in a moment like this.

He waited. The old gentleman must be playing with his scraps of paper. Why didn't he say something? Nothing could be heard but the purring of the stove. Time passed. Then Frank opened his eyes and saw the acolyte standing next to him, waiting to take him back. The soldier was already at the door.

It was over. Perhaps for a little while—until tomorrow.

They didn't nod at each other. No one here ever nodded at anyone. It must have been one of the local customs. It lent the building an impression of emptiness.

It was very cold outside, much colder than it had been over the last few days. The sky was as bright as polished steel. The crests of the roofs seemed sharper than usual.

Tomorrow morning there would be frost flowers on the windowpanes.

# 4

IT WAS funny. He had spent the greater part of his life—it wasn't an exaggeration—hating destiny with an almost personal hatred, to the point of looking for it everywhere, wanting to defy it, to wrestle with it.

And here, when he wasn't even thinking about it, destiny gave him a gift.

There was no other way to put it. Of course the old gentleman, cold-blooded fish that he was, might have had a moment of weakness and felt some pity. Or it could have been a tactical error on his part, but that wasn't very likely, since he never made mistakes. But probably it had happened on another level entirely, in that *very high* section to which Holst had addressed his request, and where someone who knew nothing at all about the whole matter had attached a note to the request meaning "yes."

Holst was downstairs! Holst was in the little room by the stove, and with him, a little behind him, was Sissy.

They were both there.

Frank hadn't been warned. They had come to collect him as if for further interrogation. In the five days or so since his mother and Minna had been there, he had been interrogated twelve, maybe fifteen times. He was almost at the end of his rope. He was so weak that his mind wandered.

Holst was there. Frank stopped short and looked at him. He had seen Sissy, too, but he continued to stare at Holst, and his feet wouldn't stir, his body wouldn't stir. The marvelous thing was that Holst didn't even dream of opening his mouth.

To say what?

He seemed to understand the question in Frank's eyes. As though in answer, he pushed Sissy forward a little.

The old gentleman must have been presiding at his pulpit. The two acolytes were standing at their posts, he was sure of that. There was the stove, the window, the courtyard, the guard near the sentry box.

In fact, there was nothing at all: just Sissy in a black coat that made her look very thin, wearing a black beret that didn't completely hide her fair hair. She looked at him. She didn't want to cry like Lotte. She wasn't overcome by pity like Minna. Perhaps she didn't even notice his two missing teeth, his unkempt beard or rumpled clothes.

She didn't come any closer. Neither of them dared to come closer. And if they had dared, would they have done it? He wasn't sure.

She started to open her mouth. She was about to speak. Finally she said—exactly as he had known she would— "Frank . . ."

She wanted to say something else and he was afraid.

"I came to tell you . . ."

He was embarrassed. "I know," he murmured.

He thought she was going to say, he was afraid she was going to say: ". . . I'm not angry with you." Or perhaps: ". . . I forgive you."

But that wasn't what she said. She kept looking at him, and it seemed impossible that two people ever looked at each other so intensely ever before. She simply said, "I came to tell you I love you."

She was holding her little black bag in her hand. Everything was happening as it had in his dream, except that the old gentleman had just meticulously rolled a cigarette and was licking the paper with the tip of his tongue.

Frank didn't answer. He didn't have the right to. He had nothing to say. He looked over at Holst. Holst wasn't wearing the gray felt boots he always wore on the streetcar. He had shoes on like everybody else. He was dressed in gray. His cap was in his hand.

Frank was afraid to stir. He felt his lips move, but he wasn't trying to speak. He was nervous—maybe, he didn't know. Then Holst stepped forward, without paying any attention to the old gentleman and the two mustachioed acolytes, and he laid his hand on Frank's shoulder exactly as Frank had always known a father would.

Did Holst think that explanations were necessary? Was he afraid Frank hadn't understood? Did he still have doubts?

The hand lay on Frank's shoulder and as Holst began to recite—he really seemed to be reciting, in a voice that was both solemn and without expression; it was reminiscent of certain ceremonies during Holy Week. "I had a son, a boy who was a little older than you. He wanted to be a doctor. Medicine was his passion. Nothing else mattered to him. When I ran out of money, he decided to continue his studies in spite of everything.

"One day some expensive supplies, mercury, platinum, were found missing from the physics laboratory. Then people began to complain about minor thefts around the university. Finally a student, coming into the cloakroom suddenly, caught my son in the act of stealing a wallet.

"He was twenty-one. As they were taking him to the rector's office, he jumped out of a third-story window."

Holst gripped his shoulder more tightly.

Frank would have liked to say something. There was one thing he wanted to say above all, but it meant nothing, and Holst might take it the wrong way: he would have liked to have been Holst's son. It would have made him so happy—it would have relieved him of such a burden—to say, "Father!"

Sissy continued to stare at him. He couldn't say whether, like Minna, she'd gotten thinner and paler. It didn't matter. She had come. She'd wanted to come and Holst had agreed.

Holst had had taken her by the hand and brought her to Frank.

"You see," he finished, "it's not an easy job, being a man."

And he seemed to smile a little as he said these words, as if he was sorry.

"Sissy talks about you to Monsieur Wimmer all day long. I found work in an office, but I get home early."

He turned toward the window so they could look at each other, just the two of them.

There was no ring. There was no key. There were no prayers. Holst's words had taken their place.

Sissy was there. Holst was there.

They mustn't stay too long. Frank probably wouldn't be able to stand it. That was all he had and all he wanted. It was his lot. He had nothing before and nothing would exist after.

This was his wedding, his own wedding. This was his honeymoon, his life—it had to be lived all at once, taken in a single dose, while the old gentleman went on rummaging among his scraps.

They wouldn't have a window that opened, laundry to hang out to dry, a cradle.

If there had been all that, then perhaps there would have been nothing at all—just Frank raging against destiny. It wasn't whether it lasted that mattered. It just mattered that it was.

"Sissy . . ."

He didn't know if he had murmured her name or only thought it. His lips moved, but he couldn't prevent them from moving. His hands moved, too, reaching out, though he stopped them just in time. Sissy's hands also moved. She controlled them by clutching at her bag with her fingers.

For her, too, and for Holst, it mustn't go on.

"We'll try to come back," Holst said.

Frank smiled, still looking at Sissy. He nodded his head, knowing of course it wasn't true, just as Holst knew it wasn't, and as Sissy probably did, too.

"You'll come back, yes."

That was all. His eyes couldn't take it anymore. He was afraid he'd faint. He hadn't had anything to eat since the day before. He'd hardly slept in a week.

Holst went to his daughter and took her arm. "Be brave, Frank," he said.

Sissy said nothing. She let herself be led off, head still turned toward him, eyes fixed on his with an expression that he had never seen in human eyes.

They hadn't touched each other, not even their fingers. It hadn't been necessary.

They left. He saw them through the window, against the white background of the courtyard, and Sissy's face was still turned toward him.

Quick! He was going to scream! It was too much! Quick!

He couldn't keep still any longer. He walked toward the old gentleman, opened his mouth. He was going to gesture wildly, say something loud and furious, but the sounds wouldn't emerge. He stood paralyzed.

She had come. She was there. She was in him. His. Holst had given them his blessing.

Destiny had given him a gift, and now, by an absurd aberration, with unheard-of generosity, it handed him another. Instead of interrogating him, which was no doubt what was supposed to take place, the old gentleman got up and went to put on his hat—it had never happened before—and Frank was led back to his room.

---

He owed it to himself not to sleep on his wedding night, and they didn't disturb him.

It was better that he couldn't feel his exhaustion anymore, that he was so calm when he got up, so sure of everything. He waited for them. He looked at the window across the way, but it hardly mattered if they came before it opened.

Sissy was in him.

Civilian in front, soldier behind, he came along, and though they kept him waiting, he didn't care. It was the last time. It had to be the last. And there must have been a new light in his eyes, because the old gentleman looked up and then paused, taken aback, before studying him uneasily.

"Sit down."

"No."

It wasn't going to be a seated session, he had decided that.

"First, I should like to ask permission to make an important statement."

He would speak slowly. It would give more weight to his words.

"I stole the watches and I killed Mademoiselle Vilmos, the sister of the watchmaker in my village. I had already killed one of your officers, at the corner of the blind alley that leads to the tannery, in order to take his automatic, because I wanted one. I did things that were much more shameful. I committed the worst crime in the world, but that has nothing to do with you. I am not a fanatic, an agitator, or a patriot. I am a piece of shit. Since you began interrogating me I've done everything I could to gain time, because I simply had to have more time. Now it's over."

He spoke without taking a breath, almost as if trying to imitate the old gentleman's icy voice. At times, though, he sounded more like Holst.

"I know nothing about whatever it is you're investigating. That I swear. But if I did know something, I wouldn't tell. You could interrogate me as long as you wanted, but I wouldn't tell you a word. You can torture me. I'm not afraid of torture. You can promise me my life. I don't want it. I want to die, as soon as possible, in whatever fashion you choose.

"Don't resent my talking to you like this. I have nothing against you personally. You've done your job. As for me, I've decided to stop talking, and these are the last words I'll say to you."

———

They beat him. They brought him down two or three times to beat him. The last time, they stripped him naked in the room. Then the men with mustaches went to work, but without excitement and without animosity. They had been ordered, no doubt, to hit him hard, to knee him in the balls, and he had blushed when for an instant he had thought of Kromer and of Sissy.

He had nothing to eat but soup. They had taken away the rest.

It wouldn't be long now. If they didn't hurry, it might happen anyway.

He still hoped they'd take him to the cellar. It was his old obsession with wanting to be treated differently from other people.

There was always the window above the gymnasium, the window that might have been his window, the woman who might have been Sissy.

At last they made up their minds, one morning when it had begun to snow again. The sky was so black and lowering that it seemed they were running ahead of schedule. They had gone to the other classroom first. He hadn't thought it would happen like this. Then, leaving the three men they had selected on the walkway, they opened his door with a shove.

He was ready. No use putting on his overcoat. He knew all about it. He hurried. He didn't want to keep the others waiting in the cold. In the half-light he tried to make out their features, and it was the first time he felt any curiosity at all about the men in the other classroom.

They made them march in single file along the walkway.

Funny! He had turned up his collar like the others!

And he had forgotten to look at the window, he had forgotten to think. He would have all the time in the world afterward.

*Tucson (Arizona)*
*20 March 1948*

# AFTERWORD

$W$HAT IS noir? The old saw about pornography applies: You will know it when you see it. Varying in temperature from downbeat to gloomy—in other words, below freezing in either case—varying in locale from urban ghettos to squalid little towns controlled by political machines, noir is actually surprisingly unvaried. Think betrayal, think murder, think secrecy and crookedness, and you're pretty much there. But for much the same reason that the most threatening street in the red-light district may support a plush, safe bar or even a business-class hotel, noir's grittiest page-turners are sometimes inhabited by heroes who are strangely—heroic. Raymond Chandler's protagonist, the private eye Marlowe, to whom the word "hardboiled" has been so often attached that it's now stuck to his shoe like chewing gum, is actually a softy: compassionate, even ethical in the bourgeois sense. He doesn't mind being nasty to stuck-up rich bitches or hiding the occasional dead body; all the same, he preserves what strikes this reader as a comically dated horror of drugs and pornography, he avoids sexual gratification on the job, and, above all, he'll never betray a client, much less a friend. Loyalty! Decency! As technology and corporatism impel us more and more to treat one another like things, those two words approach irrelevance, except between intimates, and sometimes even then. This is why with each passing decade, Marlowe's corpse decomposes ever more rapidly into a skeleton of outright sentimentality. To some readers he already seems as quaint as Fenimore Cooper's Deerslayer.

A couple of centuries from now (assuming that there will still be human beings to stain the snows of this earth), Simenon's protagonist Frank Friedmaier may be considered more or less repellent than he now appears, depending on the sensibilities of that age, but he's hardly likely to suffer Marlowe's fate. In fact, he is almost inhumanly horrific. Chandler's novels are noir shot through with wistful luminescence; Simenon has concentrated noir into a darkness as solid and heavy as the interior of a dwarf star.

How has he done it? Part of his artistry consists of limiting Frank's life and crimes, not to mention his whole world, to a scale as petty as a prison yard, thereby bringing Hannah Arendt's old phrase, "the banality of evil," to life. And of course Frank's evil is banal not to us, which would have meant that he bored us, but to Frank himself. Oh, no, he scarcely bores us; on the contrary, some of his doings are almost unbearable to read of. But what he does approaches pointlessness. The crimes of an inmate of Marlowe's world have their objects; the plot unfolds more logically than life itself. *Dirty Snow* is no improvement on life itself. This is why Frank reminds me less of Marlowe than of some Chekhov character, a provincial mediocrity condemned to swelter in his own dullness. Now magnify dullness until all possibilities are frozen and filthy. *Dirty Snow* is the aptest title I could imagine.

One fundamental question that this book raises is: Does every human being seek to evolve, even if unknowingly? Is Frank abnormal in this regard, or are his mother's whores and his own thuggish acquaintances more than they seem? In my own bread-and-butter work (I am a journalist) I travel to nasty places. Based on what I see there, it seems to me that brutality and immiseration compel the human majority to exhaust itself in what my interpreter in the Congo kept calling *the struggle for life*. In the world of *Dirty Snow*, that struggle occupies most people. The tenants of Frank's building hate him not only because he is hateful and because they disapprove of his mother's business, but also because they are cold and hungry while he isn't.

Chekhov encourages us to believe, and I myself prefer to believe, that within us all hides a spark of something more than mere consciousness; that spark is called potentiality, and its common failure to become what it could have been is tragedy. Another place this theme is worked out is *Middlemarch*, George Eliot's longish nineteenth-century masterpiece where the characters live at some remove from noir: there Lydgate sets out to revolutionize the field of medicine but corrupts himself with a foolish marriage in which his social-climbing wife runs up ruinous bills; Dorothea marries pedantic Mr. Casaubon because she longs to devote herself to her husband's great scholarly work, only to find that his project is the feeblest phantasm. What about the struggle for life? And yet even if everybody could be sufficently well housed and fed, most of us would be lucky to approach Lydgate's level of aspiration, and disappointment.

Thanks to his mother, Frank doesn't have to worry about the struggle for life at all. He possesses the freedom to aspire to be more than he is. He's at Lydgate's level. What makes *Dirty Snow* so haunting is that unlike Lydgate or Dorothea, or even Chekhov's three sisters who only know that they are unhappy and keep vaguely dreaming about going to Moscow, Frank never articulates what it is that he is looking for. Furthermore, the spark in him is not very nice.

To get right down to it, Frank despises what he gets. Without understanding himself or the world in which he finds himself, he sets out to pollute everything. Marlowe might have gotten dirty, but he aspired to be an agent of truth and even salvation, although sometimes he only accomplished finality. Frank for his part is nothing more or less than an agent of corruption.

But how intensely human he is! Here is Simenon's genius.

Frank wants to be recognized. He wants to be *known*. He scarcely knows himself, or anything else worth knowing. But if he can somehow stand revealed to the gaze of the Other, then maybe he will achieve some sort of realization. Don't you and I want to be more real than we are? And wouldn't it be convenient if somebody else could help us get there? All we have to do is move to Moscow or marry Mr. Casaubon.

This theme is very subtly articulated at first; certainly it remains almost invisible to Frank himself. The plot begins on page one with Frank's desire to be noticed. To fulfill that desire, he will commit a meaningless murder.

Frank's "friend" Kromer (I use the word because Simenon introduces him as such; I use the quotation marks because of course Frank has no friends in any human sense) once strangled a woman with whom he was copulating because she dared to hope that he was making her pregnant, and because, worse yet, "she had kept getting more tender and clinging." So it follows that Kromer wouldn't have killed her if he hadn't been fucking her; and the relationship between sex and death becomes still more pronounced when Simenon remarks:

> And for Frank, who was nineteen, to kill his first man was another loss of virginity hardly any more disturbing than the first. And, like the first, it wasn't premeditated. It just happened. As though a moment comes when it's both necessary and natural to make a decision that has long since been made...
>
> For weeks, perhaps months, he had kept saying to himself, because he had felt within himself a sort of inferiority, "I'll have to try..."

Frank's story is far more shocking and squalid than Dorothea's, of course. It is up to you to decide whether it is more or less "tragic." The gap between Dorothea's aspiration and the far more limited reality which marks her best effort is measurable. In Frank's case, both the goal and the achievement remain at such a low level, so close to the desperately brutish struggle for life, that it's necessary to ask: Which is worse (and obviously I'm not speaking here in an ethical sense) Dorothea's gaping failure or the sickening meanness of Frank's potentiality?

Let's just suppose for a minute (in which case *Dirty Snow* would be an entirely different book) that Frank chose to express his identity by joining the Resistance (I capitalize this in World War II form because *Dirty Snow* is despite itself a World War II novel). After all, the occupiers are ruthlessly oppressive, and violence against them would be justified. All right, so we've supposed it and it's inconceivable. Why? Dystopian novels usually create some sort of opposition between tyranny and its victims, in order to highlight the wickedness of the former. Even Orwell's *1984* endows its hero and heroine with sensitivity, in order to appall us with the ultimate destruction of that sensitivity in the torture chambers of the Ministry of Truth. But as we rotate our telescope through Frank's universe, we seem to find an awful lot of people who don't express any sensitivity at all. The best of them—Holst, Sissy, old Mademoiselle Vilmos whom Frank robs and murders—are no better than atomized. The rest are simply brutes.

Frank's first victim, the Eunuch, is typical of *Dirty Snow*'s environs, which is to say of the struggle for life. This fellow scarcely deserves our pity at all. He compels the prostitutes at Timo's to eat and drink; he finger-fucks them in front of others; he lays down his gunbelt on the table as they eat. To Frank, none of these acts are particularly interesting or relevant (like Marlowe, he's seen it all), but all of the sudden, in what he slyly pretends to be a non sequitur, Simenon articulates Frank's thoughts for him as follows: "So wasn't it natural that—since he had to kill someone sometime—he would think of the Eunuch?" Of course, nobody really does think of the Eunuch, not Simenon, not us; we're not even present at his murder; he's nothing but another nasty placeholder, a two-dimensional piece of work who's promptly swallowed up in the dirty snow. We don't care. He's nothing.

But the decision to slay him, unlike the erotic decision to which it has been normatively compared, goes far beyond callous bravado to outright self-destructiveness. To kill a member of the occupying forces would be nearly suicidal under any circumstances; to kill him without any particular motive is—well, it's certainly peculiar. And this is what makes Frank such a haunting character. The struggle for life alone cannot explain him. Frank doesn't know what he's about, and it is a measure of his sickness (and his world's) that all he can think of to do in order to discover himself is to commit acts of violence and betrayal.

Frank for his part proposes a more rational explanation for the crime: if he gets the Eunuch's gun he'll be able to impress a certain Berg, another non-friend whom he doesn't care about. Ayn Rand once wrote: "You have to flatter other people whom you despise in order to impress other people who despise you." It's beyond that: Frank has to flatter someone to whom he's indifferent in order to impress someone who's indifferent to him, and he knows all along that even if Berg is impressed, Frank will remain indifferent to that, too. In short, the motive is absurd, in keeping with the deed.

Here my editor advises: "Avoid this word" (absurd) "as carrying too much baggage? Also, the idea of the absurd suggests the 'motiveless crime' of Gide's Lafcadio, and this crime isn't motiveless, it just isn't explained by the reasons Frank supplies." But what if Frank wants those reasons to be absurd? If so, why would he?

We cannot ever ascertain whether Frank sets out to be caught, but he is certainly willing to increase his chances of getting caught in order to experience something or learn something, though he doesn't know quite why. Why else would he *want* Holst to see him lie in wait for the Eunuch? "Had Frank perhaps coughed out of childish impulse? That was too simple, too pat." We're told that the idea of Holst's knowing that Frank is the murderer "excites" Frank, that there's a "secret bond" between them. The exchanged gazes between the man and the boy come to take on a deeply intimate, almost erotic character for Frank, much like his impulse to the murder of the Eunuch. Holst is the one he murders the Eunuch for. (Why not say so? He didn't do it for Berg.) Holst is the one he fondles Holst's daughter for.

In short, Holst could be described as the key to Frank's soul. What exactly does Holst "mean"? We'll never know. (Love, kindness, fellowship; Frank rages against all these. Holst seems, insofar as we can tell, to be a decent and perhaps cultivated man. Why then does Frank not murder him?) Like so many other characters in this novel, he's delineated partially and sparingly. And in passing I want to call attention to another measure of Simenon's artistry: the enigmatic relations between Frank and Holst tease the mind; yet they take up an astonishingly small proportion of the page count.

What precisely do we know? Simenon reminds us explicitly that Frank lacks a father—that's the gist of it; Holst for his part (as we learn during their meeting in the prison) evidently sees Frank as a filial surrogate, for he compares him to his own son who stole mercury and platinum to finance his studies; the difference, of course, is like the difference between Frank and Dorothea: Frank has no goal, no studies apart from his own perverse search for self-awareness, of which he can scarcely be said to be aware; and he squanders the proceeds of his crimes. (The similarity is that both Holst's son and Frank commit suicide.) Frank's desire for Holst to be disbursements is more important to them than the murder of the Eunuch. Still, maybe it was the murder which impelled them to bring him in. Well, what's the difference? If that crime didn't in and of itself lead to Frank's arrest, it commenced a string of in-your-face follies which eventually did doom Frank. All of them were vile, and all were meaningless. So why do we need to know?

Who turned him in? We can't be sure of that, either. Maybe no one; maybe the authorities were watching him all along. Probably not his mother, but we can't entirely dismiss her. With good reason, she fears his lethal anger and coldness, which might be cause for saving herself; she's an exploiter who's callously disregardful of her girls' health (the episode with the whore whose "plumbing" gets damaged by Otto is especially telling); she has an understanding of some kind with the inspector, who might be Frank's father; she turns her brothel into an information-gathering apparatus for the occupiers. One of the nastiest characters in this book, she turns country girls into whores, then, once they've become stale and blowsy, demotes them to household drudges and finally kicks them out; Simenon remarks that the girls arrive thinking they've found haven in her warm, food-rich apartment. She "knew how to train them." To be sure, she loves Frank, or believes that she does; and she caters to him; indeed, she is a major factor in his spoiling. She has fed him with the corruption he regurgitates, which is why, as I said, *he wants to be hated*—a surefire way to get others to *see* him, to be real, to actually catch the eye, like a blot of fresh red blood on the dirty snow. Indeed, most people do hate him. Therefore, the question of who might have turned him in can be answered: Anybody and everybody—except the two who had most cause: Holst and Sissy.

What do we know about Frank? Almost nothing. What is there to know? The same.

Given all that it does not say, *Dirty Snow* succeeds quite surprisingly in being a classic bildungsroman, a novel of development. By the end, Frank is asking himself: "Were they going to make him the kind of offer Lotte had accepted? ... What would he do if they asked him outright? ... What would Holst do?"

But this is not quite the great moment of moral redemption which we tend to encounter in the bildungsroman—or is it? Calmly, defiantly, Frank informs the interrogator: "I am not a fanatic, an agitator, or a patriot. I am a piece of shit ... I want to die, as soon as possible, in whatever fashion you choose."

What makes *Dirty Snow* so depressing and so true is that Frank is a piece of shit who does deserve to die. In the end, he has learned to know himself; nothing more is left to him. Like the Nazi war criminals at Nuremberg who admitted to their crimes, he has achieved the only kind of heroism which is still open to him: he admits that he is ruined and evil through and through. He stands by himself. His moral and intellectual development, such as it is, has been the explicit assumption of the evilness which he has long since arrogated.

When the book first opens he has not killed anyone; he has not committed the worst betrayal of all, the seduction and proxy rape of Sissy. Nor, I repeat, was there ever any need for him to do these things. When I had only read a few pages of *Dirty Snow*, Frank reminded me of Camus' protagonist in *The Stranger*, who kills for no reason. But all around him a cruel and evil occupying force from some unnamed country is oppressing and killing. Frank is less "absurd" than the Stranger, less out of place. In spite of his privileged existence, he too is contaminated by the terrible struggle for life. The only experience available to people in Frank's country, so it would seem, the only form of maturing and growing, is being corrupted. And all that Holst's proxy fatherhood can give

Frank in the end is empirical validation of his own badness. There's destiny for you! No wonder Frank hates it. Can anything get much worse than this?

—WILLIAM T. VOLLMANN

# TITLES IN SERIES